P9-AQY-788

The Lighthouse & Me

History, Memoir, & Imagination

Jeffrey Burke

The Lighthouse and Me

© Copyright 2017, Jeffrey Burke

ISBN: 978-1-63381-124-9

All rights reserved. No part of this book may be reproduced in any form or by any electronic or mechanical means, including information storage and retrieval systems, without permission in writing from the author, except by a reviewer, who may quote brief passages in review.

Cover

Original oil painting by Jeffrey Burke, inspired by a photograph by William Brehm.

Designed and Produced by

Maine Authors Publishing
12 High Street, Thomaston, Maine 04861
www.maineauthorspublishing.com

Printed in the United States of America

To the lighthouse

Acknowledgments

My deepest gratitude for the "lighthouses" throughout my life: Pete Seeger, Mahatma Gandhi, Dr. Martin Luther King, Jr., Bob DeWitt, Sr., Ted Hoskins, Lou and Joan Burrell, Lloyd Wells, Richard Komp, Jim Climo, the Camino de Santiago, the Fourteenth Dalai Lama, and my good wife, Judi. Fondest appreciation to so many sources of Island lore: Billy and Bernadine Barter, Sally Greenlaw Bowen, Jim Greenlaw, Harold VanDoren, and the people of Isle au Haut. I would have been way off course without the guidance of my overly sensitive readers: Judi Burke, Kathie Fiveash, and Harold VanDoren. Keeper Ted Panayotoff provided authoritative lighthouse history fact checking. Landscape architect Peter Burke rendered the two captivating maps. His eight-year-old son, Ezra, drew the maps' artful little symbols. Skillful camera work by Billy Brehm converted a pile of dog-eared documentation into fascinating images. Most of all, thanks to all the innocent/guilty folk—living, dead, and imaginary—who provided the facts, fiction, and fairy tales during this long journey to understand lighthouse magic.

The campaign to save the lighthouse is hardly ours alone. This renaissance will never be complete without the dedication provided by these island friends.

Town of Isle au Haut Lighthouse Committee

Lisa Turner
Alison Richardson
Marshall Chapman
Kathie Fiveash

Jeff Burke
Bernadine Barter
Martha Greenlaw

Friends of Isle au Haut Lighthouse, 501c3, Board of Directors

Matthew Costello
Jeff Burke
Jennifer Greenlaw
Allan Toubman
Diane Valillee
Linda Greenlaw
Garrett Aldrich
Donna Hopkins
Bill Clark
Wendell Chamberlain

Experts Aiding Our Lighthouse Restoration

Alfred Hodson, Resurgence Engineering
Mike Johnson, Maine State Historic Preservation Office

And finally, thanks to both Rachel Harris and the folks at Maine Authors Publishing for making me do things right.

Contents

Author's Historical Note

From its beginnings in 1906, the United States Lighthouse Service referred to this lighthouse as "Robinson Point Lighthouse Station"—this was the operational name used throughout the years the station was staffed with government lighthouse keepers. Since 1934, when the tower was automated and the remainder of the station sold to private owners, both the station and the tower have most commonly been referred to as the "Isle au Haut Lighthouse." Nowadays, almost all references use this newer title, including government agencies, guidebooks, fishermen, and the people of Isle au Haut. To provide consistency and to avoid confusion, "Isle au Haut Lighthouse" and "Isle au Haut Lighthouse Station" are used throughout the entire book.

"Shine on me...
Shine on me...
I wonder if the lighthouse
Will shine on me."

—Traditional Negro spiritual

Prologue

In 1986 my wife, Judi, and I moved into the old lighthouse station on Isle au Haut, with our youngest son, Matthew, and our Great Dane, Maggie. For the next 26 years, we threw ourselves into restoring the old buildings and cultivating a hideaway inn on the outermost fringe of America. The Keeper's House Inn became a refuge where travelers could relish virgin coast, feast on lobster chowder, and gain a deeper perspective of their lives, and the world whirling around them.

During the course of those years, many remarkable events occurred. Guests and travelers—as well as our employees and ourselves—altered their lives here, and made life-changing decisions: to get married; to get divorced; to join a monastery; to rob a bank; to quit a job; to opt for compact fluorescent light bulbs and unbleached toilet paper. The inn hosted plays and concerts and a hundred celebrations, all with accolades and gratitude piled on Jeff and Judi.

This recognition was appreciated, of course, but the fact is we had little to do with how we got here or the unfolding of these events. This experience fell in our laps by chance. Somehow we were anointed by fate to spend time on this rock, two fleeting guests in a long legacy of people living in towers of guiding light——an experience that goes back to the beginning of time…and deep into future ages.

The opportunity to live at this lighthouse station was welcomed by the previous occupants, too, bringing good times—and bad—to the Robinson and Greenlaw families, and the lighthouse keepers and their families who first lived in these buildings. Understanding the attraction of this site is elusive; there's something mysterious that makes a lighthouse more than a common dwelling.

Maybe it's in the rock, I wondered, *or the ocean currents that caress the shore, or the surrounding legions of spruce and cedar, or the ever-*

tumbling clouds that bring on the weather, all crowned by a dome of sky so high, so mighty, it only begins up there, mingling with the planets, the suns, the Aurora Borealis, the glittering tiara of stars.

But back then, in 1986, I couldn't quite understand what made the lighthouse so compelling.

* * * *

Twenty-eight years later, in the summer of 2014, as chairman of the town's lighthouse committee, I was invited by the Isle au Haut Historical Society to do a presentation on the history of our lighthouse station. The townspeople gathered at the town hall for the occasion, with punch and oatmeal cookies provided. Harold Van Doren, the society's president, screened historic photographs unearthed from the bowels of the society's archives, while I rattled off a procession of names and dates and lighthouse trivia. Our presentation was followed by a lively discussion, and it was the consensus of all present that I, Jeffrey Burke, should forthwith produce a complete written narrative of the story, jumbled together in a plastic binder to be stored on the shelves of Revere Memorial Library.

After the program, I complained to Harold.

"I can't do that," I said. "The lighthouse is in terrible condition. I have to raise tens of thousands of dollars and twist a million arms to repair it. I don't have time to write a book!"

Harold flashed me his knowing look: raised eyebrows arched, creating a field of furrows across his forehead.

"Well," he said, "Might be a handy way to raise some cash for the restoration."

"I'll think about it," I said.

* * * *

The next day, I caught up with Harold in front of the post office.

"Look, bud," I said, "The problem is I don't want to chronicle the names and dates of all the lighthouse keepers. Boring statistics make me wince: the number of pounds of flour a lighthouse keeper's wife uses, how many steps to the lantern room, the weather log for a hundred years—I'd go bonkers!"

We crowded into the Lilliputian post office hunched on Town Road's shoulder and began spinning the dials of our P.O. boxes.

"But you are considering it, right?" asked Harold, his pointer landing on its final click.

"Maybe. But only if it includes the magical, hair-raising stuff."

"Ghost stories?" prodded Harold.

"More than that," I said. "You got your hurricanes and murders, too. Shipwrecks and pirates, debauchery, and Indians, and prowling Nazi submarines, energy forces, galactic interventions. Sure, the mundane's gotta be included, but it's the bumps in the night that give it spice. That's what proves lighthouses are magic."

"Magic?" said Harold. "Hey, you can't get away with presenting history as magic!" He extruded the circulars, bills, and papers from his box and cradled them in his arms. "I mean, if you're gonna rely on magic, your book's credibility is gonna go up in smoke!" We strolled back into sunshine.

"Guess you're right," I said. "But if I write this thing, maybe in the process I'll come to understand the mysterious allure that lighthouses have."

Hearing that, Harold stopped midstep, turned, and faced me. "By gorry, now, you might be on to something!" he said.

"The only problem is, if this is to raise money to save the lighthouse, it's an awful big project, a whole lot of time."

Harold's eyes twinkled. "Well, my friend," he said, "you better get started."

* * * *

I'm no academic. Please don't expect this effort to be tethered with footnotes, indexes, and those sorts of things. Let's rely, instead, on the island tradition of storytelling, the memories and beliefs my neighbors share, along with a requisite smattering of factual matter——just to give it credence. Mostly though, let's acknowledge intuition, fairy tales, and imagination——the juicy stuff that gets the heartbeat racing. Don't worry. I promise I'll include the usual lighthouse stuff: the biographies of the lighthouse keepers, the dates of the restorations, the history of the fishing folk, their failures and victories. And a bit about the workings of lighthouse technology—you'll get all that, too. Maybe a poem or a scary story, and some fuzzy old photographs, some maps and charts and drawings that are sure to quench your lighthouse thirst. I'll tell you about our lives here as well, and how we came to retire, and pass on the stewardship of the lighthouse station to the next destined fellow.

* * * *

When I sketched out this **PROLOGUE,** Judi wanted to get her say in, too. She took a moment off from her bread making to offer advice.

"Now Jeffrey," she said. "Don't get carried away; you know you tend to exaggerate."

"Why not jazz things up a bit," I said. "Lighthouses are special, after all. They deserve a tad of creative texture, like your perfect blueberry gallette, or the arty swirl on the frosting you make."

"Yes, Jeff, but you need to be honest. You can't just make things up. Stick to the proven recipe if you want your concoction to turn out right."

"But Judith, it's the chef's spirit that makes cuisine tasty. And it's the writer's imagination that makes a story soar, prods the reader's consciousness, prompts one to swim against the current, or raise the battle cry. You can't generate that kind of response with mere names and places and dates on graves."

She wiped her hands on her apron, her flow of red hair moving in waves around her narrow shoulders.

"Get off yer high horse," she said, "and learn to control your syntax, too, and ease up on the fancy words. Fabricated babble will only drive your readers nuts."

"I'd never pen anything phony, Judith. Just a tad of embellishment, that's all a story needs. Besides, even 'made-up' stories spring from a seed of truth."

"You've got to be kidding!"

"Great works—and not-so-great ones, too—stream from the brain and heart. Every great painting and every tearful lament began as a flash of thought."

She turned from the kitchen counter to face me. Her pale blue eyes were filled with fifty-five years of knowing me. "That's wacky, Jeffrey. You better get yourself a professional editor," she said. "Just to keep you grounded!"

"I have a plan for that."

"Which is?"

"A panel of three friends as readers. To give it credibility, to satisfy you doubtful sorts."

"What's wrong with a real editor?"

"That'll happen, too, for the trickier English stuff."

Judi looked skeptical. "Okay. So who's the panel?"

"Harold, of course, for starters. He's the island history buff, lugs around more minutiae than Wikipedia. Plus he's written two books about the island's characters and knows the importance of getting human stories into the script. And Kathie, too. She's a stickler for scientific fact. Her book on island nature was a Maine Literary Awards winner in 2015. And she has soul, knows how to get those heart strings zinging—just what I need to legitimatize my machinations."

Judi seemed unconvinced. "And I suppose for the third reader you've earmarked the town drunk...or your fairy godmother."

"Nope."

"Then who?"

"You, my sweet!"

Judi returned to her bread making, giving the dough a final punch before sliding it into the oven, a warning poke to accentuate the doubts she had about my writing. But I'm not allowing my dear wife's discomfort to hold me back. Besides, the relationship between the two of us is part of this story, too.

Judi: Editor at Work. Oil portrait by the author, 2010.
Photography by William Brehm.

* * * *

As I finish up this manuscript, we are still here on the island, retired and living near the lighthouse in a cottage in the woods, still engaged with the new inn proprietor to show him the ropes, still committed to caring for the lighthouse. Bricks and mortar, I can do. Stories I can tell. I'm even learning the agonizing necessity of how to write a restoration grant proposal. It's a tricky job, however, to explain the strange and powerful allure of a lighthouse—but that's what this book will try to do.

And most importantly for me, it helps me understand how this lighthouse changed my life.

Chapter 1

Something in the Rock

Climb to the top of Duck Harbor Mountain on a clear moonlit night. Rotate around to view every compass point. Flickering like fireflies, seven lighthouses pierce the darkness. *Imagine: If you could climb a thousand feet higher, fifty flashing beacons might sparkle on the seascape around you.*

Observe also—while perched there high in the sky—the mountain masses awash in the sea, with their serrated peninsulas slashing southward. And islands are everywhere, squat and tall, forested and barren, rough and raw, or polished smooth as marbles. It's an obstacle course with ominous consequences for any erring sailor. Add to that the rise and fall of the tides, each hour altering the dance between safe and risky: neap tides and spring tides and bore tides and drain tides. Then there's the weather to consider: *Imagine a seventy-mile-per-hour gale slamming you sideways, pushing, tossing, heaving your boat, bit by unstoppable bit toward some lurking gnarl of sea-foamed granite. The fog presents additional perils—you are disoriented in it! A January nor'easter can be even nastier. Instead of passive blindness, that winter menace assails your vision with blasts of icy crystal that cake the eyelashes, decks, and rigging.*

No wonder we find our waters prickled with lighthouses; they are our best hope for maneuvering our way through this labyrinth.

Why is Maine's lighthouse coast so dramatic?

Professor Marshall Chapman knows the answer.

He first came to Isle au Haut in 1986, the same year Judi and I arrived to open the inn. At the time, Marshall was a graduate student at the University of Massachusetts, writing his thesis on the Island's geology. He'd often visit the lighthouse station to examine the odd bedrock where the tower stands. After boring core samples, labeling them and depositing them in his field pack, he'd arrive at the kitchen door looking hungry. We shared a lot of coffee and muffins.

I found him one day crawling around the base of the lighthouse, chipping at the rock with his geologist's pick.

"Hey, bud, what's the genesis of this weird looking rock?" I said, nudging the stone with the toe of my sneaker.

Marshall rocked back on his haunches and pushed his hat back a smidgen.

"That's precisely the info I'm after. This grainy gray stuff here," he said, tapping his pick at the bedrock. "This is volcanic tuff—brittle, hard, almost impossible to penetrate. I use a diamond core drill for the job. Later, I can date it, compare it to other samples, try to trace its source."

"How old is it?"

"Depends on your perspective," he said. "These atoms, these molecules, they stretch back four and a half billion years."

"Whoa!"

"Yep," he said. "Back to the Big Bang."

Marshall took a pull on his coffee mug, settling down to enlighten me. After the Big Bang, he explained, the elements contained in this rock were the result of a third- or fourth-generation supernova, a gigantic exploding star whose debris careened through space. Before, there was nothing, only a wisp of gas here, a dusty particle over there, spread out so thinly that space appeared as clear as bottled water. The force of the supernovas was so powerful, so hot, they smooshed together the vast expanse of gas and dust, accreting everything into blobs of white-hot plasma. In this neck of the woods, the sun became the largest. The resultant fireballs that we now know as planets were much smaller and solidified faster. The smaller ones closest to the sun formed a scabby crust, and the larger ones farther away remained more vaporous, more dusty and gassy. So, even though the earth back then was a primordial sea of fire, it included the parental atoms of everything that eventually morphed into both bedrock and gold, augmented by eons of meteorite blizzards that added a dash of water.

"At least that's the way I tend to understand it," he said. "Other geologists disagree in certain aspects."

"Yep," I said. "Of course things have cooled down a tad since then."

Marshall tied it all together. "That was just the origin, of course," he said with a chuckle. "Since then, we've spun through many ages, countless convolutions in geology, a cavalcade of changes: the eventual appearance of humankind and the grand assemblage of matter that forms the world today as we know it."

I stood there listening to Marshall's geology lecture and daydreaming. Stabilizing myself on the jagged ledges with one hand braced against the lighthouse, its solid mass thrust from the bedrock like some timeless petrified oak, a realization suddenly struck me: *The granite beneath my fingertips, the clay used to mold the tower's brick, the sand refined into lantern room windows, the minerals for cement, wire, paint—everything in this tower (including dust motes and seagull spatter—even me, standing here leaning against it)—had evolved from matter created during the Big Bang and its raging supernovas.*

"As for this *particular* rock," Marshall resumed, bringing my attention back to the stuff beneath our shoes, "it was formed just four hundred million years ago, simply another shakeup of the atoms and molecules that were already here."

I envisioned a hellfire of magma back then, a cauldron of molten material seething away.

"Before this stuff erupted to the surface," Marshall said, eyeing the cold stone beneath us, "it still had unmelted hunks of mineral debris suspended in it." He used his pick to point out dark blobs in the gray rock, as clearly defined as chocolate chips in cookie dough. "Eventually, things got so hot the crust of the earth couldn't contain it. She blew! Somewhere around here there's a vent that spewed this stuff into the sky, millions of tons of it. Fell in leaden downpours. The xenoliths (the undissolved black blobs), became entombed in stone, as the tuff cooled and hardened."

Marshall went on to explain that he was exploring remote corners of the island trying to locate the ancient vent, but he thought it was probably buried by more recent geologic action or too far offshore to ever be found.

"Where we are standing," said Marshall, "this rock remained under water for millions of years." He explained it wasn't until the relatively recent ice ages that things began to change. As the earth cooled, seawater eventually transitioned to ice and snow. Year after year, that snow and ice became compressed and swelled to mile-high thicknesses: the continental glaciers. It happened at least four times—the last one only 22,000 years ago. Each time the climate cooled, the ice built up, sliding slowly like behemoth bulldozers from north to south, scouring, gouging, tearing at the bedrock, and creating a ravaged earth strewn with transported boulders.

"And that's how the land became shaped the way it is today?" I asked.

"Yep. Then, following the last ice age, when the glaciers stalled and the ice melted, the seas swelled and flooded all the lowest spaces, leaving the peaks protruding, the islands and ledges we see out there."

"Must have been a nightmare for any prehistoric fellow trying to paddle a raft from one dry spot to another," I said.

Images came flashing to me of Neanderthals scrambling from caves to ignite bonfires atop strategic locations, to guide fellow hunters and fishermen home. Our first lighthouses!

* * * *

These days you'll find scads of lighthouse lovers touring Maine's coast. Armed with binoculars and bag lunches, they pursue their passion aboard chartered ferries or by land in sport utility vehicles. From the expansive facility at Portland Head (the first lighthouse completed by the new republic in 1791) to the tiny range lights that dot Maine's rivers, pharologists (those who study lighthouses) scale tower steps and click their cameras. They'll check off their list at each station they visit, get their Lighthouse Passports stamped and feel grateful they've visited all the towers erected, perhaps unaware that these existing structures aren't the only lighthouses ever built. There may have been others unknown to today's lighthouse aficionados. For example, the high slanting ledges here at Robinson Point have always provided a perfect lookout for seafaring folk—both contemporary and prehistoric: The Red Paint People, for instance. Those seafaring folk certainly had sufficient skills to build a guiding tower.

Chapter 2

Finding the Way on Water

After school, on a balmy Isle au Haut afternoon in 1996, Leland Small skidded his bike into the Island Store parking lot, propped it against the loading dock, and clambered down the embankment to the water's edge. His dad needed a pound of hamburger and a can of tomato sauce, but it would be awhile before the storekeeper returned to open for the pre-supper crowd, so Leland had the opportunity to poke through the clutter of beach stone and search for treasures. He began to roll over larger stones and rake his fingers through finer ones. *"Wouldn't it make sense," he might have mused, "that some ancient seafaring native might have picked this very spot to chip rocks for arrowheads?"*

As he brushed away a pocket of pebbles, an odd smooth stone emerged. Unlike the vast array of common beach rubble here between the tide lines—the raggedy fractured tuff, the sea-sorted tidbits of metamorphic matter, the occasional shard of sea glass (once whole and functional as a bottle for Moxie or illegal rum), fragments of mussel shells, periwinkles, and whelks—here, mired in the gravel at the feet of Leland Small, lay exposed a stone unlike any other. A fine-grained rock, it measured as long as his boot and almost as wide. His fingertips found it smooth as a mackerel, as perfectly proportioned as a Fabergé egg, tapering from wide to narrow, with the broader end cleaved evenly on two sides to form an arcing cutting edge. Symmetrically, it was perfect.

Leland knew this was neither spear tip nor arrowhead. He had a dresser drawer full of those fond treasures and was knowledgeable about their dark flint, their jaggedly edges and irregular lash notches. No, this was something distinct, something he'd never seen.

Using both hands, he cradled the damp stone like a newborn baby, escorted it back to his bicycle, and nestled it into the basket, tucked in with his lunch box and books.

"I gotta get it to the 'historical people,'" he said out loud. "I better go find Barbara."

* * * *

Leland had found a wood-shaping adze left by the Lost Red Paint People. Barbara Brown (one of the volunteers with the island's Historical Society) lugged it up to the curator's office at the Maine State Museum in Augusta. A swarm of anthropologists examined it. Probably five thousand years old, they said, honed from quartzite and perfectly milled, definitely the work of the "Lost Tribe." They hoped to retain the discovery in their warren of stodgy buildings, but Barbara was adamant.

"It belongs on the island," she said.

Al Gordon fashioned a sturdy lexan box with an oak base to house it, and the Isle au Haut Historical Society pledged care and protection forever. They locked away the treasure in the clunky tin cabinet they use to store their artifacts. On special occasions, Leland's treasure is hauled out and displayed—you're even permitted to stroke it.

* * * *

The familiar tribes of Algonquian Native Americans in Maine (the Penobscot, Micmac, Passamaquoddy, Maliseet, and Abenaki) had been established here for ten thousand years and were at the pinnacle of their civilization when European colonizers arrived. But the Red Paint People became known to anthropologists only within the past two hundred years. Unlike the Algonquian tribes, they had vanished three thousand years ago, leaving neither bartering tribesmen nor warring bands to greet the new foreign arrivals.

As the colonial farmers began to topple forests and turn the soil to plant corn and squash, as settlers excavated river banks to build mills and villages, as the interlopers expanded disturbance of the supposedly virgin soil, a surprising discovery developed: Multiple burial sites were found that had nothing in common with those of established Algonquian tribes. Found solely along the shore and the major coastal rivers, these strange pits were characterized by a bed of red ocher layered with finely crafted woodworking tools, fishing implements, and bits of human bone. But despite the abundance of these burial sites, no links to any fishing village locations have ever been found. Where did these long lost people live? Where did they go?

Their precision stone chisels, augers, and concave polished scoops are highly sophisticated, suggesting that these water-oriented people must have been skilled in boat building, and the fishermen among them savvy enough to be working offshore, catching swordfish and seal—maybe even whale. Anthropologists believe the Red Paint villages must have been built right on the shores—unlike their upland woods-oriented kin—perhaps within reach of obliterating hurricanes. Any trace of those ruins disappeared long ago when sea levels rose.

Carbon dating shows that identical artifacts throughout northern Europe match the same timeline as those in Maine. Stonehenge may have been part of their world. The Red Paint People may have been so adept at their seafaring skills that traffic across the North Atlantic could have flourished centuries before Columbus ever hoisted a sail.

Archeologists agree that the red ocher burial sites were, in fact, reburial sites. Perhaps the Red Paint People dug up old remnants and reinterred them in higher grounds because of rising seas, while they continued to inhabit their vulnerable seaside villages. Colossal storms may have been their end. Another theory for the disappearance of the Red Paint culture postulates that the seabottom fault line laying parallel to the coast of Maine may have violently shifted 5,000 years ago, causing sudden reactions, perhaps massive tidal waves that swept ashore and washed away Red Paint populations.

Leland Small's adze discovery proves that during the era the Red Paint inhabited this coast, they reached all the way to Isle au Haut. *I can envision how they must have paddled by Robinson Point. Did they have a sentry here on the rock, someone to monitor the mood swings of the sea, someone to kindle a warning blaze or send smoke puffs climbing? And their tribal carpenters (the ones with keen-edged adzes, chisels, and plumb-bobs), did they fashion more than just boats? With all their fishermen out to sea beyond this promontory—might they not have erected some signpost to guide their providers back, possibly using Leland's adze to fashion a primitive beacon right here at Robinson Point?*

* * * *

After the Red Paint People disappeared, Algonquian tribes filled the void they left. These tribes were characterized by their similar languages and migratory patterns, navigating their canoes with the seasons to be where food was most plentiful: upstream in the winters where shelter and game were more accommodating, and downstream in the summers, to fish and gather berries, dig clams, and harvest sweet grass for baskets—and escape from black flies and mosquitoes. These migrations continued well into the era of European colonization.

The Penobscot are the primary native people who have lived in the area that includes Isle au Haut. The name "Penobscot" is a simplified version of the original native name, "Penawapskewi," which translates to "Stony Part" or "Descending Ledges," in reference to the Penobscot River, which sustained the tribe. Early contact with explorers and settlers was sometimes peaceful, sometimes barely tolerable, sometimes horribly bloody, and as the colonist's appetite for land expanded, so did the level of conflict. Worst of all, between 1616 and 1619, fully 85% of American Indians in this area succumbed to invasive European diseases.

When Seth Webb settled briefly on Kimball Island adjacent to Isle au Haut in 1780, and when Pelatiah Barter planted permanent roots here in 1792, these relatively recent immigrations seem only a bump in time when compared to the ages the Penobscot have been here. Certainly new settlers disrupted native patterns, but on Isle au Haut the two cultures coexisted with no recorded incidents of confrontation. Documents in the Historical Society archives attest to occasional collaboration between the islanders and Indians. Just as the Wampanoag taught the first Pilgrims how to plant and raise corn on Cape Cod, so too, the Penobscot showed the new arrivals here how to trap duck and harvest clams. Many old photographs and recorded comments attest to a "live and let live" philosophy, right up to the mid-nineteen-forties, when the Penobscot ceased their summer visits.

Billy Barter, an Isle au Haut fisherman and direct descendant of Pelatiah Barter (the Island's first year-round settler), remembers the last Penobscot summer encampment near the trail to the lighthouse. Billy's neighbor, Aubrey Greenlaw II, refers to it explicitly later in this book (*The Legend of Joe Pete Notch*). And down by Duck Harbor, Jim Greenlaw (Aubrey's brother) recalls his grandmother showing him the remnants of wigwams left on the shore. Even though the Penobscot no longer paddle to Isle au Haut, manifestations of their past linger everywhere: in the shell middens where summer wigwams clustered, in the scattered arrowheads found by beachcombers, and in splashes of DNA blended into the veins of Maine hunters, lobstermen, hairdressers, cops, and chiropractors. In spite of European domination, slaughter, revolution, industrialization, timbering and tourism, as well as rivers dammed and seas almost depleted of fish, the Penobscot Nation today still stands proud, ensconced on sovereign tribal land up the mighty river, still at the "Descending Ledges."

* * * *

Seth Webb, Pelatiah Barter, and other coastal settlers faced additional conditions more hostile than Native Americans. Uncharted waters plagued by jagged rock and shifting tides greeted them. Most of all, newcomers found life challenging without a ready infrastructure of roads and towns and aids to navigation.

As with most emerging settlements, these new arrivals established their enclaves along the edges of water. An open door to the sea, a sheltered harbor, a crook in a river where hunting and fishing and trapping were easy: These were the sought-after sites for colonies, trading posts, and shipping and fledgling industries powered by water wheels and teams of oxen. In the northeastern part of the Massachusetts Bay Colony (eventually to become the State of Maine) there was plenty of space for everyone. Three thousand miles of coast made up the twists and turns of this shoreline cut by eight major rivers, not to mention the immeasurable distances that rimmed the thousands of islands.

Timber was the first important resource to be exploited. Native trees, both hardwood and soft, abounded everywhere, ready to be felled and hewn for sailing ships, and construction lumber for coastal and river villages.

The truest and tallest trees in Maine's North Woods were mandated by law to be harvested for masts for the King's Navy, dragged by oxen to the river's edges and floated downstream, loaded on clippers, and ferried back to England. The islands, where every tree was close to water, were particularly conducive for timbering, with an ever-growing fleet of schooners ready to carry the logs to the nearest mainland sawmill. Even today, rusty anchors from those timber schooners are sometimes snagged by lobster boats, hauled up and lugged home to adorn a patch of lawn.

Other schooners were built with flat bottoms, so they could be run aground at low tide, wherever hardy farmers had managed to carve out a space in the woods sufficiently large to grow a few rows of corn and squash. The beached ships were loaded, and when the tide returned and the schooners rose, off they went to market.

Fishing, too, was abundant. Cod, flounder, hake, and haddock filled the kettles in every New England kitchen. Shellfish were equally plentiful, although our ubiquitous lobster was generally considered a garbage creature, more suitable for paupers and prisoners.

But one thing was clear, be it saw logs or fish, turnips or pelts of beaver, everything moved by water. Sailing ships were constructed by the thousands. Small craft, too: dories and skiffs, friendship sloops, every imaginable floating contraption crafted to tend to the burgeoning population. Just as importantly, this new water-oriented economy provided employment for a huge percentage of Maine's people, not just the captains and mates and seamen, but also the cargo loaders, shipbuilders, and their families and neighbors. Farmers, lumberjacks, and exporters of fur and fish also relied on the flotilla to deliver their products to the nearest village, or overseas to the motherland. Tradesmen used the water, too: merchants, tinkers, blacksmiths, and such, all plied their trades from barges, canoes, schooners, and skiffs.

While individual entrepreneurs characterized our growing colonies, more collective needs soon became apparent. There was an urgent need to develop a regional approach for dealing with commercial issues, first and foremost the marine transportation system. Navigation technology and safety had become paramount. Thousands of lives and untold tons of vessels and merchandise had been lost. Back in Europe—and around the world—established marine cultures had developed sophisticated tools to aid their shipping industries. Accurate navigation charts, tridents and telescopes, improved sailing methods. All these resources took leaps forward in worldwide development. But one key element was missing along this colonial coast: There were no lighthouses.

For a struggling coalition of colonies with few resources and little unity, the establishment of early navigational aids presented a major challenge. But the bootstrapping colonists were a people of ingenuity. Crude aids existed right from the beginning: stone pillars, a scraggly dead tree to mark a harbor entrance, early maps to show the deadliest ledges, shore-side fires on stormy nights. When "thick-a-fog" rolled in, many seaside communities intuitively gathered along the shores with cooking pots and cowbells and any available device to beat or clang to direct sailors to where dry land awaited.

Someday a lighthouse would come to Isle au Haut. But back at the end of the nineteenth century such a necessity still seemed unlikely. *Can you imagine, back then, a clutch of fishermen, captains, and boatswains huddled around the forge in Haskell Turner's blacksmith shop, bemoaning the fact that no harbor light had come to Isle au Haut?*

"We need a lighthouse in the winter, to lead the groundfish fellows

Camden Public Library
Camden, Maine

in," said Spencer Robinson.

Haskell lit his pipe and pontificated. "Those Washington boys don't understand the risks we take out here."

"Yep," said Captain John Barter, a direct descendent of Pelatiah. "It isn't like they don't know how to do it; lighthouses are nothing new—just look at the rest of the world! Why, us seafaring folk been building towers since the dawn of time."

Captain John knew what he was saying.

Chapter 3

Precursors on the Water's Edge

The Tower Of Pharos

Although we might visualize ancient lighthouses as small crude structures, that was not always the case. In fact, the most magnificent lighthouse of all time, the 450-foot Tower of Pharos, dwarfed the dimensions and longevity of any modern tower.

In 300 BC, Alexander the Great established the largest trading port of the world, located on the Mediterranean next to the western edge of the Nile River Delta; it was named Alexandria in his honor, and the Tower of Pharos he built there was the leading architectural accomplishment of the time. It was constructed with massive limestone blocks and lead to seal the joints. Alexander's engineers designed a 600-foot ramp, supported by stone arches, that climbed from the mainland bank to a point a third of the way up. (Interestingly, these proportions mirror almost exactly the ramp and tower at Isle au Haut, but ten times larger.) The tower had a square base, ninety-eight feet by ninety-eight feet. An octagonal midsection with a winding ramp inside was wide enough to accommodate a horse-drawn wagon for supplies and firewood. This section was capped by yet another smaller cylindrical tower fitted with a winching contraption to haul supplies the rest of the way up to the beacon room. There, an open fire raged, backed by a twenty-foot concave bronze disk that concentrated the firelight in a beam that radiated twenty-nine miles out to sea. Crowning the tower, a statue of Poseidon gazed vigilantly over the Mediterranean.

The Pharos tower also provided a landmark destination for travelers of the day, and sported viewing galleys complete with that era's fast food vendors and tourist shops. The Tower of Pharos is considered one of the Seven Wonders of the Ancient World and stood intact, and in operation, for almost 1400 years, until a series of earthquakes between 956 AD and 1323 AD finally shook it down.

Monuments to the rich and mighty or glorious historical events dominate the Seven Ancient Wonders list. The Pharos lighthouse, however, was the only practical one, built solely to serve and protect the interests of civil society.

Boston Harbor Lighthouse

In 1718 only 70 permanent lighthouses existed throughout the world. In that year the Massachusetts Bay Colony (which included all the territory that would become the State of Maine) constructed the Boston Harbor Lighthouse, the first major lighthouse in the Western Hemisphere. Located on Little Brewster Island in Boston harbor, the tower was maintained by a one cent per ton tax on all incoming and outgoing ships.

Only a few months after the tower was lit, the first light keeper, George Worthylake, along with his wife, daughter, and two seamen, were drowned when their tender overturned, an ominous sign for the tower's future. This traumatic experience shook the colonies and was most dramatically memorialized in a poem, *Lighthouse Tragedy*, written by a young fellow named Benjamin Franklin.

Remarkably, the second keeper also drowned, also in a dory accident. The third keeper managed to survive without tragedy. It was he who inaugurated the first fog signal to be used at an American lighthouse; in 1719 a cannon was delivered to the site and supplied with enough gunpowder to fire constantly during long periods of inclement weather.

During the Revolutionary War, the Boston Harbor Lighthouse was often at the center of the rebellion. Occupied by the British most of the time, the colonists lodged several assaults against the lighthouse—the second one led by George Washington, himself. He managed to burn down the wooden structures around the tower, but the Brits maintained control over Little Brewster until the last breath of the war. Then, while withdrawing from the bay, they left behind a keg of powder with a slow burning fuse. As the Brits sailed away, the lighthouse was blown to bits. Rebuilt twelve years later, it remains today, and, in 1998, was the last lighthouse in the United States to be automated. Symbolic volunteer lighthouse keepers still man the station.

Saddleback And Execution Rock

In 1849, while busy Isle au Haut remained without a maritime beacon, a mile across the bay a lighthouse was erected on unpopulated Saddleback Ledge. Saddleback was known as one of the hardest places to land a boat anywhere in the nation. In fact, no dock was ever built there. Instead, a shoreside davit was used to hoist freight and keepers ashore, swinging them onto the rock from craft pitching just off the ledges.

Native Islander Charlie Bowen remembers, prior to 1960, "On summer days the kids from Isle au Haut used to take an outboard out to Saddleback. The Coast Guard fellows marooned on 'The Rock' there were always happy to swing them ashore—the kids usually delivered freshly baked cookies sent by their mothers."

The ingenious and prolific architect for this difficult location had been Alexander Parris (who later became influential in founding the American Institute of Architects). With this successful station crowning his résumé, he was selected several years later to design an even more-challenging station to be located at the mouth of Long Island Sound. Ledges there had wreaked havoc on hundreds of ships sailing into New York Harbor. Parris designed a structure similar to Saddleback Light: squat and spread at the base, narrowing dramatically as it rises, its sloped sides shaped to resist direct hits from the seas. He also selected the specific site, a slash of forbidding stone with a history to match its name: Execution Rock.

Some say that name was chosen because of the lethal threat the Rock posed to passing ships—scores of hulls had been ripped asunder by keen-edged ledges, with many sailors lost. Other accounts posit a much darker origin. As a measure to quell upstart revolutionists during colonial times, King George's soldiers rowed the condemned out to the site at low tide and chained them to the rocks. The tide turned and did its work on the helpless renegades.

Fate dealt the British a round of retribution. When General Washington retreated from Manhattan, one of the Royal Navy's pursuing ships ran aground on that very same rock. Every sailor and soldier perished.

With British bones mixed with those of their colonial victims, the waters lapping Execution Rock became even more cursed after the lighthouse was built in 1849. Two fires, unexplained to this day, broke out at the station and random drownings and ship disasters continued. Then, during the Roaring Twenties, a serial killer by the name of Carl Panzram terrorized the nearby mainland with home invasions, thieving, vandalizing, arson, torturing, raping, and murdering. Using a 45-caliber pistol stolen from the home of former president William H. Taft, Mr. Panzram executed at least 21 people, luring them to his yacht in New York Harbor for grizzly dances of death, weighting their corpses with rocks, and hefting the bundles overboard a hundred yards from Execution Rock. Lighthouse beams lit the finales of his ghoulish games.

Even with its morbid history, in 2007 Execution Rock Lighthouse was renovated and became a thriving bed-and-breakfast, just like the Keeper's House Inn here on Isle au Haut. If ever a lighthouse was mired in blood and darkness, Execution Rock surely was.

Fortunately, others came into being that projected more positive light.

The Statue Of Liberty

It's probably the most recognized monument in the world. It evokes liberty and freedom more eloquently than any speech ever written. It reaches 305 feet high, 100 feet higher than any other American lighthouse. In 1886 it came to tower over the banks and counting houses, the centers of commerce, the mansions, museums, and arching bridges that formed the face of New York City. It's the Statue of Liberty, America's most-loved structure. It was never intended to be a lighthouse, but political expediency at the time came to override the requirements of shipping and engineering experts. The history of its erection in New York Harbor is almost as complex as the struggle for liberty itself.

The key actor throughout this drama was the statue's creator, an accomplished French sculptor/engineer and inexhaustible promoter, Frederic Auguste Bartholdi. Originally he hoped to build a version of *Liberty* in Egypt on the banks of the Nile River, but the project fell through due to his inability to consummate a deal with the Arabs. In 1871 his attention turned to America. He hoped we would see the benefits of scooping up his creation, what with our lofty republican ideals and the recent erasure of slavery. And the nation had held together even through civil war. Weren't these reasons aplenty for the United States to host this symbol of freedom?

In 1874, to build support for his brainchild, Bartholdi founded the Franco-American Union, a populist movement on both sides of the Atlantic. The Union raised over a million francs from its European supporters. In the U.S. there was enough support for the monument that Bartholdi was able to win a patent for his design. This enabled him to manufacture scores of miniature statues, which were sold to raise funds to launch the enterprise.

Bartholdi campaigned tirelessly across the nation. From coast to coast, numerous expositions showcased elements of his grand vision. Working together with the prominent French engineer, Alexandre Gustave Eiffel, who later designed the Eiffel Tower, they erected models of *Liberty* in Paris and other cities. In this way, Eiffel was able to demonstrate his revolutionary techniques for elaborate steel understructures that supported the plates of the statue's outer layers.

Although the statue was a gift from the people of France to their American cousins, the two governments added support by partially funding the project. President Ulysses Grant offered federally owned Bedlow Island (later renamed Liberty Island) as a location for the statue. The subsequent president, politically savvy Grover Cleveland, recognized how popular the statue was becoming. He demanded it be modified to serve as a lighthouse.

Bartholdi and Eiffel embraced the new idea: Wouldn't the lighthouse theme add frosting to the fund-raising cake? They quickly modified *Liberty*'s hollow torch to accommodate electric lighting. She would be the first American lighthouse to burn without bonfires, whale oil, or kerosene.

An American architect, Richard Morris Hunt, was enlisted to design the pedestal, a mammoth base providing almost half the monument's height. Hunt was no novice: he had also designed the façade and Grand Hall of the Metropolitan Museum of Art.

Meanwhile Bartholdi traveled the nation, doing his best to promote the project. He and his supporters appealed to the usual expected donors: the country's millionaires. The results were paltry. Apparently, the wealthy felt little call to support a monument to universal liberty or a welcoming symbol for the millions of immigrants flowing in at that time. The reception center on Ellis Island was adjacent to Liberty Island, and the statue was the first thing these new arrivals saw. What a glorious greeting it was: "Libertas," named for the Roman goddess of freedom, officially titled, "Liberty Enlightening the World," her torch held high to guide the newcomers in, her tablet inscribed with July 4, 1776, the chains of bondage around her feet broken. On the eve of the America's Progressive Era, these were unsettling images for those who were profiting from the labor of the unorganized and powerless.

Without the patronage of the wealthy, could the dream materialize?

The French had agreed to provide the statue, and the Americans to finance and construct the infrastructure, including the massive pedestal. In 1883, an auction was held in New York as one way to raise funds. For that occasion, American poet Emma Lazarus penned a moving piece, "New Colossus," contrasting the significance of *Liberty* to the giant statue of the sun-god Helios, erected in the harbor of Rhodes by the ancient Greeks during the third century BC to memorialize their military victory over the ruler of Cyprus.

Not like the brazen giant of Greek fame,

With conquering limbs astride from land to land;

Here at our sea-washed, sunset gates shall stand

A mighty woman with a torch, whose flame

Is the imprisoned lightning, and her name

Mother of Exiles. From her beacon-hand

Glows world-wide welcome; her mild eyes command

The air-bridged harbor that twin cities frame.
"Keep, ancient lands, your storied pomp!" cries she
With silent lips. "Give me your tired, your poor,
Your huddled masses yearning to breathe free,
The wretched refuse of your teeming shore.
Send these, the homeless, tempest-tost to me,
I lift my lamp beside the golden door!"

Lazarus's words popularized the meaning of the Statue of Liberty: it would herald a haven for immigrants. And although the poem received an appreciative welcome, it wasn't until 1903 that the words were cast in bronze and fixed to the reception area inside the pedestal. But even with the wide-reaching appeal of Lazarus's poem and the booming sales of Bartholdi's miniature statues, there remained a huge financial gap before the pedestal could be constructed.

Joseph Pulitzer stepped forward, editor of *The New York World*, one of the more idealistic publishers of the day. His editorials began to appear in the pages of the newspaper, promoting the statue as a symbol of the soul of the nation. Donations began to trickle in. Soon the trickle became a flood. From schoolchildren, new emigrants, working and poor from across the nation, the money kept arriving. Hundreds of thousands of contributions were received, many for a dollar or less. Although Bartholdi raised enough to finish the pedestal, it fell short of the funds needed to satisfy his highest expectations; he had wanted the statue to be plated with gold leaf. Thomas Edison was disappointed, too; he had offered to rig the statue so she could talk, broadcasting patriotic speeches across lower Manhattan. Without those fancy accoutrements, the monument was completed on schedule.

The day of the unveiling occurred on November 1, 1886. Cannons blasted. Extravagant fireworks filled the sky. There were dignitaries aplenty. The gleaming copper goddess dominated the cityscape, her fiery torch promising freedom and liberty for all. But any observant celebrant present that day must have noticed that among the dignitaries invited, there were no women. With the exception of Bartholdi's French wife, only men occupied the seats on the dais, gave the speeches, and garnered the plaudits, credit, and fame.

Suffragettes rebelled. Crowded into launches, they plied the waters surrounding the celebration with banners and chants demanding recognition, but the rumble of cannon fire and pompous speeches drowned their voices. Thirty-three more years would pass before the suffragettes' central mission would be accomplished: In 1919 the Nineteenth Amendment to the Constitution was ratified, giving full suffrage to American women.

Another distraction also affected the statue's inauguration; the event had been marred with embarrassing failures in the lighting of the torch and the overall illumination of the monument. President Grover Cleveland wanted that corrected. He knew he could rely on the efficiency of the country's experienced lighthouse professionals to get the job done right. Two weeks after the unveiling, he ordered that The Statue of Liberty be placed under the administration of the U.S. Lighthouse Board, as an official aid to navigation, complete with agency lighthouse keepers, and provisioned and financially managed by the Lighthouse Board. There was a problem, however: The Board hated the idea.

A lighthouse was serious business, and the Board had standards. Establishing a new lighthouse was always the culmination of a long planning process. The siting, the specifications, the unique characteristics of each tower had to be painstakingly calculated. The idea that some layperson, some politician, some *president* could simply up and declare a particular property be a registered aid to navigation! Blasphemy, they said. For instance, the fact that *Liberty's* torch was held 305 feet above sea level, the highest in the nation, in no way met the requirements of the Board; the height of every lighthouse is unique, based on the topography of the site, the dominant fog and cloud conditions, the surrounding environment, and the specific reason for the site. (Channel marker? Navigation aid? Marking a dangerous ledge?) The idea that a president could declare this monument to be a Registered Aid to Navigation may have been appealing to the public, but it was an insult to lighthouse science and tradition. However, Cleveland was a popular president, so it was done.

The man to become *Liberty*'s first lightkeeper was a professional mechanic and electrician by the name of Albert Littlefield. He and his wife lived adjacent to the statue in a separate building, which also housed Littlefield's assistant keepers and their families. The first order of business for these new caretakers was to get the lights working reliably. At that time all things electric were a grand experiment. A fledgling power company had installed the original system. In its place, Littlefield installed a series of nine electric arc lights in the torch, their wattage generated on site by a gasoline generator. The exterior spotlights were refitted as well, so Liberty's face was highlighted artistically, not cast with shadows the way she had been at the time of her inauguration. In spite of the professional operations afforded by the Lighthouse Board, the Statue was run more like a tourist attraction than a typical lighthouse station. The climb to the torch was difficult, requiring the stream of visitors to have the abilities of mountain goats and contortionists. More than one ankle was turned, more than a few legs broken. Additionally, the long arm of the statue leaked profusely. Water and ice penetrated the leaded copper windows in the torch, and oxidation ate away at the steel infrastructure, causing safety concerns. In 1916, the arm and torch were permanently closed to the public.

Littlefield and his keepers served reliably until 1901 when the War Board took control of the memorial, and the keepers were relieved of their duty. No longer would "Liberty Enlightening the World" officially be an Aid to Navigation. In 1932, under Roosevelt's New Deal, responsibility for the Statue of Liberty was transferred to the freshly-created National Park Service, where it has remained to the present. The original torch that had served as a lighthouse was removed altogether and replaced in 1986 with a solid, sculpted watertight flame. Bartholdi would have been happy: the flame is finished in gold leaf.

Regardless of our modern concepts about the message of the Statue of Liberty, her creators and sponsors never intended her to be a welcoming symbol for immigrants. At the time, the 1880s, the central dynamic the French and Americans shared was an appreciation for their revolutionary heritages: the American Revolution for independence (which was supported by the French) and the French Revolution against the monarchy (heavily inspired by the American experience). These were both essentially republican revolutions, movements against the constraints that bound their peoples to privileged property and economic systems controlled by the wealthy. Individual freedom, universal suffrage, liberty, *justice for all* were not frequent words in the parlance of the time, in spite of Patrick Henry's famous century-old declaration, "Give me liberty or give me death." Mr. Henry may have been sincere, but he wasn't really talking about the women of the colonies, the landless, the slaves, and the impoverished and oppressed of the world, nor, a hundred years later, were Bartholdi and his fellow entrepreneurs, nor the well-intentioned membership of the Franco-American Union.

Certainly, Bartholdi's colossal sculpture deserves recognition as an exquisite piece of art, beautiful and inspirational, and Emma Lazarus's poem put into verse evocative moving propositions. The good deeds of Pulitzer, the contributions of a chain of presidents, the donations that poured in: These were all manifestations of the appeal of "Liberty Enlightening the World."

But what would the results of this "enlightening" be? The towering statue greeted hundreds of thousands of immigrants passing through the Verrazano Straits. They watched speechless, overwhelmed by the intangible power of hope and imagination, perhaps sensing that life can be good for us, *all* of us. Over the passing decades, the millions of tourists that visit Liberty Island or fly over in helicopters or international flights or cruise through her shadow on ferries or stand on the shores of lower Manhattan gaping—they too feel the buzzing, tingling, all-encompassing charge of hope and goodwill that surges through their bodies. Go there yourself, if you haven't already, and you too will know what I mean. It's no wonder that *Liberty* served as a lighthouse.

* * * *

Throughout the nineteenth century, across the nation and around the world, lighthouses sprouted up to match the growth of travel and commerce. As the country's economy flourished, development moved into the heartland of the country, but population still centered on proximity to water. Then, with the advent of steam-powered boats and more sophisticated navigation tools, the emphasis on lighthouses began to lessen and the pace of their construction slowed.

By the turn of the century, spider webs of roads, railways, and trolley lines connected every street corner in America to the national transportation system. Railroad spurs were laid to factories and shipping ports. Railway stations became the hub of most every American town. Thirty years later, thousands of miles of concrete topped the old dirt roads that served the burgeoning nation, with the "horseless carriage" the preferred mode of family transportation. At Kittyhawk, North Carolina, the Wright brothers toyed with flying machines. By 1914, the diesel engine had been developed to the point that it propelled both U.S. and German submarines.

Overnight, it seemed, transportation had become so diversified that lighthouses, while still an integral link in the country's transportation system, no longer held the singular importance they had when everything moved by water. As the nineteenth century drew to a close, only a handful more would be built. The last complete family lighthouse station constructed in Maine would be on Isle au Haut.

Chapter 4

A Boat Ride with Harold

In order to understand why a lighthouse station was established on Isle au Haut, let's take a look at the surrounding area, and review its local history. There's no better way to do this than to take a boat ride. And no one is a better guide than Harold Van Doren, our maritime legacy buff and president of the Isle au Haut Historical Society. Strap on your PFD (personal flotation device) and bring along a sandwich if you like, while I recount my own recent sea tour with Harold.

* * * *

It took Harold all summer to get his boat in the water.

First it was the motor: it wouldn't go. He had to replace the starter, the plugs, this and that and the other thing. It was the end of August by the time we got the boat down to the Town Landing and eased her down the ramp into the water, whereupon Harold discovered his mooring was missing and had to procure another. Several more months went by.

Early in October we finally got the telephone call.

"How's about we take a voyage?" said Harold, his cheery voice cajoling. "Ruthie's putting together a snack. We can cruise around the island; seas are flat, nary a breeze out there, perfect time to picnic on Eastern Ear."

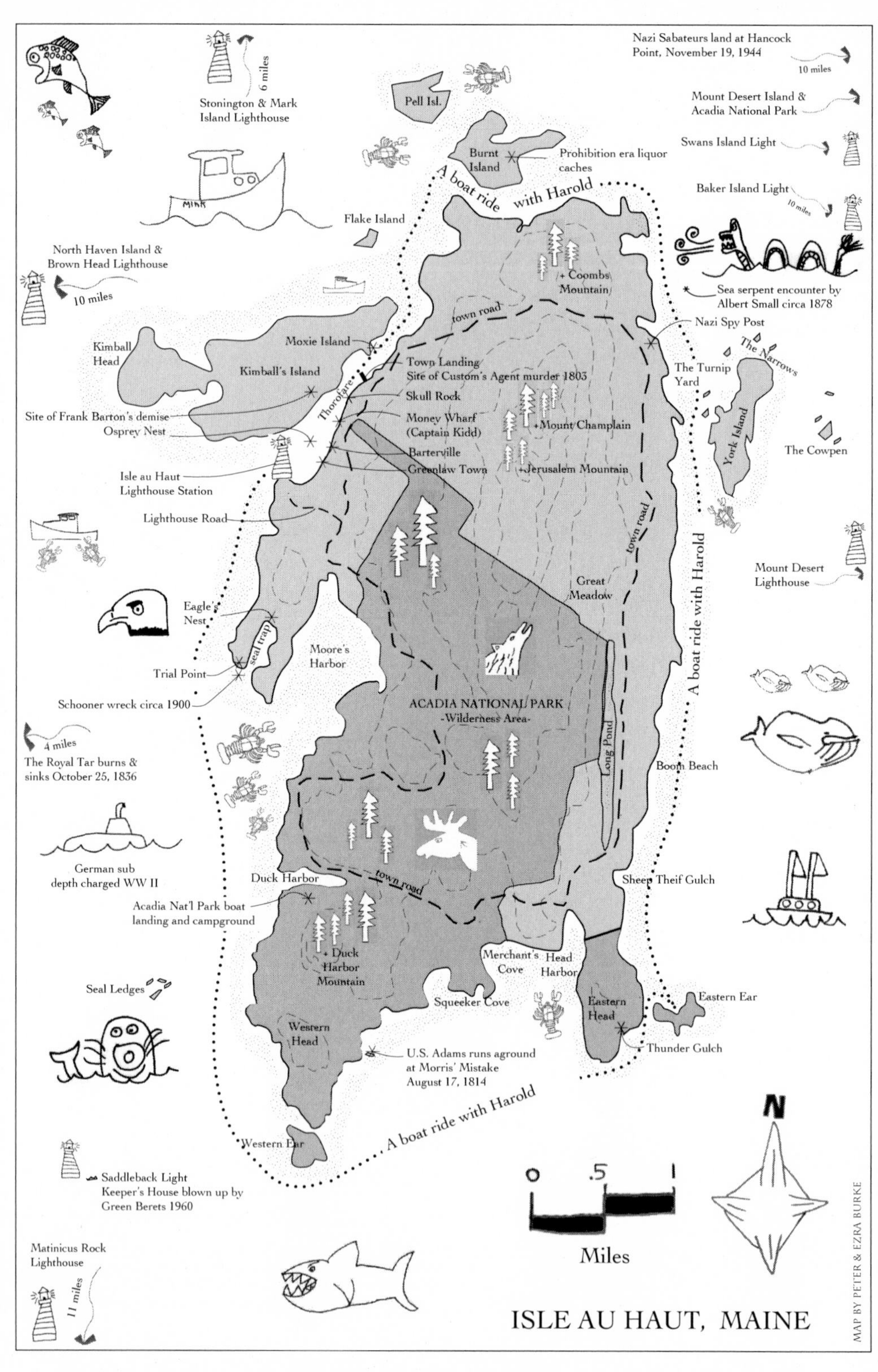

Circumnavigating the Island with Harold. Cartography by Peter Burke, Landscape Architect. Artwork by Ezra Burke.

"Of course," said Judi. "I've got some brownies here. I'll bring them along."

"Meet at the landing in an hour?" said Harold.

"We'll be there," said Judi.

Harold's boat *looks* fast. It's streamlined and shiny, has a big engine hunkered on the transom, and lots of doodads and gadgets. But he rarely runs it more than half throttle. He says the engine's a little "iffy." And besides, he explains, the hull design is queer for these waters, that the something-or-other doesn't match the whatchamacallit. So, actually, a cruise with Harold is pretty slow, which is fine with Judi and me. She doesn't like to go fast, and I enjoy a slower pace, too, so Harold and I can jabber about the passing sights.

We cast off from the Town Landing and turned into the coming tide, striking a course toward the lighthouse. To our starboard side, Skull Rock squatted on the shore, an erratic granite boulder that hinted at foreboding possibilities for mariners heading out. Just beyond Skull Rock, we saw the remnants of an old stone wharf, a crude assemblage of boulders that had once supported a landing spot for early fishing boats.

"That's Money Point," said Harold, nodding at the abandoned stone bank. "Some say Captain Kidd once bottomed out *Adventure Galley* there to let the tide run out so his crew could patch her bottom."

"Yep, John Blaisdell told me about that," I responded. "He said there are tales of scallop draggers plowing up gold coins right there. Maybe more buried somewhere near."

"Well, I suppose every coastal town in Maine has a similar story—Captain Kidd and buried treasure. Still, I guess the old scoundrel did haunt these parts," said Harold.

That jibed nicely with other stories I'd heard. Captain William Kidd was born in Scotland in 1645, and spent his early life at sea employed by the Royal Navy. England was at war with France back then, but it wasn't only the king's warships that boasted heavy firepower: many armed ships of the day were mercenary craft, privateers commissioned to capture the enemy's merchant craft and bring home the loot, the privateers retaining a percentage, of course, to finance the ship and crew. Captain

Kidd's first capture was a beauty: the frigate *Blessed Mary*.

With a bountiful victory behind him, Kidd established himself in the New York Colony where he hobnobbed with the local bluebloods and English aristocracy, found a wealthy widow to marry, and hatched plans for a glorious career. Privateering was a very respectable vocation back then—as long as you worked for the *right* side. Kidd's closest ally was the Lord of Bellomont, a successful entrepreneur who soon rose to be appointed governor of the New York Colony. Kidd sailed back to England where he cultivated additional friends among the ruling elite, particularly among the wealthy investor class. The results: Kidd was outfitted with a 34-gun privateer christened *Adventure Galley*, a crew of 150, and a royal commission to roam the seas in search of enemy treasure. Even as he departed England, Captain Kidd proved controversial. On the way out of the Port of London, the *Adventure Galley* sailed past the king's ships protecting the entrance, whereupon his crew lined the gunnels and "mooned" the royal sailors.

Things didn't go smoothly after that. His captures were few. He had leadership difficulties. On several occasions, large cliques of his crew turned against him. In one case an insubordinate gunner confronted him. Kidd responded by seizing an iron bucket and striking the fellow dead.

Months went by without a capture. Frantic to harvest bounties—and often at the behest of a desperate crew on the verge of mutiny—Kidd made some bad choices for targets, plundering ships whose investors were English. Upsetting his financial backers, he soon was labeled a traitor, a pirate, and a wanted man. He sought to clear his name in New York where he thought he maintained considerable backing, even revealing the location of gold and silver plunder he had buried, in hopes of wriggling his way free. This gave credence to the possibility that there may have been other buried caches. Afraid of the repercussions of standing behind a reputed pirate, even Bellomont turned against him. The British arrested Kidd in 1700 and held him in prison under conditions so severe he went half loony.

The following year Kidd was shipped to England in chains. His trial became a sensation: the traitor pirate versus the moneyed classes and the royal crown. He was found guilty of murder and treason. The sentence? He was to be hauled off to Execution Dock and hung by the neck until dead. Unfortunately, the first attempt failed when the rope broke, requiring a second effort. For the following three years his moldering corpse dangled in an iron cage over the harbor entrance, a warning to any privateer who went against the system.

Harold, Ruthie, Judi, and I eased past Money Point and out of the harbor and cruised past the parsonage, past the spindle where in the spring the osprey scolds us from her nest, past Billy and Bernie's bungalow (she ambled out on the deck to wave), and past the cluster of Greenlaw homes. At the lighthouse, Harold twisted the wheel to port, and we slid along virgin shore, barren of rooftops and power lines.

About a mile down the coast, Harold moved offshore, coursing a wide berth around the Trial Point Ledges. Here lay the secret entrance to Seal Trap, a mysterious pocket of calm water, where, if you were a pirate or contraband runner or latter day "coyote," you could hide from the spyglasses of the old Revenue Service, The U.S. Coast Guard, the State Marine Patrol, the County Sheriff, and the Immigration Control Enforcers. A jagged row of tidal ledges on each side of the passage guards the narrow mouth to the hideout, like a set of shark jaws, ready to tear apart the underbelly of any encroaching boat. It gives me the willies every time I pass here, even when giving wide berth as Harold does (he's a very cautious sailor).

"Scary place to navigate," I say.

"Yep," says Harold. "More than one old sailing ship ran aground here, back before the lighthouse was built." He took a hard look at the chart between us, just to make sure we weren't overlooking some nearby hidden ledge.

I remembered stories of coastal villages around the world, where opportunistic locals on the watch for easy pickings would build fires along the shores on stormy nights to misdirect passing ships. They would run aground and be plundered.

I asked Harold, "What would have happened back then, Bud, if a ship had foundered here? Knowing the island, I expect everyone would have come running to the rescue?"

Harold gazed over at the ledges. "Back then folks on these islands lived pretty close to the bone. Had to take whatever they could: a crate of tobacco, a barrel of rum. What would you do, matey, if you didn't have a thing?"

"Gulp!" I said.

Harold's face turned gloomy. "According to George Wasson (historian, writer, artist, sailor), there's a big black spot in the Island's history regarding shipwrecks; many happened right here—and wreckers rushed in like flies on a corpse."

But not all ship disasters resulted in looting. Jim Greenlaw tells of an incident back at the turn of the century (before the lighthouse was built) when, during a raging winter storm, a fishing schooner ran up here on the Trial Point ledges. As the pitching ship shook them into the sea, the four fishermen aboard grabbed for any handy flotation. One fellow hung on to a wood crate that housed a hand-cranked fog signal, enough buoyant matter to keep him afloat until he could flail his way to shore. The others, luckily, also made it. Sopping wet, the four dazed seamen made their way through snow banks and blasts of arctic air to the Robinson Homestead, where young Lillian Hamilton Robinson was home alone baking biscuits and knitting. By then the poor fellows were sheathed in ice, barely able to speak, jaws chattering, fingers numb with frostbite. She hustled them inside, and for two weeks she nursed them back to health, feeding them and keeping them warm and comfortable. Finally able to travel, the four arranged passage back to the mainland on a lobster smack bound for Castine. Having rescued nothing during the shipwreck, they had neither coins nor goods to offer in exchange for the food, lodging, and care Miss Lillian had so generously provided. Before they left, one fellow hiked back to Trial Point to find the crated fog signal that had saved his life. He gratefully presented it to Lillian.

Today, her grandson, Jim Greenlaw, still protects that artifact in his modern-day house built on the cove a few hundred yards from where his grandmother's farmhouse once stood. The foghorn remains in perfect working order, perched high on a shelf over a bay window that looks across Robinson Cove, past the pasture and the burned-down houses' tumbled foundation stones, the icy water and jagged shore, where now the lighthouse rises above the treetops.

I wondered how many ships and lives the lighthouse has saved since that almost fatal wreck on the Trial Point Ledges.

* * * *

"Right over there," barked Harold, over the throb of the engine, breaking into my reverie. "That's where the *Royal Tar* went down."

Harold had the boat parallel to the Western Ear, the southernmost tip of the island. Off to our starboard side, beyond the ghostly silhouette of Saddleback Lighthouse, the Fox Islands stood gray against the marbled sky. Between here and there the sea spreads out, deep and wide and all-encompassing. Somewhere below us rests the wreck of that unfortunate ship.

It happened October 25, 1836. She'd hauled anchor four days before in Brunswick, Nova Scotia, and fought ugly weather all the way down on her voyage to Boston. The night before she had sheltered in the Fox Islands Thorofare, just across the bay from Isle au Haut. The *Royal Tar* was a side-wheel paddle steamer with schooner rigging. She carried her regular crew of twenty-one seamen. Her cargo, however, on this particular outing, was anything but regular: a fully outfitted circus, complete with elephants, horses, various other critters, performers, circus wagons, and a gaggle of performers' children—seventy-plus passengers in all. To accommodate the extra cargo, two of the four lifeboats had been left behind, a profound mistake on this day, given the tumbling seas and the howling blow.

To make matters worse, a lazy engineer had failed to keep watch over the boilers. The water level had dropped, and the boilers overheated. Beneath the animal cages, the ship's interior burst into flame. Panic ensued as the fire spread rapidly, fanned by the incessant wind and the wealth of combustible provisions. Captain Thomas Reed ordered pumps into action, but their futile stream couldn't keep pace with the spreading inferno. Sixteen soulless seamen lowered one lifeboat and fled off toward Isle au Haut. Captain Reed rose to the occasion and maintained control over those remaining. Somehow, he managed to get the other lifeboat filled and lowered. With the *Royal Tar* now consumed in flames, the remaining passengers began to leap into the water, screaming and thrashing. Seeing the smoke and flames, the U.S. Revenue cutter, *Veto*, made her way to the site and was able to rescue the few still aboard, including Captain Reed. This second lifeboat also made it to Isle au Haut. There were thirty who drowned, including ten children. All the animals perished, too, except for a pair of exhausted horses that clambered ashore on Vinalhaven.

In the panic to evacuate, no thought had been given to saving the ship's safe: the bill of lading listed many gold and silver coins. The abandoned and burning *Royal Tar* drifted easterly across the bay toward Isle au Haut with no one there to witness the spot where she finally went down. The safe was never recovered. Unlike the uncertain treasures that Captain Kidd may have buried, the booty of the Royal Tar was fully documented, investigated, recorded in court documents and local newspapers. *That sunken safe full of treasure is still somewhere nearby, mired in seaweed and muck, maybe right below us here as Harold's boat chugs by.*

To the south, we catch a hazy glimpse of distant Matinicus Rock Lighthouse, grasping onto a knob of rock untouched by any sign of plant life. Here, in January 1856, during a freakish northeast storm, a seventeen-year-old girl named Abby Burgess became a hero. She was assistant keeper to her dad, Samuel Burgess, who had rowed to Rockland to replenish the station's stores. Abby's brother was somewhere off on the horizon hauling lobster traps. Alone with her invalid mother and two younger sisters, she felt the winds mount in the unexpected assault. The four females retreated into the granite tower. In no time, monster waves rose up and swept the Rock bare of everything not bolted down. Her father and brother were forced to remain in safe harbors, so Abby labored alone for three long weeks to keep the lighthouse shining.

* * * *

Harold maneuvered the boat around the tip of Western Ear and cut across the mouth of Head Harbor, aiming for the Island's Eastern Ear. Abreast the narrow passageway between Eastern Ear and Isle au Haut, the seas slopped over a massive shield of time-smoothed granite.

"Morris's Mistake," he said.

Harold gestured with a tilt of his head at the watery threat. He clutched the wheel with both hands, his fingers tightening, as if the mere sight of that rock had tripled his vigilance.

"So, that's the infamous ledge," I said. I'd often heard of it but never knew just where it was.

"Yep. Named after the unfortunate Charles Morris, captain of the *USS Adams*, launched in 1799 as a part of John Quincy Adams's plan to dramatically expand the navy."

"Why 'unfortunate'?" I asked.

"Started out with a bang, he did," said Harold. "Morris had become a naval hero early in the War of 1812. After recovering from a near-fatal saber wound, he was given command of *Adams*. Chasing and hitting British ships—that was his mission."

Harold paused, as if there was a shift in his sentiments regarding the naval officer.

"So," I prodded, "what happened then?"

"He chased the Brits around, captured a few small ships, but never scored big. In 1814, he got his orders to return to Washington. The *Adams* needed repairs. On August 17th he was working his way down the east coast during a heavy storm with a few British prisoners on board. Lost in pea-soup fog and a hundred miles off course, he skirted the edge of Isle au Haut and ran aground on that ledge."

"Oops!" I said.

"Hit wicked hard. Lifted the bow right outta the water and fractured her bottom."

"Now that's what you call an aptly named landmark!"

Harold nodded. "Ayuh," he said. "But despite the nasty weather, Morris was somehow savvy enough to free the ship on the rising tide."

"What about the prisoners?" I asked.

"He turned them over to some local fishermen—the Knowlton

brothers—who escorted them across the bay to the Castine jail. Morris tried to sail on to Boston, but the *Adams* was leaking so badly she barely managed to limp up the Penobscot River toward Hampden."

"So, he got away?" I asked.

"Not exactly," said Harold. "British ships chased her up there, burned her to the waterline. Not only that, but the crew and the local militia fellows fled in the face of the swarm of landing British soldiers."

* * * *

After running through the Gut, on the lee side of Eastern Ear, Harold circled a few times at slow throttle, testing with a small anchor for a piece of decent holding ground. With two hooks secure in the bottom (I told you Harold was a cautious sailor), we got to shore in the skiff and had a delightful lunch. I snoozed a bit while the three of them chatted. Back on board, Harold eased us back toward Isle au Haut.

We crept along the Turnip Yard, a stretch of coast riddled with hidden ledges, a place where more than one lobsterman has ripped apart a keel. Some say back in the late 1880s this stretch of sea had even nastier threats.

"Sea serpents," said Harold. "They were popping up all around the globe back then—here as well. Albert Small was hauling from a dory right about here; one came up right beside him—six feet of the critter right out of the water, its snaky head staring at him as if it were gonna ask for directions—that's the way Albert's son, Leon described it to me."

"You're kidding," I said.

"Day-yah. Said his dad turned the boat toward it and the thing slithered off through the Narrows."

I asked if people believed him.

"Hard to deny it," said Harold.

He explained how sightings of sea serpents were common between 1840 and the end of the century. The British Navy authenticated several, one in 1848, another as recently as 1980. In the

Chesapeake Bay, many sightings were chronicled, and in New England, too. Interestingly, unlike yeti sightings and UFOs, the descriptions of sea serpents were always the same, from Japan to Gloucester: serpentine creatures, as long as a hundred feet, as big across as a Swampscott dory, with unblinking python eyes.

"The one Albert Small bumped up against right here in the Turnip Yard, maybe wasn't as big as *that*, but it sure fitted the classic description."

I looked alongside Harold's boat, just to make sure we weren't being stalked.

"Did they...bite?" I asked.

"No actual attacks on ships or swallowing of scuba divers, at least not according to any credible sources," Harold said.

We crept north, now sighting a few rooflines of summer homes that dot the east side, facing across the open ocean. *If the earth were flat as a map and you had a telescope, from here you could see Nova Scotia, Spain and Portugal, the Rock of Gibraltar, Morocco, Guinea and Liberia, Gabon and Angola all the way to South Africa, a distant wedge of the Antarctic, a bit of Brazil, the coast of Venezuela, with the sweep of Cuba filling out your field of vision.*

To our right, we slipped past the ledges of "Holbrook's Battery." Harold says the only Holbrook he knows of that ever ranged these parts had been Elmer Holbrook, the first keeper of the Isle au Haut Lighthouse Station, so it's anyone's guess, Harold said, how this hunk of rock might have picked up that name prior to Elmer's arrival. I later combed through the albums of remembrances housed in the Revere Memorial Library and found mention of one Elisha Holbrook who arrived here early in the 1800s and built a log cabin on the east side of the island, probably just ashore of Holbrook's Battery.

York Island, Burnt Island, we passed them all, a veritable obstacle course of immovable rock, the ribs of the earth jutting through the waters, a hard-ass reminder of who's really in charge here. As we rounded the north end of the island and passed by Point Lookout nearing the end of our journey, I couldn't help but review our voyage with Harold, *thinking about the centuries of shipwrecks, lost lives, and crippled bodies that lay strewn in the wake of history. How odd, it seemed, that during all that time, while life-saving stations and lighthouses were being constructed by the hundreds all around the nation's rim, at the turn of the century, on Isle au Haut not even a flashing light had ever been erected.*

I decided to find out why.

Chapter 5

A Lighthouse for Isle au Haut

Every lighthouse in America was created by an act of Congress. That meant lots of economic and political finagling, and long delays. Petitions were common, of course, and studies had to be done, the pluses and minuses listed. Meanwhile, arm twisting, payoffs, and heated competition raged between thousands of ports and dangerous spots that all cried out for attention. In spite of the slow, messy process, one by one, our nation's lighthouses were fought for and built—all twelve hundred of them.

There were early lighthouse stations built during colonial times. Portland Head Light was the first to go up after the formation of the new national government, back when Maine still remained a sparsely populated corner of Massachusetts. Completed in 1791, Portland Head Lighthouse was no primitive stack of stone; the proud new nation wanted to strut her maritime presence for the entire world to see. What better way to make the statement than to erect the most modern, technologically advanced lighthouse possible? Portland Head Station also demonstrated how beautiful a lighthouse could be.

Up and down the coast, America's aids to navigation became established, keeping pace with the nation's expansion. The Carolinas got tall lights to guide offshore shipping. Massachusetts and Rhode Island got

59TH CONGRESS, } SENATE. { REPORT
1st Session. } { No. 800.

FOG-SIGNAL STATION, ISLE AU HAUT HARBOR, MAINE.

FEBRUARY 8, 1906.—Ordered to be printed.

Mr. FRYE, from the Committee on Commerce, submitted the following

REPORT.

[To accompany S. 4095.]

The Committee on Commerce, to whom was referred the bill (S. 4095), to establish a light and fog-signal station at or near Isle au Haut Harbor, Maine, having considered the same, report thereon with a recommendation that it pass without amendment.

The bill has the approval of the Commerce and Labor Department, as will appear by the following extract from the annual report of the Light-House Board for 1905. The bill referred to therein passed the Senate in the Fifty-eighth Congress.

Isle au Haut Harbor, Isle au Haut Thorofare, Maine.—The following is a copy of a letter, dated February 1, 1905, from the Secretary of Commerce and Labor to the Senate Committee on Commerce:

"This Department has the honor to acknowledge the receipt of a letter, dated January 28, 1905, from your committee, inclosing a copy of Senate bill No. 6929, 'To establish a light and fog-signal station at Robinson Point, Isle au Haut Thorofare, Maine,' on which suggestions are asked touching the merits of the bill and the propriety of its passage. In reply this Department begs leave to state that the Light-House Board, to which the matter was referred, reports that in its annual report for 1903, and again in its annual report for 1904, it recommended that an appropriation of $14,400 be made to establish a light-station with a fog-bell at this place.

"The following is an extract from page 24 of the Board's annual report for 1904, in which the recommendation appeared:

"'Lower East Penobscot Bay and the water seaward for a distance of about 10 miles outside of Saddleback Ledge light-house are claimed by fishermen to be exceedingly good fishing grounds, and are frequented by fishing vessels ranging in size from 10 to 100 tons burden. Haddock are caught here from March till May; haddock, cod, and hake from May till October, and cod from October till January. The most profitable fishing is during November and December, when northeast snowstorms are apt to prevail and are often of great severity. The trawls set by fishermen, which often contain several thousand hooks, can not be suddenly left without material loss or disadvantage, and when storms or night approach the vessels often need to remain on the grounds till the last moment, when it is of the utmost importance that they be able, quickly and with certainty and safety, to make a s cure harbor. Isle au Haut Harbor is the best harbor convenient to these fishing grounds, and is so convenient in distance and has such good holding ground and is so well sheltered, especially from all the worst winds, northeasterly and easterly, from which shelter is most needed, it is highly valued and much frequented by fishermen. A light-station with a fog-bell, struck by machinery, would guide fishermen into this

harbor when they could not find it without such aid. It is estimated that these could be established here for $14,400, and the Board recommends that an appropriation of this amount be made therefor.'

"The Board's estimate of the cost of establishing this light and fog-signal station is $14,400, while the sum appropriated in the bill is only $14,000, which appears to be insufficient, as the Board states that it fails to see how the station can be established for the lesser amount, and the Board suggests, and in that suggestion this Department concurs, that when the bill is so amended as to appropriate $14,400 it be passed."

O

1906 Congressional Record announcement of the appropriation to fund construction of the Isle au Haut Fog Station. Photo restoration by William Brehm.

carefully calculated lights to guide ships into tight harbors. And Maine got super-strong lights to cling to its storm-prone shore, fortress-like structures carved into the bedrock, drilled and pegged with fat iron bars, cemented and battened down with tons and tons of granite. Even more prolific, the shores of the Great Lakes blossomed with hundreds of lighthouses. In 1821, Ohio's Lake Erie welcomed the first.

By the 1850s, west coast lighthouses had taken root in the high mountainsides that gazed over the Pacific, completing the flickering string of sentinels that rimmed the nation's edges. This was no shotgun pattern of random structures. However, each station had a carefully calculated function in the overall scheme of navigation. But they were birthed, one by one, contingent on the urgency of the situation, and on the economic/political clout of the region. At the bottom of the priority list waited an isolated hump of wooded rock awash in the Atlantic Ocean: Isle au Haut, Maine.

* * * *

When Portland Head Lighthouse was built in 1791, the Treasury Department had also founded a new Federal agency, the U.S. Lighthouse Establishment. It was charged with cobbling together a unified system for all navigational aids. Back in those days, maritime commerce was a major source of income for the new nation, and lighthouses played a key role in the operations of the Treasury Department's Revenue Service. In this initial attempt to coordinate the nation's lighthouses, the loosely knit Lighthouse Establishment did its best to tie together the helter-skelter local operations.

Over the following sixty years the burgeoning merchant trade came to demand a more tightly organized system. In 1852, as a replacement for the Lighthouse Establishment, the United States Lighthouse Board was born. It was a hard-nosed federal panel of professionals that operated in quasi-military fashion. Snappy order and efficiency came to rule our chain of lights, then growing by dozens every year.

The foremost advancement in lighthouse technology during this revolutionary era had been the Fresnel lens. Developed by Agustin-

Jean Fresnel in France in 1823, this breakthrough in optics featured an artful mechanism using concentric glass prisms to concentrate and direct a source of dispersing light (oil lamps) into a single beam, providing a much brighter signal that could be seen from a greater distance. All across Europe the new lens was rapidly implemented, with a resounding decline in maritime disasters.

Here in America, the old Lighthouse Establishment had waffled over the value of the Fresnel lens, categorizing them as foreign contraptions that cost too much. Tons of freight and hundreds of lives must have been lost because of our failure to adapt the new device. But the new U.S. Lighthouse Board immediately began installing Fresnel lenses to replace the obsolete compendium of optical devices. By the outbreak of the Civil War, the transition was complete. Unfortunately for American industry, that stubborn thirty-year delay meant that our nation's entire inventory of lenses had to be imported from France. No American manufacturer had ever developed one.

In other areas, too, the Board broke ground with advanced and novel construction for more effective lights, fog signals, and communications, administering the upgrades with ironhanded efficiency. All around the continent's rim, throughout the Great Lakes, and up and down the navigable rivers, a vast array of beacons, foghorns, markers, buoys, and supply systems came into being. Of the twelve hundred lighthouses built, no two looked alike. From humble wood-frame island stations like Pumpkin Island to sprawling brick and granite mansions like Rhode Island's Block Island Station, their presence graced the nation's shores like an arcing string of Christmas lights, marking the Maginot Line, the warning defense that defined the scary zone between dry land and Davy Jones's locker.

* * * *

There had been early appeals for a station on Isle au Haut. The first we know of occurred in 1837 when a petition was filed with Congress. But nothing much happened, regardless of numerous shipwrecks and considerable loss of life. In 1855, with the new and more aggressive Lighthouse Board in control, it was acknowledged that there was "a need for a lighthouse" on Isle au Haut. That year, however, it was deemed that nearby Spoon Island had a more urgent situation. In yet a further reversal, six months after that it was determined that Saddleback Ledge (just off Isle au Haut) was an even more suitable location. That's where the money went.

Isle au Haut incorporated in 1874, lending weight to the island's ability to speak up for its needs. By the 1860s, the town had reached its highest population ever—up to 300 year-round souls. Concurrently, the Point Lookout Association had been formed on the northern tip of the island. This was an influential core of summer folk that brought additional muscle and bargaining power. These new developments may have been influential in the march towards winning a lighthouse station.

The U.S. Lighthouse Board included a lengthy discussion of the situation on Isle au Haut in its 1902 Annual Report. It cited the "rich fishing grounds" here, and pointed out that our Thorofare was "the most convenient harbor of refuge for fishing trawlers" and noted that Robinson Point was the best possible site for a station.

Still—despite shipwrecks and loss of life, the sunken tons of cargo, the fogbound shore where townspeople waited for familiar prows to emerge through the veil—nothing ever happened.

Eventually, it was politics that made the difference. The period between 1890 and 1906 saw mounting pressure from the increasingly organized coastal communities and their commercial supporters: the New England fishing industry, the men of commerce, and the shipbuilding yards. Most of all, it was the rapidly expanding numbers of maritime voters that caused the shift. In 1904, U.S. Congressman Edwin Burleigh listed a lighthouse for Isle au Haut as a central plank of his Republican campaign. Burleigh was a popular politician who served many decades in public office, including a term as state treasurer, a term as governor, four terms as congressman, and later as U.S. senator. Credit goes to him for pushing through the legislation on February 8, 1906. President Theodore Roosevelt signed Senate Bill #4095 into law:

A Fog Signal Station
For Isle au Haut Harbor, Maine.

"Lower East Penobscot Bay and the waters seaward for a distance of about ten miles outside the Saddleback Ledge lighthouse are claimed by fishermen to be exceedingly good grounds, and are frequented by fishing vessels ranging in size from ten to one hundred tons burden. Haddock are caught here from March to May; haddock, cod and hake from May to October, and cod from October to January. The most profitable fishing is during November and December, when Northeast snowstorms are apt to prevail and are often of great severity. The trawls set by fishermen, which often contain several thousand hooks, cannot be suddenly left without great material loss or disadvantage, and when storms or night approach the vessels often need to remain on the grounds till the last moment, when it is of the utmost importance that they be able, quickly and with great certainty and safety, to make a secure harbor. Isle au Haut Harbor is the best harbor convenient in distance and has such good holding ground and is so well sheltered, especially from all the worst winds, Northeasterly and Easterly, from which shelter is needed. It is highly valued and much frequented by fishermen. A light-station with a fog bell, struck with machinery, would guide fishermen into this harbor when they could not find it without such aid. It is estimated that these could be established here by $14,000, and the Board recommends that an appropriation of this amount be made therefore."

* * * *

By the end of 1906, the US Lighthouse Board had surveyed and purchased a two-acre plot from Charles Robinson for $400. The Army Corps of Engineers built the entire lighthouse station during the following season.

The first workers who skiffed ashore dynamited a cellar hole for the keeper's house. Because the exposed shoreline had no protected area for a dock, a second crew hand-pounded holes in the ledges and

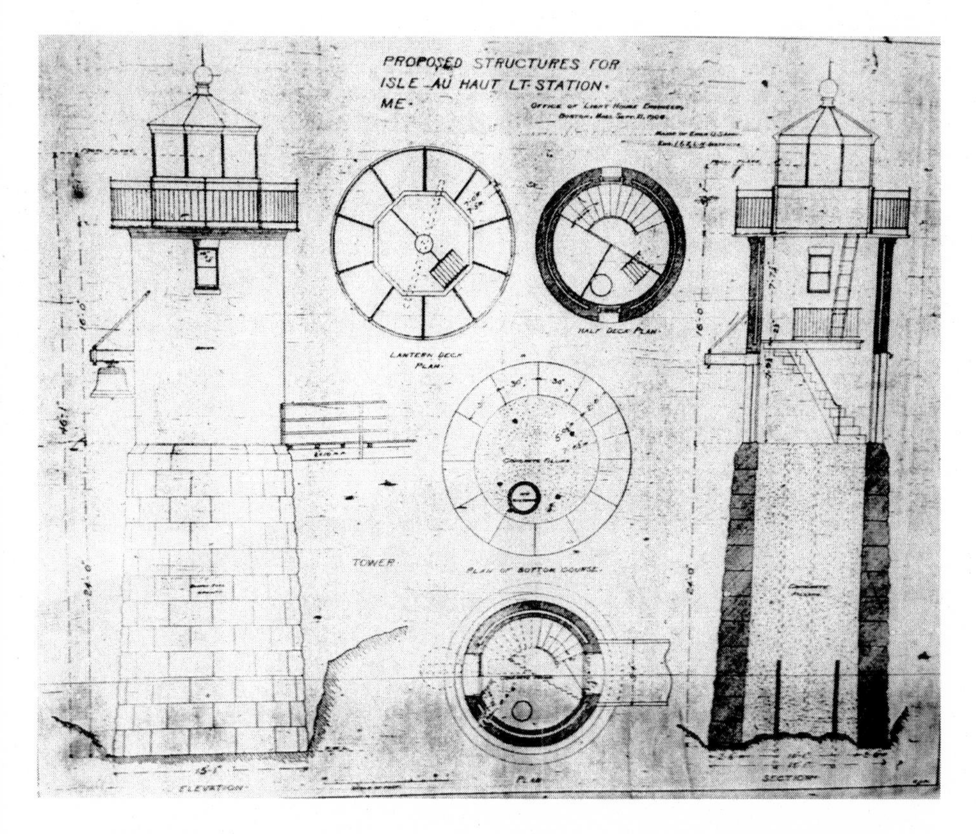

Original blue print for the construction of the Isle au Haut Lighthouse. 1906.
Photo restoration by William Brehm.

drove iron loops into the rock where the soon-to-arrive stone sloops could tie to the cliffs. These steel "staples" were of such high quality that they remain today with their original diameter, unscathed by more than a century of pounding surf and gnawing ice. The bedrock here at Robinson Point is exceedingly hard. When we came along in 1986, Bradley Burns, our well driller, managed to bang a hole only 120 feet deep. Geologist Marshall Chapman had similar frustrations drilling for geological core samples, using a mere one-inch bit. "Damn wicked hard!" Bradley had cursed, with Professor Chapman later echoing the mantra.

The granite blocks for the tower's foundation average 30 inches thick, two feet high, and 30 inches across—that's about twelve cubic feet each. At 175 pounds per cubic foot, each block weighs over a ton. Each was cut and finished with slanted ends, all calculated to fit snugly in ascending concentric circles. The stone sloops that delivered the blocks used the iron staples in the shore for tying points, and used deep-water moorings to stabilize their position. Davits aboard the ships then swung the blocks into place, each eased down into a fresh bed of mortar. Twelve courses of block gently taper upward to 24 feet above sea level. The interior of this cylindrical base was then filled with concrete and broken stone, with a smooth 20-inch diameter hole reaching from bedrock to the foundation's top, thus creating a traveling space for the soon-to-be installed fog bell weights. Topped by a flat slab where the brickwork would start, this platform served as a landing point for building materials for the rest of the station. Then, sixteen feet of brickwork was added on this base, with a spiral staircase inside to access the lantern room on top. The whole works were secured to the bedrock by a series of deeply driven iron rods leaded into the bedrock, like connective tissue, linking stone and brick to the spine of the earth.

Since the Isle au Haut Lighthouse Station was Maine's last link in its chain of sentries, it was also the most technologically advanced. Lighthouse features had developed rapidly under the U.S. Lighthouse Board. They were always ready to try something new, to improve safety, navigation, and construction quality. The Isle au Haut Lighthouse Station became an adventure in innovation.

Unique Features of the Isle au Haut Lighthouse Station

Brick lighthouses are normally built with a single wall of masonry, of varying thickness, depending on the circumstances. But here on Isle au Haut, the Army Corps of Engineers opted for an exterior wall of two wythes (courses) of brick, with a second wall inside. These two walls were separated by a one-inch air space, sort of like a vacuum thermos bottle. The theory was that this void would be an insulating space that might keep the tower a bit warmer, protect it from condensation, make it stronger, and modulate the forces of wind and sea. The interior wythe was built with five courses of brick, then one course of wood block, followed with five more courses of brick, another of wood, and so forth, up to the floor of the lantern room. Vertical lath was nailed to the wooden blocks, providing a good holding ground for a thick coat of stucco that would be painted pure white, as pristine as any parlor.

The huge fog bell had to be the most visually dominating feature of the Isle au Haut station. Starting in the 1850s, these bells became common at most lighthouse stations. Mechanical striking systems made tending them easy. In the past, the keepers had to pound on the bells with giant hammers, or yank ropes tied to the clappers. These new systems were basically giant clockworks powered by falling weights. The keeper would use a built-in winch to hoist up the weights and the thing would bang away for six hours before needing another winding. Cogs were inserted in the gears to program each fog station with a distinctive pattern of soundings, so an approaching ship would never confuse one station for another.

The Isle au Haut bell tolled once, then, twenty-nine seconds later, it sounded a double ring, then a single stroke again twenty nine seconds later, and so on. The 20-inch cylindrical cistern (24 feet deep) down through the granite base provided space for the weights to rise and fall. This became common operating equipment for many Maine lighthouse stations.

What made the Isle au Haut fog bell unique was the bell's specific location: it hung from a beam cantilevered from the side of the tower, suspended over the water. It was a beauty, forty-two inches in diameter, fifteen hundred pounds of brass, with a clear hearty ring pitched to the key of G. Other stations housed their bells in separate detached small buildings, on weight towers on the shore shaped like metronomes, safely away from the reach of the sea. But on Isle au Haut, there she hung, exposed to the leap of storm seas, flaunting her rugged beauty, ringing out peril any time fog rolled in. No other fog bell in Maine was so heroically positioned.

* * * *

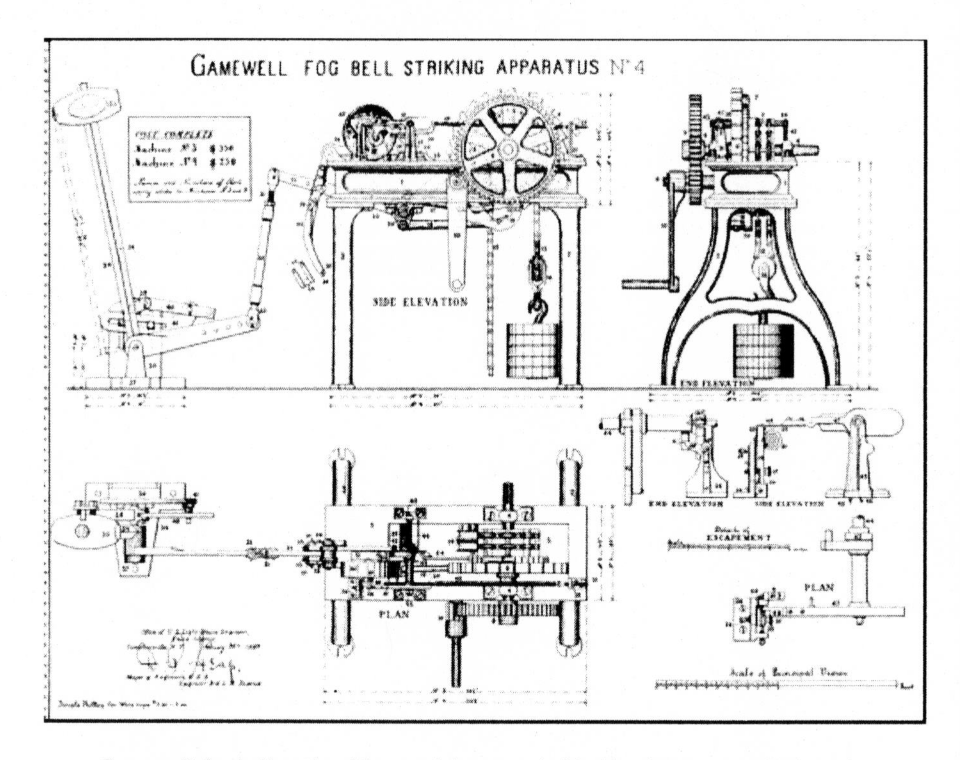

Gamewell fog bell striker. This model was probably like the one installed inside the lighthouse. Unlike the stacked 100-pound weights shown at the lower right of the machine, our weights traveled up and down in a thirty-foot well sunk down through the tower's base. Photo restoration by William Brehm.

In the construction of the keeper's house, carpenters used *balloon framing*. This method has the wall studs traveling all the way from the base plates to the rafters, no matter how many floors. On the other hand, a building that's *platform framed* means that the first floor is framed and sheathed over with the base for the next floor, and so on, rising until you get as many floors as you need. Lighthouse architects loved the idea of balloon framing—uninterrupted framing gives the building more stability in the face of powerful winds and provides more rigidity to prevent shifting and cracking of interior plaster walls and stucco exteriors.

Another advantage of this feature must have pleased the keeper's family: balloon framing provided an exquisite heating conduit. The cellar housed a gigantic coal boiler, with two-inch hot water pipes running to every nook and cranny, feeding heat to cast-iron radiators. Balloon-framing leaves the walls hollow, all the way from cellar to attic, with no interruptions to stem the flow of rising hot air from the toasty basement. So, the house not only had hot water radiators in every room, but all the exterior walls filled with warm air, a double whammy against winter's cold. In 1907, this was an unheard-of luxury for a place like Isle au Haut.

These days, however, any building inspector would scream "foul" if ever he came upon such an out-of-code travesty—a wall with no fire barriers inside is a rapid conduit for fire, providing oxygen and air flow to allow an errant flicker to explode into conflagration.

Along with heavy winter storm sash for every door and window, asbestos added yet another heat-saving advantage. All the pipes and the boiler were caked with a thick coat of it. Later on, when Judi and I bought the place, the health threat posed by asbestos had been fully proven. One of the first things I did was to rid the house of this toxic material. We had just opened the inn and had no money; it was impossible to hire a professional outfit. I decided to do it myself. I picked up a fancy respirator with goggles over at the Stonington shipyard. Coupled with an L.L. Bean rubber-hooded raincoat, a pair of fisherman's oil pants, snow boots bought at a rummage sale, and long yellow dishwashing gloves, I was ready. It's the dust that's dangerous, I was told, so suit up good and water down the insulation. It took fifteen extra-large garbage bags to hold the soggy muck, and a dozen times over with a wet/dry vacuum to suck up the remaining fuzz. Its final destination: the Hazardous Materials Landfill up in Hampden. That was thirty years ago, but I still worry every time I cough.

I didn't need to deal with the radiators: they were already gone. I heard that one of the prior keepers had taken his family off-island for some holiday celebration, leaving the station alone. Unexpectedly it froze that night, breaking all the radiators. When the keeper reported the circumstances to his District Inspector, he was told, "Get yourself a woodstove, mister, and get started chopping timber."

Jim Greenlaw has an alternative opinion; he thinks the U.S.

Lighthouse Service ripped the radiators out and sledge-hammered them back when the station was automated. With no budget to maintain the scores of vacated keeper's houses and no personnel on site, these buildings faced very real threats from vandalism, personal liability accidents, fire, sometimes even squatters. The Lighthouse Service—and the Coast Guard after it—pragmatically implemented measures to limit those complications.

* * * *

Every keeper's house in Maine is painted white. The original Isle au Haut facility was no exception. Uniformity, visibility, and tradition all demanded oodles of pure pigment. But oddly, when Judi and I first came to investigate the lighthouse in 1985, the three gable ends of the keeper's house no longer passed muster; some irascible fellow had painted them blue! While at first it appeared a tasteful choice, the robin's egg hue soon evolved into a curse; you can read all about that in a later chapter, "A Lesson from Jamie."

The 1907 construction also featured a unique water system. Because the station was erected on solid rock, there would be no well dug or drilled. Instead, the keeper's house was fitted with a massive water cistern that occupied half the cellar. A network of gutters, downspouts and flumes captured roof rainwater and fed it to storage. Later, when we bought the place from the Greenlaw family, Aubrey Greenlaw II pointed out the "scuppers," 90-degree fittings that received the rain from the downspouts and directed the flow through the sills on its way to the cistern.

Aubrey explained, "Normally the scuppers would be rotated downward, so any drizzle or condensing fog coming off the roof would rinse the shingles and leave the runoff outside, so the cistern didn't get contaminated with spruce pollen and seagull droppings."

I marveled at how vigilant these keepers had to be—it wasn't only pirates, hurricanes, and shipwrecks that demanded attention.

"Then, after a good rain had started and the system had a chance to cleanse the roof, the keeper scampered outside and 'turned up the scuppers,' connecting the downspout to the flumes that fed the cistern.

For the duration of the storm, all water was collected."

"What happened if the cistern ran dry?" I asked, wondering about the volume of water needed to cook, drink, and wash the dirty faces of a tribe of lighthouse children.

"Never a problem," said Aubrey. "With the vast supply system of the U.S. Lighthouse Service, in no time at all, there would be a tender here, equipped with pumps and hoses, and water to fill the cistern."

* * * *

Those early lighthouse keepers also existed without benefit of any utilities. Lighting came from kerosene lanterns. A hand pump in the pantry pulled cistern water up to the kitchen. *Imagine the scene with the lightkeeper's children lined up for Saturday bathing. First, the keeper's wife used the pantry pump to suck the water up from the basement. The kerosene cook stove would have been used to warm it. One by one, the keeper's kids got soaped and scrubbed. Beneath the pantry sink, a cast-iron drain ran under the foundation for trickling used water overboard.*

No toilets existed back then, but the carpenters had crafted a sweet Victorian "backhouse" behind the woodshed, charming as any Mother Goose cottage, and crisply painted. Inside: a bucket. *I envisioned the proverbial Sears Roebuck catalogue there on the bench beside it.*

The kerosene needed for cooking, warming bath water, filling lanterns, and for fueling the lighthouse beacon was dependably delivered by the supply ships of the U.S. Lighthouse Service. The kerosene was stored in a fireproof oil house located a few hundred feet away from the other buildings, where the keeper would fetch it as needed. The oil house sported a slate roof topped with a lightening rod, a double masonry wall to protect the volatile contents, and, I understand, an unofficial second bucket for any urgent family member unable to wait in the "backhouse" line.

Other attendant buildings built during that summer of 1907 included a barn and a boathouse. The barn was a small post and beam structure, sized to house workspace and storage, located in the lee of the keeper's house.

The boathouse, constructed directly on the shore, measured 16 by 30 feet, with a set of steel rails running out the seaward end, where dories could be launched and hauled using a beefy two-man winch bolted to the floor at the other end of the building. The floor was slanted, to ease launching and to allow the runoff of seawater whenever freight or boats were pulled inside. A heavy-duty wagon (about the size of a small bathtub) was provided for off-loading coal, barrels of kerosene, and all manner of supplies. Workbenches ran along each side of the boathouse; here the keeper had space and tools to tend to the maintenance needs of all the station's gear and buildings.

In 1907, no deeded access wound its way the half mile across ledgy land to the town road. This station was designed to be serviced from the ocean, and only a dory was provided for the keeper's transportation. If the keeper's family wished to visit the village or send their kids to the island school, they had to row into town…or scramble along the rugged shore.

To finish off preparations, the Lighthouse Board had delivered standard issue supplies to furnish the house, right down to a pivoting flour barrel stored beneath the kitchen counter. In the space of a single calendar year, the entire lighthouse station had been surveyed, constructed, and furnished. From fog bell to flour, everything was ready.

The only missing element: a lighthouse keeper's family.

Isle au Haut Fog Station, Circa 1908. Photo restoration by William Brehm.

Chapter 6

The Holbrook Years: 1907–1922

On the farthest fringe of Maine's Penobscot Bay, Matinicus Rock Lighthouse Station stands awash in deep, cold water, a barren spit of stone without a patch of soil to nourish any greenery. Renowned as the most cursed assignment a keeper could incur (latter-day Coast Guardsmen dubbed it "Alcatraz"), this is where Francis Elmer Holbrook landed, with his wife and four young children. They served here as keepers from 1898 through 1907. Matinicus had gained notoriety long before the Holbrooks arrived, when Abby Burgess kept the light burning here during the infamous storm of 1856.

Francis "Frank" Holbrook's family was no less heroic. He hailed from nearby Swan's Island, born and raised with a genetic understanding of things aquatic. But once stationed on Matinicus, even he eventually tired of the cramped space and the extreme isolation. Hearing of a new station being erected on nearby Isle au Haut, Frank Holbrook applied for a transfer. He was awarded the position as head keeper, with elevated pay of $540 a year.

The Holbrook family arrived on Isle au Haut in December 1907, with the finishing touches to the keeper's house still incomplete. The floors had just been varnished and remained tacky, so the Holbrooks slept on the floor of a neighbor's house the first several nights.

By Christmas Eve everything was ready. The children's modest clothes were hung in freshly painted closets. The aroma of simmering stew seeped from the virgin kitchen. As evening approached, Keeper Holbrook adjusted the wick of the lighthouse lantern, made sure the oil reservoir was full, and gave the windows a final wiping. When the sun dipped low across the bay and crept behind the Camden Hills, the first keeper at the new lighthouse lifted his eleven-year-old daughter, Esther, high enough so she could light the wick.

Esther's predilection for lighting the lantern may have been passed to her through quantum physics; those two Matinicus Rock keepers' daughters, Esther Holbrook and Abby Burgess (spaced fifty years apart) must have shared the same bed and chamber pot, way out there in the middle of the ocean. Perhaps their energy mingling in time and space produced dutiful girls of similar virtue.

In 1988 I visited Esther Holbrook Robinson in Rockland, Maine, at the senior citizen residence where she lived. She was ninety-one by then, but fastidiously neat, slim, agile, attractive. She offered me refreshments, and proudly showed me a framed photograph of the Isle au Haut Lighthouse that graced the living room wall of her tiny apartment.

"Thought I'd died and gone to heaven," she said, referring to the day she arrived from Matinicus Rock. "My lord, it was the prettiest place on earth!" She meant it, too. I could tell by the tone of her voice, the way she nodded her head, remembering.

"What was it like back then, for a little girl?" I asked.

"We all did everything together. The children, the adults, everybody. The town hall was the social center."

"Winter must have been pretty tough." I said.

"Oh, no, dear," she said. "That was the best of all, the skating on the pond, the fun at school, I wouldn't trade it for the world. Especially Christmas, that's when the Flying Santa arrived. We'd be nervous as cats awaiting. Then you'd hear the plane and he'd circle around a bit, taking measure, you know, before he dropped the package. Always something for each of us, even Mom and Daddy."

"But wasn't it cold?" I said.

"Not so bad when I was little. But later, after I married the boy next door and we set up housekeeping just up the shore, boy did we get a whopper in the winter of thirty-five. I remember clearly because that was the year after they closed the station. Sea froze all the way to Stonington. Ice so thick you could drive a truck across it, temperatures near thirty below, snowed thirty inches in February alone. I remember that—the thirty inches—that was some kind of record. I believe the low temperature was a record, too."

"Who was the boy next door?" I asked.

"William Robinson—my husband, Bill, for forty-seven years. He was the young neighbor boy. I watched him build the concrete walkways at the lighthouse station, the ones that connect all the buildings, you know. I was only a teenager then, but boy, did I have my eye on *that* one!"

I was aware how many larger tracts of land on this side of the island had been settled by the Robinson family: Alphonso, Charles, Spencer, maybe others. It was her husband's cousin, Charles, who sold the lot where the government built the lighthouse. That's why it was known as Robinson Point.

Nearing the end of our conversation, Esther smiled and paused to reflect.

"Bill died five years ago. I'm not alone though. I have my two daughters, grandkids, friends, and more, lots of kin still on Isle au Haut, all descended from my Dad, Francis Elmer Holbrook, the first keeper of the Isle au Haut Lighthouse Station."

One of Esther's daughters, Dorothy (Dot) married a local fisherman, Irville Barter from Rich's Cove. For many years they ran the local grocery store and raised a pair of sons, Wayne and Billy. Wayne became the lead ranger for the island annex to Acadia National Park and was one of the original members of the Isle au Haut Lighthouse Committee. Billy is my neighbor and the patriarch of all the Island lobstermen.

During the 1907 to 1922 tenure of Elmer Holbrook as keeper on Isle au Haut, no famous shipwrecks or deadly hurricanes hit the shores here, although during World War I German submarines were busy in deeper waters sinking U.S. merchant ships.

Perhaps the biggest event that affected Holbrook's years at the Isle au Haut station was the remarkable 1910 transformation of the federal administration of lighthouses. During America's Progressive Era (c. 1890–1920), which coincided with the administrations of Theodore Roosevelt, William Howard Taft, and Woodrow Wilson, the nation was infused with confidence, modernity, and a progressive attitude that bred massive changes in society and politics. With each step forward, there were backslides too, caused by entrenched powers and a Supreme Court that lagged far behind the changing nation.

The steely, professional military-types on the U.S. Lighthouse Board had functioned with tight discipline regarding their mission, like generals supervising a battlefield. District inspectors conducted surprise inspections of lighthouse stations. Consequences of faulty maintenance or lax record keeping could be severe. Obedience was mandatory, and there had never been much consideration of the rights of the Board's employees, in particular the nation's lighthouse keepers. By 1910, when the nation had amassed over twelve hundred lighthouses and many more auxiliary aids to navigation, the payroll list was gigantic: not just lighthouse keepers, but also logistics crews, warehousemen, technicians, administrative employees, maintenance yard workers, and tender crews. Lighthouse ships had crews as well, and there were fleets of trucks with drivers and mechanics, secretaries in office pools, employees by the thousands. The Lighthouse Board ruled them all with rigid vigor.

Imagine, for a moment, that you are a dinner guest at the Holbrook's lighthouse table. How would the mealtime chatter proceed? I'm not suggesting that lighthouse families were part of Marx's industrial proletariat, but these were literate people. Keepers were required to be able to peruse the sheaves of government rules. Education for their children was always provided, and stations with multiple keepers often had their own teachers. But with the nation tossing in a sea of change and civil unrest, there certainly had to be some interesting conversations over the mashed potatoes at the Holbrook house; the folks working under the U.S. Lighthouse Board had some of the most intransigent bosses of any government agency.

* * * *

So in 1910 the U.S. Lighthouse Board, out of sync with the momentum of the Progressive Era, finally rose to the top of the reform agenda. It was disbanded. In its place a new agency arose, The United States Lighthouse Service. This organization was more representative of the country's empathy for its people and was led by civilians rather than generals.

President William Howard Taft appointed George R. Putnam as the first commissioner of the new agency (not to be confused with another George R. Putnam, husband of Amelia Earhart and noted publisher and explorer). During Putnam's administration (1910–1935), the number of aids to navigation doubled from 12,000 to 24,000. There were sixty ships (some as long as two hundred feet) that supplied the twelve hundred lighthouse stations, and maintained the bell buoys and lighthouses. Thirty anchored lightships stood sentry in crucial places where no lighthouse tower could survive. For keepers like Frank Holbrook who manned the lights and the thousands of support staff all across the nation, Putnam's years at the helm were a blessing. He vastly improved their working conditions and benefits, health care, wages, retirement—all the populist issues that drew support during the Progressive Era.

The new U.S. Lighthouse Service was big business. In addition to all the personnel employed, the required logistics provided a bonanza of sales for the country's factories—every tool and piece of gear for maintaining the lights, all the furnishings for the keeper's quarters, dinnerware and dories, the timepieces the keepers kept in their vest pockets, the hats and uniforms, flue brushes, teaspoons, lamps, and buckets. Designed and manufactured to order, all these supplies arrived on a flotilla of tenders. If it didn't rain, a tender would arrive to fill the Holbrook's water cistern. Even though Elmer Holbrook's salary of $540 per year seemed meager, it was a pretty good deal considering that most of the family's needs were provided by the Lighthouse Service, and a year-round paycheck on Isle au Haut was something few civilians could boast.

Technological advances surged in this period as well. The electric power grid spread rapidly across the country, and by the time Elmer Holbrook moved on in 1922, more than half of the nation's lighthouses had been electrified. Other innovations revolutionized the keeper's job:

devices that switched a new light bulb into service whenever an old one failed, radio beacons that announced their positions to approaching ships, new electronics that could turn lights and fog signals on and off, monitors that detected whether or not a gaslight lighthouse burned safely. All this new gadgetry permitted the automation of some of the lighthouses, and the abandonment of many ancillary station buildings.

Pay rates went up for keepers. Elmer Holbrook must have been particularly delighted in 1918, when he read about the new Retirement Act that would provide him with a pension. At the age of 63, in 1922, he took a year off and left the island. He lived to the age of eighty, safely sheltered ashore on the mainland. His daughter, Esther, who on numerous occasions had lit the lantern and wound the fog bell winch, remained behind, already married to William Robinson and raising two daughters of her own. As you'll find out later, her descendents here are many.

With their usual efficiency, when the departing Holbrooks moved on, the Lighthouse Service didn't let our station go unattended, not even for a day.

Isle au Haut Lighthouse Station – AKA as Robinson Point Lighthouse while it was staffed with US Lighthouse Service personnel. The gentleman seen at lower right on boardwalk may have been Elmer Francis Holbrook, the lighthouse keeper. Photo restoration by William Brehm.

Chapter 7

The Smith Years: 1922–1933

From the 1930 U.S. Census, Isle au Haut, Maine:

Smith, Harry...Head Light Keeper
Smith, Minnie E...Wife
Smith, J. Elliott.. Son, Deckhand
Smith, Roland H. .... Son, Deckhand
Smith, Roger R...Son
Smith, Donald C. ....Son
Smith, Carla I. ....Daughter
Smith, Helen E..Daughter
Smith, Barbara F. ....Daughter
Smith, Murdock B. ....Son
Smith, Fred W. ....Son
Smith, Thomas M. ....Son

With his wife and ten children in tow, Harry Smith arrived on Isle au Haut in 1922 to replace Elmer Holbrook as the keeper of the lighthouse. Imagine the locals' eyebrows arching: "Who is this guy? With all the time he spends bedding his wife, how does he ever find time to trim a lantern wick?"

The record shows he did.

From 1910 until 1912, he was listed as an assistant keeper at the

Rockland Harbor Breakwater Lighthouse. In 1919, while stationed as head keeper at the hard-duty Boon Island Lighthouse Station ("The Rock") from 1916 until 1920, he and his crew rescued a crew of seven from the *Hazel C. Ritcey* after she struck hard against a ledge and sunk. Boon Island was the kind of duty station where simply being there forced one into becoming a survivalist. Before the lighthouse was built in 1710, the British ship *Nottingham Galley* ran up on The Rock. Survivors languished for weeks before resorting to cannibalism. Assignment on an intimidating island like that was the kind of duty that honed the skills and temperament of any lighthouse keeper. We can be sure the family of Harry Smith was strengthened by his assignments.

When the Smith family was transferred to Isle au Haut in 1922, one thing more than any other showed how Keeper Smith's life would be easier than the one he left on The Rock. Instead of laboring through the night sounding Boon Island's 1,200-pound fog bell by hand, on Isle au Haut he'd find the process powered by machinery.

The Smiths moved into the keeper's house when Helen was only four. Harold Van Doren recalled a chat with her when she reminisced about her first impression when she moved here.

"I'd never seen a tree before," she'd said. She had claimed a baby spruce for her own on the day she arrived and proclaimed, "This is mine—and don't nobody take it!"

Like Esther Robinson (the lighthouse keeper's daughter before her), she grew to feel at home here, and like Esther, her father often called on her during her adolescent years to light the lantern or get the fog bell tolling.

By the time her father was transferred to Two Bush Island Lighthouse in 1933, she had grown into a full-fledged young woman, and had made the acquaintance of Maurice Barter, a good-humored fellow from the other side of the island. Once again, like Esther Holbrook before her, Helen fell for an island boy. Instead of tagging along with her reassigned dad, at the age of sixteen she stayed behind and married.

She and Maurice had three daughters who grew up on Isle au Haut and went to the one-room schoolhouse. After grade school, the Smith kids daily took the mail boat down Merchant Row to the High School in Stonington. Later, Helen served for many years as the island's postmistress. Of the ten children of Harry and Minnie Smith, she had been the only one to stay, and the only one to be buried here.

In 1987, a year after Judi and I arrived on the island, one day I stopped at Helen's post office to see what waited in my box. There were no telephones on the island back then, so it wasn't just U.S. Mail we collected. Any islander was free to slip notes, reminders, and invitations, anything, into your post office box. Even a forgotten school lunch or a left-behind potluck platter could be relayed through Helen's transfer station. In later years, the mainland post office bureaucrats tightened down on Helen. A hand scribbled note on her window now stated, **"ALL ITEMS MUST HAVE STAMP."**

Helen's diminutive figure sat behind the barred grill that separated her from the public. Always cordial and helpful (they say her rosy outlook was cultivated by radio preachers), she readily passed along local gossip and prognostications on the coming weather, her jaws working ceaselessly trying to hold her dentures in place.

"Jeff, I have a request of you," she said, her chompers clacking like castanets. "We're all so pleased that you and Judi have brought the lighthouse back to life, me and Maurice, my brothers and sisters."

"It's been our pleasure," I said. "What can we do for you?"

Her thoughts burst loose, as if they'd been percolating for ages.

"We'd love to have a reunion," she said. "Not all of us are still around, you know, but me and my brothers and sisters want to have a get-together at the lighthouse, just a little tea and pastry, and time to sit and reminisce. Oh, we would *never* bring liquor or anything like that!" she assured me (I chuckled to myself, knowing Maurice wouldn't agree with *that* restriction).

"We'd be honored," I said. "Let's do it."

A few weeks later the Smith siblings arrived with spouses and children. They wobbled up the lighthouse hill, some with canes or crutches, others slightly more nimble. Helen and Maurice led the way with their daughter, Scamp. They spent the afternoon clustered in the front yard of the keeper's house, facing the tower. There were jokes aplenty, an occasional tear, and exaggerated tales. We joined in too, Judi and I, and were the recipients of many questions.

I had a question, too. During that first year at the station I had painted every inch of woodwork inside the keeper's house. Even though, by historical standards, it wasn't very old (only about eighty years at that time), it left me puzzled: the trim in the house was unscathed. I wondered, if one keeper had five children crashing around, the next with ten, how could the woodwork still be so pristine?

Of the still-surviving clan, Fred W. ("Bill"), seemed to be the spokesman. He paused, staring out to sea. The sagging skin around his eyes seemed to tighten. First he surveyed the faces around the family circle. He licked his lips, squinted just a little. Then, like a jury foreman delivering a unanimous decision, he answered.

"Well," he drawled, "Pappy…he run a *really* tight ship!"

All around, murmurs acknowledged Bill's summation.

* * * *

Although the Smith reunion at the lighthouse may have raised nostalgic memories of the twenties and thirties, we can be sure that during those times other trends and forces were at work, forging the futures of lighthouse keepers, families, fishermen, and future infantrymen all across the nation. But Maine, in particular, became the flashpoint for two major struggles: the Ku Klux Klan and the Prohibition-era rumrunners. Keeper Smith may have been only an observer for the first of these, but the second must have been a constant worry.

* * * *

In the wake of the tragic and bloody First World War, America had become isolationist. "Nativist" thinking was everywhere.

"Be on the lookout for foreign enemies and evil influences bound to destroy our nation," was the message.

"America first," rang the clarion call.

"We can't be sucked in again by rapacious outside forces."

When Mainers looked around their white Protestant state, it didn't take long for the threat to become apparent for many. From across the northern border, a tidal wave of invaders poured: French-Canadians—foreign-speaking, strikebreaking, job snatching. Catholics!

A barber from Columbia Falls named F. Eugene Farnsworth wasted no time. Joining with the broad national rebirth of the Ku Klux Klan, Farnsworth jumped on the populist bandwagon, crisscrossing the state and cultivating the xenophobic fears left in the wake of the Great War. "We have to halt this invasion," he preached.

While the Klan in the Deep South primarily targeted African-Americans, Maine mill towns and industrial areas focused their anger on the new low-wage labor force that poured down through the north woods and across the seas from "papist" Europe. The perceived aggression was so threatening that Maine became the most fertile ground outside the Deep South for Klan ideology. In 1923, Farnsworth and his followers organized thousands of new converts to parade down Main Street in the little town of Milo in the middle of the afternoon. This was the first time in the nation that the Klan displayed its forces openly in broad daylight. Photographs of the extravaganza show columns of hooded citizens flowing through the town. The Klan's Maine ranks had swelled to over 20,000, maybe even 50,000, according to some sources. The same scene was repeated in other towns. City councils and churches, lady's sewing circles, and civic service clubs all rushed to join the movement. Membership had become fashionable.

In 1924, the dominant Maine Republican Party hoped to elect a moderate for the next governor, but the Klan, now at its zenith, was able to help win the nomination for Ralph Owen Brewster, an avowed supporter of theirs. With Farnsworth fanning the flames of bigotry and fear, Brewster won the nomination and went on to win the general election. The democratic nominee, William Pattangal, had campaigned on a fiercely anti-Klan platform, but was unable to prevail against the populist tide.

Southern states reveled in the Klan's reborn power, resulting in a huge resurgence of lynchings and *de facto* segregation. After the South, Maine led the rest of the nation in Klan marches and pro-Klan tea parties and luncheons. Although there were no lynchings in Maine, anti-Catholic animosity had been present for decades, exemplified in Ellsworth, where in 1854 a Klan mob had tarred and feathered Father John Bapst, the local Catholic priest.

Just two years after the pro-Klan Brewster was elected Governor, Mainers were called to the polls for a special senatorial election. This time the Republicans nominated Arthur Gould, a liberal who actively campaigned on an anti-Klan platform. Democrats flocked to support him. He won in a landslide—every county and city voted his way. In that year of 1926 the Klan's appeal had begun to lessen as the economy boomed and Klan promises proved hollow. Besides Gould, other sane voices had gained force, led by liberal Republicans former Governor Percival Baxter and Representative Clyde Smith and his wife, Margaret Chase Smith, who had all vigorously opposed the Klan. Governor Brewster lost his bid for reelection.

In spite of Brewster's loss and the Klan's diminishing popularity, Brewster went on later to become a U.S. Senator, and a close ally to the red-baiting Joseph McCarthy during the 1950s. Interestingly, in 1949 Margaret Chase Smith—who by then had become a Congresswoman—also ascended to the U.S. Senate. During her first year in that Chamber, she became the brave voice that ultimately faced-down the hysterical and frightening accusations of Senator McCarthy.

> *"The right way is not always the popular way. Standing for the right way when it is unpopular is a true test of moral character."*
>
> —Margaret Chase Smith

Margaret Chase Smith had played a crucial role in the history of the Isle au Haut Lighthouse Station, which will be noted in the next chapter.

* * * *

Were there ever any "nativist" sympathies for the Klan on Isle au Haut? Probably, like everywhere else. But we may never know; isolated in Penobscot Bay, no KKK parades and no bonfires surrounded by hooded fanatics ever played out here. But in the 1920s, down on the Town Landing and outside the Island Store, there were cues of fishermen and knitters, jabbering about other sorts of invaders: Prohibition-era rum-runners, moonshiners, and arks awash with gin and whiskey. With no federal presence here, only one ill-suited federal fellow was ostensibly charged with stemming the flow of liquor: the island's lighthouse keeper.

In 1920, Congress had passed the Eighteenth Amendment to the Constitution, prohibiting the manufacture, transportation, and sale of intoxicating liquors. It must have been the idealism of the Progressive Era, the belief that society could be perfected, wholesome living dictated for every man and woman. Churches, The Woman's Christian Temperance Union, politicians, even the Ku Klux Klan, all had pushed and preached to create the "perfect" nation. The Volstead Act was cobbled together to put teeth into the prohibition movement. Realizing the futility of the effort, President Wilson vetoed the Act. But the very next day he was overridden by both the House and Senate. Before the Congressional Record could even be printed, Al Capone and thousands of others like him had set to scheming ways to earn a fortune by meeting the unquenchable thirst for booze.

Eliot Ness and his crew of "untouchable" agents spent years and made thousands of raids in Chicago, trying to dry out that city's labyrinth of bootleggers, saloons, and distilleries. New York City was said to have 10,000 "speakeasies." Most towns and small population centers like Isle au Haut succumbed easily to the gushing flow of alcohol. Dutifully, the Feds declared major action against the tide of smugglers who assaulted America's beaches with barrels of whiskey, gin, and rum.

While thousands of agents fought the land battle to no avail, the U.S. Coast Guard was charged with interdiction on the seas. Two new fleets of ships were designed and built to ply the rivers and coasts, waging the "Rum War" in a futile attempt to keep the public from imbibing. Interestingly, neither the Eighteenth Amendment nor the Volstead act made it illegal to consume alcohol; only its manufacture, transfer, and sale had been prohibited.

The U.S. Lighthouse Service would not be incorporated into the Coast Guard until 1939, six years after the ill-conceived Eighteenth Amendment was repealed, but lighthouse stations and their attendant services were very much a part of the government's effort to enforce prohibition while it existed. What did that mean for poor Harry Smith, Keeper of Robinson Point Lighthouse Station on Isle au Haut?

Expecting Harry Smith to stem the flow of liquor to the island was like expecting the Little Dutch Boy to use his thumb to plug Holland's leaky dikes. As the outermost ring of defense, it was the thousands of islands and small coastal harbors that were expected to repel the assault of armadas of whiskey-laden vessels. Most often, small, fast boats ran cases ashore to any remote outpost where a wharf existed. The local distribution point was often the sheltered space beneath the local Town Landing. Other favored landing spots were small, protected coves, places like Isle au Haut's Head Harbor. Those cute little lobster smacks (fashioned to come and carry a fisherman's catch to market), may well have unloaded a case of Irish whiskey or moonshine for local consumption. George Wallis and his wife, Alice, who spent summers over on Burnt Island, loved to recount tales of caches of liquor hidden among the boulders and bushes, and the eternal search by islanders to find them.

Not all booze was imported. Islanders are inventive people, capable of cobbling together whatever is required to meet their personal needs. Billy Barter remembered his dad describing the dandelion wine brewed by Charles Robinson in the shadow of the lighthouse.

"Musta been sometime in the twenties," said Billy. "Dad and Gordon and Phyl Alley used to purse seine for herring over ta Marsh Cove. Phil had an old single-lung dory back then, I guess. Got a few fish at times, but sometimes they'd drag around and get nothing." Billy shuffled his feet in the gravel remembering. "Coming back in past the lighthouse one evening, they figured on stopping by Charlie Robinson's place. Charles beckons 'em ashore. Yells out he's got a 'refresher' to share. It was early summer (that's when the herring run) and Charlie been snapping dandelion greens, jest what he needed for makin' his famous homemade wine. Dad told me it was the worst awful swill he ever stomached. 'Green,' he said, 'green as pea soup.' Hardly able to get it down, but I guess they did. They cast off from Charlie's pier and made for the Town Landing. Didn't hardly get to the spindle before the cramps started coming." Billy slapped his thigh twice and erupted in a howl of laughter. "Guess it was quite a mess, all three of 'em together. Musta let the tiller loose a while, drifting there in the Thorofare, three bare fannies stretched over the washboard, spewing green goo into the brine."

* * * *

Life at the lighthouse station and around the Island may have been much like that in any American home during the "Roaring Twenties." The Ku Klux Klan had risen and fallen. Prohibition collapsed soon after. Everything had settled down. But things changed dramatically after late October of 1929; a dark, unstoppable calamity swept across the country.

It made its way toward Isle au Haut.

Chapter 8

The Great Depression

The 1930s

"When Wall Street took that tailspin, you had to stand in line to get a window to jump out of," heralded the feature in the *New York Courier*. It was October 24, 1929, just a few weeks after Black Tuesday when the Great Crash rocked Wall Street and the country plunged into its worst-ever depression. So startled by the report, few readers paused to notice that the author of that column was nationally syndicated humorist Will Rogers. He had penned the scene to paint an impressionist picture of that black day on Wall Street, unaware that his words would be repeated as the truth far into the future.

In fact, in those weeks following the crash, only two individuals actually leapt from Wall Street buildings. One of them splattered on the sidewalk adjacent to the hotel where Winston Churchill was staying. Churchill duly recorded the incident in his personal papers. Other suicides did occur due to financial ruin, but the preferred method generally chosen was gunshot or asphyxiation. Regardless of the methods selected, cases were few compared to suicide rates during previous years.

In the wake of the financial disaster came bread lines, foreclosures, dust bowl migrations, and all the other sad events that era bring to mind. Our parents and grandparents passed on to us their own personal stories of sacrifice and lean times. While only a few stockbrokers actually leapt from windows, so too did few other folks succumb to drastic resolutions. Everyone was preoccupied trying to survive.

Hard times were nothing new for more remote pockets of the country. Communities like Isle au Haut were less linked to the booming, wildly reckless, all-consuming madness of the Roaring Twenties. The island way of life had *always* been based on self-reliance and sticking together as a community. Public handouts and bread lines were foreign. Unlike those living in the more industrialized sections of the nation, Mainers primarily lived outside the cities, on little farms and in fishing communities, logging camps, and mill towns that still had ties to the bountiful resources of sea and earth. When Franklin Delano Roosevelt ran for president in 1932, challenging Republican incumbent Herbert Hoover by heralding his "New Deal" promise, Maine was one of only two states (Vermont was the other) that rejected FDR at the ballot box.

"We can take care of ourselves," Mainers professed.

Not much changed as the Depression lingered. For four straight Roosevelt elections, Maine and Vermont never voted Democratic. Roosevelt once snickered, "Well, as Maine goes, so goes Vermont."

Of course on Isle au Haut and all across Maine (and Vermont, too!), there were crippling effects from the Depression. Cash was scarce. Lobster sales were decimated. As with all luxuries, our trademark crustacean only found its way to the tables of the wealthy. Tourism shriveled along the coast and through the pastoral inland valleys. Although hardworking farmers and fishing folk rarely liked to acknowledge the economic importance of "folks from away," now they bemoaned the loss of those needed dollars.

The good times during the 1910s and 1920s had siphoned off a large chunk of the island's population. The richer life on the mainland, the ease of fishing with power boats, the opportunities for education—all this and more lured many native islanders to the mainland. The island's population dropped from 102 souls in 1920 to 89 in 1930 (despite the addition of the twelve new Smiths at the lighthouse). Between 1930 and 1940 the local numbers inched back up to 97. Perhaps folks opting to live here found the hardship softened by a supportive community. The Depression may have even stiffened their steadfast self-reliance. As far as Helen Smith and her siblings at the lighthouse were concerned, everything was hunky-dory.

"We kept plugging away," she told me when I visited her and her husband, Maurice, in their snug little house on the East Side of the island during the winter of 1987. "There wasn't a lick of difference from one year to another." Maurice sat in his rocker by the woodstove and nodded.

With the economy in tatters, Roosevelt launched his renowned "alphabet soup" of agencies to get the nation back on track: The Works Progress Administration (WPA), the Tennessee Valley Authority (TVA), and a dozen others, including the Civilian Conservation Corps (CCC), which brought hundreds of workers to Acadia National Park on Mount Desert, but none to Isle au Haut (the Island didn't become part of the park until 1944). At the same time, cuts were made wherever logical to economize and more frugally direct the flow of limited resources.

Even before the Great Depression started, lighthouse stations had become the subject of economic reform, due to their vast and expensive network of payroll, maintenance, and logistics. Early automation of some light stations had already occurred. Now, with hard times, the U.S. Lighthouse Service took a long look at their inventory and, with presidential prodding, determined which lights would stay and which would go. Soon, the Isle au Haut lighthouse station would be shuttered and auctioned off, along with six others in Maine.

But unlike the other six, which were decommissioned and ended up as summer homes for wealthy bidders, ours had the puzzling distinction of being split in half: the keeper's house, boathouse, and ancillary buildings would be sold, but the lighthouse itself would remain under U.S. Lighthouse Service control. It would be automated and continue with its mission as an aid to navigation, but without the watchful eye of a lighthouse keeper.

In 1933 Keeper Smith and his family were transferred to Two Bush Lighthouse Station, just across the bay, where his skills would be used to help ships and lobstermen find their way around Vinalhaven Island.

It must have been sad that day, during the deepening Depression, when the townspeople gathered to send off their lighthouse keeper and his gaggle of children (less Helen, who stayed behind with Maurice Barter). The Islanders knew that, this time, there would be no replacement, no one to get the fog bell tolling when "thick-a-fog" rolled in. With no wealthy bidders, what would become of these elegant buildings, the pride of Isle au Haut? But regardless of the empty station, the Lighthouse Service had plans to keep the lantern burning.

Automation had grown rapidly over the previous two decades. Pharology (the study and science of lighthouses) had developed technologies that found solutions to almost everything. They could rig a tower with everything needed to keep a light automatically burning, even on a distant sea-bound ledge devoid of roads and power lines. When the lighthouse tender arrived to batten down stations that no longer had keepers, they brought with them a clever device to replace the kerosene lantern: automatic acetylene lamps.

By the turn of the century, acetylene lighting had become a popular, efficient, and economical form of illumination for places where electricity wasn't an option. It could be used in homes off the grid, for farmers, for miners and cavers, indeed for anyone out in the dark who wished for lighting more reliable than a candle or flaming tar torch. Even automobiles and motorcycles became equipped with acetylene headlights.

Calcium carbide provided the base material for this inexpensive gas. Acetylene could be produced with nothing but a barrel of carbide pellets and a dripping garden hose. Union Carbide devised more sophisticated systems, bought the patent for the gas's manufacture, and went about brightening the homes of rural America.

The U.S. Lighthouse Service immediately recognized the advantages of this new technology. Light buoys by the hundreds were outfitted with acetylene lamps. For remote lighthouse stations like Isle au Haut that had no power grid to supply them, gas was a wondrous solution. There were precautions that had to be taken: acetylene is exceptionally explosive. Scores of miners had been killed and houses reduced to smithereens when low-hanging vapors from gas leaks met with still-smoldering coal clinkers or flipped-aside cigarette butts.

At first, acetylene gas was generated onboard Lighthouse Service tenders and then pumped into holding tanks on site for buoys, lighthouses, and lightships. In 1905, a Canadian tender named *Scout* had a terrible explosion while producing the gas, which killed the ship's captain and crew. The same tragedy occurred in American waters in 1913, when the USLHS tender *Hibiscus* suffered a similar explosion. After that, generating acetylene was done ashore, where conditions could be more closely controlled.

Acetylene gas, like many gases, can be compressed and stored in cylinders. Perfect for isolated lighthouses (it burns much cleaner and brighter than propane). A tender could pass by on a scheduled basis and hook up the requisite number of cylinders, like the local milkman exchanging bottles. But unlike many other gases, the volatility of acetylene increases radically as the volume diminishes in a compressed cylinder, making a less-than-full cylinder increasingly explosive. In the 1920s, Swedish scientist Nils Gustof Dalen discovered a technique of using a spongy cylinder liner called AGA (the namesake of Dalen's employer, the Gas Accumulator Company). This material expands and fills up the increasing void as the volume of gas diminishes, hence eliminating the elevated hazard. He also found that a smidgen of acetone blended in with the gas permitted much higher pressure; the compression could be increased a hundredfold with no additional volatility. And better still, a measure of stinky, sulfured stuff could be blended in, so the average nose could detect escaping gas.

But it took a freighter full of bottles to fuel a lighthouse station. That problem was solved by another Dalen innovation. Rather than let the carbide lamps burn day and night, by 1907 he had invented a nonelectric "sun valve" to turn them on and off. This device is a simple laminate strip of two dissimilar or coated metals; when the sun rises, the sensitive strip heats up—one metal side expands more than the other, causing the strip to bend sideways with enough pressure to push open a gas valve. A tiny pilot burned around the clock and ignited the gas stream released by the switch. When the sun set, the metal cooled and shrank, returning to its straightened position, and causing the valve to close. No clocks, no wicks to trim, no can of kerosene to lug up the stairs, no electricity, or lighthouse keeper needed.

Later, a mechanism was developed to make the switches stutter. This allowed the switches to be timed as needed to allow specified intervals between the on and off positions, providing the desired flashing pattern and saving 90% of the gas used by a constantly burning flame! You want the light to rotate instead? No problem—they figured out how to do that, too, with oscillating machinery powered by falling weights.

Nils Gustof Dalen had accomplished all this even though he was severely handicapped. In 1912, while working with acetylene gas, a horrible explosion had occurred—Dalen was permanently blinded. Yet his early discoveries were so significant, he was awarded the Nobel Prize in Physics that same year. He went on to manage AGA until he died in 1937, having produced over ninety patented inventions.

* * * *

Early in the Twentieth Century, The U.S. Lighthouse Service used tenders like *The Columbine* to supply and maintain its vast chain of lighthouses and navigational aids. Photo restoration by William Brehm.

When the tenders pulled away after installing acetylene lamps on those hardscrabble days in the mid-1930s, no one remained to tend those stations. But now, automatically, the lighthouses shone more brightly than ever. In place of the smoking old kerosene lanterns, the new acetylene technology provided a better source of light: brighter, cleaner, and miraculously able to keep burning for months without the daily aid of any human hand.

Among the old-timers who still remain today, only Jim Greenlaw retains some faint memory of the acetylene lantern here on Isle au Haut. He conjures images of "something about gas" and a vague memory of several tanks. Other octogenarians claim ignorance or insist the tower had been converted to batteries. But the 1935 *Description of Isle au Haut Lighthouse*, written by the U.S. Lighthouse Service the year after the lantern was automated, lists the lamp as "acetylene with a ¾ foot burner" (and a spare on hand), fed by two compressed gas tanks.

After the U. S. Coast Guard inherited the responsibility for the nation's lighthouses in 1939, their tenders did the best they could to provide maintenance on scheduled visits. Sometime during the 1950s, our gas lamp gave way to the battery contraption the other old-timers remembered. Not unlike a fifty-foot-tall flashlight—with all the inherit problems—the battery powered rigs were far less dependable than mainland grid-powered systems. Bulbs burned out. Batteries ran down. And the absence of any power line left the station with no way to recharge its batteries. Worst of all, the empty keeper's house sheltered no watchful eye or ready hand to fix a failed light.

The Coast Guard did make use of the old marine railway spot at the station's boathouse to land their skiffs, at least for a brief period. During the 1950s the pins rusted out and the skids washed away. After that, the coastguardsmen had to run a steel-bottomed skiff up on the rocks at the tower's base, heft off the weighty batteries while surf tugged at their pants, and drag the behemoths up through the rocks into the tower. Occasionally, as a result of burned-out bulbs or depleted batteries, the lighthouse stood unlit, a dead-black silhouette against a starry sky.

"Even with regular battery changes, the dang thing didn't always work," remembered Russell MacDonald. Russell was Billy Barter's constant childhood accomplice. I met him years ago, but he moved off the island and lives in Connecticut now. I reached him by telephone.

"I hauled traps on both sides of the island back then, mostly outside the lighthouse," Russell told me, his voice raspy with age. "We didn't have any fancy electronics back then, back in the fifties. We depended on the lighthouse, you know, particularly late in the season when the sun came down early. On a particularly messy night when I was heading in with a barrel of hard shells, I was looking for the light and there twern't any! Mad as a hornet, I was! No Coast Guard in sight either. So, the next day I goes up to scout around. Door's unlocked. I gazes 'round to make sure no one's lookin', scoot inside, climb up ta the lantern room, thinking, 'If those Coasties fellers ever catch me, I'll be in the brig forever.' Anyways, I find the rack of bulbs inside the lamp is all burned out. Crates of extras lying around. So, I figure, 'What the hell—a working light could save a life,' so I pop a new charge of 'em in and got myself outta there."

In the late 1970s a truly revolutionary invention was installed to keep a battery charged: a small solar panel sized appropriately to power the electric lamp. If ever there was a perfect example of "appropriate technology," this was it. Once a year the U.S. Coast Guard tender *Bridle* anchored in the Thorofare. The crew came ashore to check the battery and add fresh bulbs to the automatic carousel that changed any burned-out globe. Then they dawdled a while, washing the windows and sweeping away the dead flies littered across the lantern room floor. The Isle au Haut Lighthouse—off the grid and unmanned—now blazed more brightly and more reliably than ever before.

* * * *

The electric lantern wasn't the only change created by automation. The fog bell was a casualty too. In 1934, that old friend of the island's fishermen had been removed from its beam—like a corpse lowered from the gallows—and swung aboard the U.S. Lighthouse tender, along with the bell striking machinery that had served so well. Some folks out here have speculated that the bell might have been pilfered or shaken loose by a wicked nor'easter to rest on the bottom somewhere near. But U.S. Lighthouse Service inventories clearly indicate that the Service removed the bell and machinery at the time of automation. No records indicate where it went.

There existed back then a Lighthouse Service warehouse in Boston where bells were stored. Photographs exist showing its yard stacked with salvaged bells of every size. There they were melted down and recast, to be used again. Harold Van Doren suspects that if our bell had ended up there, most likely during WWII, it was melted down for artillery casings. Speculation about the bell's ultimate fate is justified. On nearby Eagle Island—which was automated in the '30s about the same time as Isle au Haut—fishermen, in 1963, watched Coast Guardsmen try to remove the 1,200-pound bell. It unceremoniously ended up in deep water. Later on, a local lobsterman rescued the slimy bell and hauled it across the bay, cradled beneath his boat in a hammock of chain. Today that salvaged bell is still cared for and protected on the estate of Maine artist Fairfield Porter.

There are other reasons to make one wonder whether our bell ever reached a safe resting place. At the same time the Lighthouse Service crew was automating the light in 1934, the rest of the paraphernalia and furnishings from our station were packed up and removed, with a few gut-wrenching exceptions. Villagers watched in disbelief as the coveted keeper's peapod was sawn in half on the beach and burned.

Recently, I asked Charlie Bowen if he remembered that travesty. Charlie grew up innocent and naive, until the shock of Pearl Harbor changed his life. He rushed to join the Navy. Even today, he references all history back to that dreadful date. With his long white mane drooped around his shoulders, he sat stiffly in a wicker chair on the front porch of the home he had shared with his recently deceased wife, Sally Greenlaw Bowen. A faded American flag fluttered feebly in the breeze.

"What a waste!" Charlie said. "With the hard times and all, where every scrap was valued. Ashes, that was all that remained from that pretty peapod!"

"Was it old and rotten?" I asked. "Maybe unsafe?" I leaned on his front porch railing, knowing that, at his age, I may not have many opportunities left to hear his childhood remembrances.

"Good as new," he said, his voice slow and faint. "Harry Smith babied that boat. There was an old fellow here, a fisherman who had almost nothing—may have been Hezzie Moore, or Johnny the Finn—can't remember for sure. Lived in a shack on the Thorofare. They say he was there on the beach that day, begging those "uniforms" to let him have it. He'd make good use of it, he promised, to feed the folks who were wanting. Didn't matter to them, though—numb as posts, I'd say. They burned that peapod anyway, nothing left but smoldering coals when the tide arrived to sweep the beach."

Charlie stared off toward the ocean, across the horizon, remembering.

* * * *

The Isle au Haut Lighthouse, circa 1940. The bell had been removed. Deterioration of the paint can be seen. Sometime after this photograph was taken, the bell beam was also removed and the doorway blocked in with solid brick. In the 1960s, an intimidating chainlink fence was erected over the bridge, the windows were replaced with solid glass blocks, and the lantern railing was replaced with looping steel cables. Photo restoration by William Brehm.

After the Lighthouse Service closed the station in 1934—essentially abandoning the place to the elements—the keeper's house and its attendant buildings stood alone on the cold rocky shores of Robinson Point. Occasionally a tender of the U.S. Lighthouse Service would stop by to swap out the lighthouse's depleted acetylene cylinders with fresh ones. But other than that, only an intermittent soul from town would wander out to the station, sit on the rocks, remember the Holbrooks and Smiths, and wonder if better times would ever return.

In 1936 the disposition of the buildings became resolved. Apparently, Margaret Chase Smith (who at that time had yet to be elected to public office, but was wife and aide to Congressman Clyde Smith) intervened on behalf of Charles and Lillian Robinson, making a case for selling the station back to these original owners of the land. Jim Greenlaw vaguely remembers that Congressman Edward Moran may have had a hand in it. Charles Robinson was quite ill and wasn't travelling by that time, so the deal was consummated when Charles and Lillian's daughter and her husband (Mattie and Aubrey Greenlaw—who were Jim's parents) came up with $550. The property was sold, less the speck of rock where the automated lighthouse tower stood. Ironically, Charles had sold the same two acres to the government twenty-two years before for $400. The difference? Now that nub of shore included the finest home on Isle au Haut, and a full array of beautifully maintained service buildings. Poor Charles wasn't able to enjoy it for long. He died the following year.

Jim Greenlaw was only a tyke at that time. Last summer he pulled into my driveway to say hello and chat. He recalled, "The keeper's house was barren after Granddad bought it back. Not even a rusty bedspring left!"

"What about the boathouse? Was that emptied, too?" I asked.

"Just about," he said. "Oh, a few old things remained: the big winch, of course, and the little coal car that went with it. A worn-out vent brush from the lighthouse tower remained, and a bunch of hundred-pound weights from the bell striking machinery. I used most of those to fashion a mooring for my boat back in the fifties. And the red glass filters used in the lantern room windows—you know about those."

I certainly did. Originally, those sheets of crimson glazing were used to filter seven of the eight windows in the lantern room, creating a warning signal to ships entering the harbor too close to ledges—the Marsh Cove Ledges to port, the Trial Point Ledges to starboard. The eighth window was left unfiltered, with a clear beam of light to guide ships in from the southwest. The Fresnel lens was updated in the 1950s, replaced with an extruded plastic rig with built in red sections. The old glass panels were removed at that time.

When Judi and I moved into the station in 1986, one of the first things I did was explore the keeper's house attic. Back then, one had to find a stepladder to reach the hatch up to the garret. There, cocooned in spider webs and dust, the Robinson/Greenlaw folk had tucked away those seven sheets of glass, so no marauding winter intruder would ever find them. When we built a staircase up to the garret and converted it into a guestroom, we moved the ruby treasure to a new hiding space. Unbeknownst to the current innkeeper, they remain there even today.

Other than these few artifacts left behind when the station was sold, I found it perplexing that the boathouse could have been so barren at the end of 1936. When Judi and I bought the property fifty years later from Jim and his siblings, one of my greatest thrills was to find the boat house crammed with interesting old stuff: tools, fishing gear, flotsam and jetsam collected from the sea, broken furniture waiting repair—a veritable treasure trove of projects, supplies, and mysteries. I had always assumed those piles of clutter dated back to the Holbrooks and Smiths. Jim Greenlaw corrected my fantasy.

"So," I asked, "where *did* all that stuff come from, the wealth of detritus that greeted me?"

Jim smiled serenely.

"The old tools and stuff? Most of that was lugged out here by my dad [Aubrey Greenlaw, the first]. He grew up in Aroostook County, outside of Presque Isle. He was the son of a barn builder, a carpenter, and a jack-of-all-trades—that sort of thing. That's where my mom [Mattie Belle Robinson] met him. After college, she was a nurse. During the big flu epidemic in 1922, she went up to

Presque Isle to tend the ill. She hooked up with Dad there and brought him back to the Island."

"And the rest is history, right?"

Jim smiled, thinking back. "They got married here in 1923. Raised us in Connecticut while Grandma Lillian stayed on at the farmhouse at Robinson Cove. Dad started moving his tools and gear out to Isle au Haut—that's how the boathouse got filled to overflowing. After the Depression, Mom and us kids all came back here in the summers. Dad stayed in Connecticut. Worked for the YMCA."

Hmmmm. Interesting—not the origin I had imagined, but still, the dusty souvenirs left by three generations of Robinson-Greenlaw folk would certainly carry their own stories, their own claims to be remembered as part of the station's history. Caulking irons, braces and bits, dented and twisted kerosene lanterns, two loose-planked skiffs, an old spinning wheel, paint-spattered block and tackle sets—these all had tales to tell. Not to mention the stashes of empty whiskey bottles found grouped throughout the building, like clutches of old men gossiping.

Back in those waning years of the 1930s, the lighthouse limped on alone with its fancy new automatic beacon, devoid of the voices of playing children and the daily footsteps that tramped up iron stairs when the keeper went to fill the lamp. Even more disturbing, there were no more eyes watching the sweep of sea from Seal Island to Kimball Head. Of the two extended lighthouse keeper families that had lived here, only Esther Holbrook Robinson and Helen Smith Barter remained, now busy on other corners of the island raising their own children. Except for an occasional visit from a lighthouse tender, the vacant lighthouse remained forsaken.

At the end of the 1930s, even the U.S. Lighthouse Service vanished.

* * * *

On July 1, 1939, the U.S. Lighthouse Service was incorporated into the United States Coast Guard. The two organizations, complete with their entire personnel, facilities, missions, and resources became one as a result of the Roosevelt administration's Reorganization Act of 1939. In some cases, higher level officials with the Lighthouse Service were given Coast Guard commissions, while virtually all employees of the Service continued on as civilians under the new plan, with retirement and normal attrition being the only way their numbers diminished. Actual lighthouse keepers and their assistants were given the choice of remaining as civilians or joining the Coast Guard. Hundreds of support staff and the resources of the old Service were moved into various Coast Guard district headquarters, and about half of the previously-unarmed civilian lighthouse keepers now served in more military fashion.

Although a radical departure for the old Lighthouse Service personnel, armaments were nothing new for the United States Coast Guard. The Coast Guard had been active during hostilities with the French in the War of 1812. During the Civil War, the conflicts with Mexico, the Spanish-American war, and World War I—as well as numerous minor military clashes—the Coast Guard had always had a fighting role.

But now all those unarmed lighthouse keepers, who had served for decades as friendly neighbors helping their communities in the face of challenges from the sea, were folded into the Coast Guard. The role of the keeper was altered forever. Interdiction of gun-happy drug runners and military defense of the U.S. coast was the primary mission of the Coast Guard. Tending to the centuries-old strings of aging and increasingly anachronistic lighthouses was at the bottom of the list.

Place yourself there, in the boots of an ex-lighthouse keeper in the ebbing days of the 1930s. During previous times you lived to "keep the light burning" for your neighbors and family, suffering deprivations but being rewarded by the strength and generosity of your community. All of a sudden, in 1939, you've become part of the U.S. military. Fascism is flourishing in Italy, Spain, and Germany, totalitarianism in Japan. Following the Treaty of Versailles, the German people were burdened with the full weight of reparations that crippled their economy, their lives. Hitler promised salvation. The military growth of Germany during the Depression was unprecedented, massive, all encompassing, and boundlessly aggressive. On September 1, 1939, Hitler swept into Poland. Hundreds of torpedo-laden U-boats skulked beneath the Atlantic's surface. During early 1941, Japan's Hirohito set his sights on Pearl Harbor.

If you were an ex-lighthouse keeper manning a Coast Guard station, wouldn't you be a little nervous?

Chapter 9

Meanwhile, Back at Robinson Cove

The 1940s

"Explosions rocked the house so hard the bed springs shook beneath us," recalled Jim Greenlaw, while we sat in his modern-day living room across the cove from the lighthouse station. "When the shockwaves started, mom rushed all us kids up to the second floor. We clustered together in bed like a nest of terrified ducklings. The Navy was dropping depth charges on a German sub that had snuck into the bay, somewhere right out there." He nodded toward the window.

"Good grief!" I said. "That must have been scary!"

"Yep. We had no idea what would happen! Went on for what seemed like hours, the sea-muffled thuds, and the force shaking the bed. Eventually it ceased."

I had visions of what it must have been like for those frightened little Greenlaw kids: a German crew abandoning their ruptured sub and swimming to shore, scaling the rocks in front of the lighthouse, sopping wet, with daggers clenched in their teeth, like some scary N. C. Wyeth illustration from a children's story book. And think about all those military maniacs in Berlin, huddled around their strategy maps making lists of targets. Airfields and factories would be identified, of course, and the infrastructure that allows our transportation system to work. Certainly, that included our lighthouses!

"I never realized civilians were so threatened," I said. "How was it that you were even at the lighthouse?"

Jim explained the events that had placed them here. After his granddad, Charles Robinson passed away in 1937, his grandmother Lillian carried on at the old family farmhouse at Robinson Cove, just down the shore a few hundred yards from the lighthouse. Charles and Lillian's daughter, Mattie Belle (Jim's mother), had departed with her new husband, Aubrey Greenlaw, to raise their five children in Connecticut.

Lillian Hamilton Robinson, Grand Dame of Robinson Cove. Date unknown. Courtesy of Marshall Chapman. Photo restoration by William Brehm.

Mattie Belle Robinson at Middlebury College, 1921 – soon to become Mattie Belle Greenlaw. Photo courtesy of Jim Greenlaw

Aubrey's career with the YMCA in Connecticut limited his time on the island to only a few weeks each year, but every summer Mattie Belle would make her way back to the island with all their little ones in tow. Their home for the season was the keeper's house. Once again, those walls felt the patter of running feet, the laughter and cries of a family whose roots ran deep in the rock at Robinson Point.

At the same time that Mattie Belle and her children filled the keeper's house rooms with family cheer, beneath the surface of the dark water running to the horizon prowled German submarines. In the early stages of the war, before radar and anti-sub technology were fully developed, u-boat torpedoes sped beneath the surface with deadly accuracy, sinking scores of defenseless freighters, taking with them sailors, passengers, and ordnance bound for Europe.

Early in the war, little protection existed for our merchant ships. The Axis Powers had had a huge jump in war preparations. It took a few years to mobilize the Allied forces and retool the nation's industries, laboratories, and fighting forces. Radar and depth charges became more sophisticated later in the war.

That's when events led to "the day the bedsprings shook."

"Mom scrambled up the keeper's house stairs with us kids, ushered us into the southwest bedroom, huddled us together on the old iron bed. Each depth charge the Navy dropped resonated, shaking the bed beneath us, the springs heaving and squealing. My older brothers sat on the edge of the bed, clutching hunting rifles."

"Did the Navy knock out the sub?" I asked.

"Doubtful. It would have taken a couple direct hits to actually tear a U-boat apart. Best they could have hoped for was a beating that messed up the communication systems."

Jim's brother, Aubrey Jr., once told me about other times he heard U-boats surface at night, their diesel engines humming as they laid off the island charging their battery banks. He would stay up sitting in a straight back chair at the window of the keeper's house nursery, his rifle cradled in his lap, protecting the family from any possible threat. Jim recalls that he and his brothers would rig the stairway with pots and pans and a trip wire to sound the alarm in case any midnight marauding U-boat saboteurs invaded the house.

* * * *

There are accounts of probable German incursions on the island. Harold Van Doren describes a situation that took place on the East Side.

"There was a summer log cabin over there built on a high bluff overlooking the eastern approaches to Penobscot Bay. Built in the nineteen-twenties, probably, just a modest knocked-together affair where someone could camp during the muggy months. Had pretty much gone to seed during the Depression."

"Still there?" I asked.

"Sure is. Expanded a bit since then, and the logs are getting soft. The old timers say the kids playing around there late in the war found the place stocked with foreign literature, rations, too, all in cans and packages with German labels."

"Spy post?" I wondered.

"Probably," said Harold. "All up and down the coast accounts abounded of the presence of Nazi agents scoping out targets for U-boat attacks."

German presence recurred all during the war. Just thirty miles from Isle au Haut, on Hancock Point, two German spies were landed by U-boat 1230 on November 29, 1944, directed to make their way to New York City to radio potential targets. One of the two, William Colepaugh, got cold feet and turned himself in to the FBI.

Further north in Canada's St. Lawrence Seaway, several nasty battles actually took place between U-boats and Canadian forces. Meanwhile, Japanese subs prowled the Pacific. On June 21, 1942, one bombarded the Estevan Point Lighthouse on Vancouver Island—that must have perked up the ears of coast guardsmen manning the Allies' lights! The same day, another unleashed a barrage at Fort Stevens at the mouth of the Columbia River in Washington State, knocking down the fence behind the facility's baseball diamond. Of all these pesky attacks, there was only a single incidence of a submarine being destroyed within our territorial waters: off Block Island, Rhode Island. The intact shell of that sunken German U-boat still provides an attraction for scuba divers and curious fish.

During the time Judi and I ran the station as an inn, we had a guest, a daughter of the wartime keeper at Whitehead Lighthouse Station thirty miles west of here, who described several occasions just before the war when German subs surfaced in broad daylight. Crewmen skiffed ashore with "jerry cans" in search of water, and the keeper's family would run panicked to hide in the woods while the fair-headed young sailors used the station's hand pump to fill their ten-liter jugs. Lighthouse history expert Ted Panayotoff suggests this keeper's daughter may have been mistaken: Such a risky venture "would have been foolhardy in the extreme," Keeper Ted posits.

Meanwhile, back at the lighthouse station at Robinson Point,

Mattie Belle survived the summers of the war years hunkered down in the keeper's house. Mattie Belle's tribe of five kids flourished and careened into their young adulthood during the final years of the 1940s.

After Jim Greenlaw finished high school, he returned to the lighthouse with a plan to find his fortune. It had long been suspected that the ancient rock at Robinson Point was rich with silver. In a search for it, explorers had dynamited holes in the bluff that ran down the southwest boundary of the Robinson property. There had been a mini silver rush in Maine from 1882 to 1887. A dozen or so "wildcat" mines opened, one as nearby as Castine. Harold Van Doren has an old map of Isle au Haut that shows an old silver mine near Head Harbor. Jim, full of enthusiasm and energy, saw no reason why the magical rock that had spawned a lighthouse and fulfilled so many dreams couldn't also birth a bonanza. Pick in hand, he labored that summer, flailing away at the stone. When September arrived, he picked out his most precious shimmery samples, swaddled them in burlap bags so no one would waylay him on the way to the bank, and dragged them back to Connecticut to be evaluated. While the assayer squinted through his monocle, rotating a sample, picking at it with a fingernail, "aahing" and "oohing," Jim nervously waited.

"Well..." said the fellow, "You got silver here all right...no doubt about it...the genuine thing...I'd say for every several tons of galena ore...if you're lucky...you could produce enough high-grade silver to maybe mint a nickel."

Like Jim, his brothers and sister soon finished school, got married, moved away, had kids. But one thing never changed—summers on Isle au Haut found the now-extended family sharing the keeper's house through the 1950s and well beyond.

The now-automated lighthouse continued to blink through the night—spring, summer, fall, and winter. Automation appeared to have guaranteed a continuing system of flashing beacons for our nation, but a new, unexpected problem soon threatened to extinguish them.

Chapter 10

Out with the Old, In with the New

The 1950s

As the nation and her lighthouse stations gratefully shifted from war into peacetime, the transition was rudely interrupted by the Korean conflict from 1950 to 1953. Even after that bloody affair, a worrisome malaise lingered: the fear of international confrontations with the Soviet Union. Bombs were no longer falling, but, instead, the world's conflicting powers careened into a protracted arms race, the Cold War, a new age of terrifying weapons. Faced with this looming threat, the nation's perimeter of Coast Guard lighthouse stations, air defenses, and missile silos seemed as futile as the Great Wall of China (my childhood pals and I remember scrambling beneath our desks in Miss Weaver's third grade class, preparing for atom bomb attacks). On top of that, with wartime advancements in shipboard radar and navigation, lighthouses were becoming less crucial in guiding water traffic.

While the end of these wars were joyously welcomed, the ensuing peace era came entwined with shifts in economics and culture. Our wartime factories, retrofitted to making consumer goods to fill the new suburbs with patio swings and power lawnmowers, dishwashers, Waring blenders, TVs, Schwinn bicycles, and badminton sets. We morphed from a collective wartime mentality to a consumer society craving all things new. Out with old, in with the new. "Keep up with the Joneses."

Far out on Isle au Haut, changes came at a slower pace. Harold Van Doren remembers when Bill Robinson got the Island's first TV set sometime early in the '50s. But instead of simply plugging the new contraption into a wall receptacle (there weren't any), he had to run an extension cord out to his Briggs and Stratton gasoline generator behind the outhouse. It wasn't until 1969 that Pat Tully erected the first power lines on the island, fed by a clattering old diesel generator housed down by the Town Landing.

Be it on the mainland or on an island, all across the nation everyone was swept away with acquiring the new bounty offered in department stores and catalogs. We knocked down old city centers and replaced them with shopping centers and parking lots. The faster new consumer goods became available, the faster we forgot about our nation's historic treasures disappearing beneath a tidal wave of merchandise and the "ticky-tack" suburbs sweeping across the nation.

This cultural amnesia spelled disaster for the country's lighthouses. In 1950, more than half of all stations had been automated, and the rest rapidly headed in that direction. With the keepers gone, no one remained to keep them painted, to tend to the daily effects of wind and sea, not to mention watch out for danger. Even where Coast Guard crews still manned the more crucial lights, maintenance became a pragmatic matter, with little regard for the historic character of each tower. Paint, patch, and blacktop were all that mattered. Few cared about their rich history and unique characteristics. Reverence for lighthouses diminished; their magic faded. On Isle au Haut, the condition of our lighthouse tumbled toward ruination.

It started with automation and the removal of the bell. Old photographs show the tower with the bell in place. The original blueprints expressed aesthetic proportions, with the bell as the focal point, grace and balance were designed into this working piece of art. After the bell was amputated, the wooden access doors to the bell were replaced with a flat brick barrier filling the rectangular void beneath the lintel, like an empty picture frame fitted with cardboard backing

Then came the menacing wire cage that blocked land access to the tower, with a message as strong as any found on the Berlin Wall:

NO TRESPASSING.
PROPERTY OF THE U.S. COAST GUARD.
VIOLATORS WILL BE PROSECUTED
TO THE FULLEST EXTENT OF THE LAW.

Just to emphasize the point, the historic glass-paned entry door soon came down as well. Its replacement: a solid stainless steel monstrosity, capable of repelling any vandal, with attached legal threats that made the perimeter warnings tame in comparison. The windows required maintenance, too, and the glass might break. They were torn out and replaced with tempered glass blocks, used so frequently during the 1950s in veterinary hospitals, welfare centers, army reserve bases, and county jails.

Next came the wood walkway that spanned the distance between the front porch of the keeper's house and the bridge to the tower. With no more keepers and no need to tend the light, the Coast Guard tore that out too. Then there was the delicate iron railing around the lantern room, perfectly contoured to fit the catwalk, with sculpted finials atop each newel post. It must have corroded or become a safety issue, but, instead of being repaired, it was crudely cut away with blow torches and replaced with welded reinforcing bars and woven steel cables, like something engineered to keep landing jets from careening off the decks of aircraft carriers. And perhaps most threatening, the mortar joints between the blocks of granite in the base of the tower had weathered badly.

Billy Barter remembers how that was rectified.

"Musta been back in the fifties," he said. "I was just a youngster, out hand-hauling traps from a skiff. Saw the Coast Guard tender there. Had what looked like those concrete pumps—thick hoses, you know—slathering cement all over that sparkling granite, like icing a friggin' birthday cake. What a mess, just to fill those narrow joints!"

Other neighboring lighthouses fared even worse. On Saddleback Ledge (just three miles from here, straight out in the bay to the southwest) during one night in 1960, the Green Berets landed and blew up the keeper's house. "Demolitions practice," they said. Twice more, over the next twenty years, the Green Berets would land to blow up a Maine keeper's house.

On Eagle Island, less than ten miles to the northwest, the Coast Guardsmen themselves were "just following orders" when they landed in 1964, smashed everything of value to pieces with sledgehammers, and burned down the keeper's house while pleading islanders looked on in distress.

Let's be fair here, and remember: the Coast Guard was never intended to be a historic preservation society. Their orders were utilitarian: to do all the tasks you are assigned; to protect the coast from foreign intervention; to deal with drug runners, smugglers, the "coyotes" that smuggle people in, and the rafts of refugees; to supervise and police billions of dollars in commerce; and, while you're at it, if you have the time, please keep those cute old lanterns polished.

They did do a good job on the duties at the top of their priority list. Back in those years, the '50s, the '60s, and into the '70s, to most Americans the fate of the nation's lighthouses didn't even matter. They were old and increasingly anachronistic. Besides, the rational concluded, the automated beacons performed dependably, year after year after year, regardless of the property's condition.

* * * *

Meanwhile on Robinson Point, across the low thatch of raspberry bushes and beach grass that separated the clutch of buildings from the lighthouse tower, inside the keeper's dwelling the Greenlaw family flourished. The four sons and one daughter of Mattie Belle and Aubrey now had children of their own, a new generation to play along the shore and build pirate-repelling forts facing the ocean.

Something strange happened, during those decades the Greenlaws populated the keeper's house. Unlike the rest of the country infatuated with tennis courts and patio grills, here on Robinson Point no cutesy amenities or tasteless additions were ever added. Screen porches, tennis courts, boat docks, and swimming pools never crept onto these two acres.

In fact, the Greenlaws never did anything! Decade after decade for fifty years the buildings at Robinson Point remained unchanged.

There were a few tiny exceptions, of course. The rooms left empty when the U.S. Lighthouse Service abandoned ship in 1934 were eventually replenished with the surplus furniture of the expanding family, but there must have been some strictly enforced code regarding the qualifications of any incoming orphaned ottoman or slack-legged table: It had to be old. The style, the period, the color or condition—none of that mattered, as long as the furnishings were appropriately ancient. Over the decades that followed, so much piled up that even the outbuildings became impacted with broken-down furniture and unwanted memorabilia. But it was *old* stuff; that was what mattered.

With the five Greenlaw siblings and all their kids, it must have been hard making family decisions. I remember a conversation I had with Sally Greenlaw Bowen after we first arrived.

"How did you all manage to keep the keeper's house so pristine?" I asked. She had come to have a cup of tea and see how we were doing in our new digs. "The entire house looks as if nothing has ever changed, as if the keeper's family left just yesterday."

Sally had a direct way of answering questions. She didn't beat around the bush.

"Well, things don't change very fast when you have a bunch of people that can't agree on anything," she said.

Sally had big round eyes that seemed to bulge a bit, or maybe it was those thick glasses she wore that amplified her gaze, to see right through you.

"Except for this yellow wallpaper," she said, nodding over her shoulder at the kitchen wall, a sly little smile creeping across her face. "That was the big exception."

I was very much aware of the bright yellow wallpaper. It was horrid. Little blue and red toy soldiers marched across its mustard surface, like Christmas nutcrackers on a picket line.

"The big exception..." I repeated, coaxing her along.

"Well, the plaster walls underneath were in bad repair," she explained. "Some of us lobbied for years to cover up the mess. How could you cook a decent supper in a room that shed plaster dust? This kitchen was spooky, too, with cracks wide enough to drive a Volkswagen through, cracks you could fill with spackle as often as you wished, and every spring when you came back they'd be bigger than ever. The rest of the house wasn't like that. This was the only room; we had to take action!"

She said that with so much certainty I thought she would start pounding the table.

"So, what happened?" I asked.

"We must have had a dozen family meetings. Pros and cons, all of that. But just couldn't come to any agreement. Finally, in the end, the minority position caved in." She paused for a moment, remembering back to the long-ago year when this summit gave birth to sheathing the kitchen in a gown of pukey yellow. "That gathering didn't go gracefully, though. There were conditions that had to be met, stipulations laid."

This was getting interesting. "Stipulations…like what?" I asked.

"We would be permitted to proceed on one central, irrevocable, ironclad condition: that the wallpaper not be…" She hesitated.

I could tell some old memory was coming back to her, some deep emotion welling.

"The condition was that we could hang any paper we wanted, as long as…" she struggled with the words. Suddenly, she broke into conspiratorial laughter. "As long as the paper wasn't yellow!"

* * * *

There were other minor changes too. In the woodshed an incinerating toilet appeared, a welcome change for some members of the family. This contraption used propane gas to nuke deposits made by those daring enough to sit atop its receiving chamber. Jim Greenlaw found time to replace the cedar gutters that ringed the keeper's house. Somewhere along the way the kitchen and living rooms were outfitted with gaslights fed by propane cylinders the Greenlaw men dragged up over the hill.

Other than that, nothing much about the buildings ever changed. But as the family multiplied, lives became more complicated. Siblings matured and diversified, and time went by. The island was no longer central to all members of the Greenlaw family.

By the 1980s the family's varied interests led to the realization that it was time for major changes at Robinson Point. In 1984 the property was surveyed and subdivided (the first subdivision in the Island's history). Each of the five Greenlaw siblings got their own chunk with ocean frontage. The lighthouse station retained its two acres, and this premium parcel with all its attendant buildings was offered for sale to the general public.

For two long years, the Isle au Haut Lighthouse Station remained listed. Inquiries were few, the offers, fewer. Obviously, back then, antiquated lighthouse stations hardly topped the real estate market.

Chapter 11

Lighthouse Renaissance

Was it by chance that Judi and I landed on the shores of Isle au Haut? Maybe the lighthouse station fell in our laps due to some higher power? In retrospect, I believe we just happened to be hanging out in some sort of "Twilight Zone," an era that separated one age where folks didn't care much about old buildings from another obsessed with saving structures that mattered. Imagine standing on that fault line between the two: Beneath us the earth shivered, quaked, and tumbled, and we fell akimbo into the crevasse. We emerged bewildered, clutching the title to one of the most pristine scenic lighthouse stations anywhere on earth.

Here's how it happened.

* * * *

During the nineteenth century, with unlimited elbow room and abundant resources, the American people didn't feel the burden of a heritage to protect. "Go west, young man, and grow with the country," was Horace Greely's advice. And so we did. In the wake of that migration we fostered a national consciousness weak with regard for the value of what our ancestors had built. Then, climbing out of the tumult of two world wars, we found ourselves a superpower greater than any other in history. The world had changed. In place of bombs and bullets, mass production now produced every imaginable consumer item. Old things mattered no more.

What once was the pride of the nation, our vast array of lighthouses, had lost its luster. It's no wonder that in 1960 the Green Berets were able to blow up the keeper's house on nearby Saddleback Ledge, or that folks on Isle au Haut hardly noticed when the condition of their lighthouse deteriorated, neglected by the Coast Guard in the name of efficiency, economy, and automation.

But something new was stirring, too, as the '60s moved forward. It was a time of questions and confrontations, of turning things upside down. Values were tested, altered, and tested again. Maybe demolishing old buildings wasn't so smart. Maybe a Model T was worth restoring, or a run-down old Victorian brownstone deserving of attention. How about those covered bridges and gristmills, the childhood homes of dead presidents, and the discontinued railway stations? Some began to sense that these were our story, our legacy, and worthy of protection. From the tragedy of the war years, we had rushed onward into the 1950s, flinging away everything old, all that anchored us to the past, only to realize later that there was much worthy of saving.

What America was sensing found expression with Lady Bird Johnson's report, *With Heritage So Rich*. It demonstrated her keen ability to put into words what Americans were feeling:

> "*...the truth is that the buildings which express our national heritage are not simply interesting—they give a sense of continuity and a heightened reality to our thinking about the whole meaning of the American past.*"

Her efforts inspired the National Historic Preservation Act of 1966, passed by Congress and signed into law by President Johnson. The new legislation established the National Register of Historic Places and the List of Historic Landmarks, as well as the State Historic Preservation Offices to oversee the restoration and preservation of identified properties. A national movement had emerged. Nationwide, communities and activists sprang into action to preserve old neighborhoods, civic buildings, and the historic homes of noted figures, both famous and forgotten.

A path for lighthouse salvation had opened wide.

The Shore Village Museum became the earliest manifestation. Located in an old Victorian house on a tree-lined backstreet in Rockland, Maine, this rich collection of lighthouse paraphernalia opened in the 1970s. Its founder, Ken Black, an ex-Coast Guardsman with years of service working on aids to navigation teams, personally cajoled, manipulated, and twisted arms to rescue a mountain of lighthouse artifacts including the original Fresnel lens from the Isle au Haut lighthouse.

In quick succession, four lighthouse preservation groups were founded, usually collaborating with each other, sometimes competing, occasionally warring over leadership and personality issues. All of them, however, dedicated themselves to the mission of preserving the country's lighthouses and educating the public about their history, the need to protect them, and the necessity for their restoration.

In 1983, a large group of retired lighthouse keepers established the Great Lakes Lighthouse Keepers Association, a 501(c)3 not-for-profit organization. Today it represents some two hundred lighthouse stations ringing all five of the Great Lakes.

The following year, the first nationwide lighthouse organization developed on the west coast, led by Wayne Wheeler, another old "coastie" like Ken Black, with decades working with aids to navigation. In San Francisco, Wayne established the United States Lighthouse Society with the purpose of bringing awareness of the plight of our nation's lights. His first major project was the salvation and rehabilitation of a ragtag lightship in San Francisco Bay. This Society was not only successful in saving the ship but also was key in developing a national awareness of the plight of so many of the nation's lighthouse assets. The U.S. Lighthouse Society went on to rescue and restore many foundering lighthouses—predominantly on the west coast—and founded an excellent historical and technical journal, *The Keeper's Log*. Besides the journal and preservation work, the U.S. Lighthouse Society also began to organize scores of lighthouse tours, both regional and international, a service it still provides today.

At the same time Wayne was getting under way in San Francisco, James Hyland, an Ohioan, was traveling the eastern seaboard, photographing and researching the deteriorating beacons on the east coast. With unflagging commitment, "Jay" was soon able to bring into being the Lighthouse Preservation Society, almost simultaneously with the birthing of its west coast counterpart. The United States Lighthouse Society concentrated on its quarterly journal, west coast lighthouse projects, and tours. The Lighthouse Preservation Society practiced its mission by successfully lobbying in Washington for legislation and policy changes and by popularizing the preservation movement with demonstration projects and lighthouse conventions.

Meanwhile, lighthouse tourism was rapidly growing. One of the developments that spawned this phenomenon was the publication of *Lighthouses of Maine*, Tim Harrison and Kathleen Flannigan's photo/touring book. Not long after, they founded The Lighthouse Depot in southern Maine, an emporium of everything with a lighthouse theme: books, souvenirs, tea towels, miniature lighthouse models, earrings, photos, coffee mugs—you name it. Their *Lighthouse Digest*, a monthly publication, soon followed, providing news, project descriptions, and historical pieces, primarily focused on the east coast lighthouse scene.

Initially, Tim and Kathleen's efforts were largely commercial, promoting lighthouse preservation through merchandising and literature. That emphasis changed radically a number of years later when Tim founded the American Lighthouse Foundation, yet another national organization established to protect and restore lighthouse stations, and to bring the movement to a larger public forum. In future years ALF would grow astronomically and lead the way to the restoration of dozens of lighthouses. *Lighthouse Digest* evolved into a highly polished online journal with beautiful graphics and up-to-date news on everything pharologic.

* * * *

Why were all these organizations emerging simultaneously? In Maine, sardine canneries and shoe factories were closing at an alarming rate. Dairy farms and poultry operations weathered and ceased.

The economic impact on their communities was devastating, but the effects were local, results that came with the rapidly changing world; one could explain with charts and globalization and the skyrocketing magnitude of big capital why this was happening. We were told it was out of our control. We were powerless and befuddled.

The response to the lighthouse crisis was different. As the awareness of their worsening condition grew, the public reacted. It was an intuitive response, like the American Revolution, the scramble to get to the moon, the arrival of the Beatles. This was a cause the nation understood—the guiding lights had to be saved.

* * * *

But Jeff and Judi Burke were oblivious to that raging lighthouse resurgence (we've never found ourselves astride the cutting edge of culture). We were blissfully serving organic blueberry pancakes and fair-trade coffee to our bed and breakfast guests at The Little River Inn in Pemaquid, Maine. In the summer of 1984, wandering lighthouse enthusiast James Hyland appeared at our door seeking lodging. He was touring the coast and researching the condition of Maine's deteriorating lighthouses. We became friends. The following year he learned the keeper's house on Isle au Haut was for sale. Immediately, Jay planed a visit there with the seller to see it. He asked us to tag along.

"I'd like your opinion," he said. "You two have created such a wondrous inn, the way you took an old farm and turned it into a booming success. Come along with me and have a look—maybe a lighthouse station could be converted, too."

"Holy cow!" I said. "Sounds like a wondrous adventure."

And then, just like that, he said, "Maybe you should buy it!"

Chapter 12

The Keeper's House Inn

1986–2012

"Sounds pretty risky," said my brother Steve.

"It'll never fly," said the lady at the Maine Publicity Bureau.

"We don't want it!" said Isle au Haut's First Selectman.

"Way out of bounds for our lending perimeters," said banker after banker.

I simply couldn't figure out why all these normally sane people (including my usually rational wife) couldn't see the guaranteed success of my scheme to create an inn at the old Isle au Haut lighthouse station. Sure, it was an isolated place, devoid of electricity and running water (hence, no bathrooms, not even a place to wash your feet), without a road to access the place nor a safe spot to land a boat. And it had only three rooms. And the islanders detested the tourism threat. And, yes, it would be an outrageously expensive undertaking—and we hardly had a cent.

But, unlike all the naysayers, this place was stirring something profound in me. A feeling of impending opportunity, perhaps. My lifetime of frustration sensed a breakaway opening that no one else could see. I had played the saxophone for fifty years, but the ability to play the blues still eluded me. The sirens of art had called me to dabble with paint and craft unwieldy wood sculptures that never sold. And my life till then had focused on seeking a utopian community where folks could live their dreams: communes and social revolution, changing the world to be free of defects. These efforts never bore fruit. But here, standing on the shore of the lighthouse station, surrounded by sculpted hill and rock, and the orchestrated rhythms, smells, and sounds of the sea, and the pristine beauty of the lighthouse with her message of hope and safety, I saw a huge unpainted canvas, primed and ready for a multi-dimensional brush. Nature and architecture, art, music, food, conversation, humanity, could all be blended together to create a theatrical masterpiece, where any visiting soul could have their moment on stage. Never in my life had I sensed such possibility.

The only folks besides me who thought my idea had merit were the Greenlaw family, the sellers of the property (who had no other offers to date). In fact, they liked the idea so much they offered to carry a second loan for us. Fortunately, a few other generous believers emerged from our past to loan us $9,000 for a down payment. With this little shudder of momentum, a maverick banker finally took notice and wrote us a mortgage.

We were in business.

Now all we had to do was build a half-mile road and a boat landing, create a sewage disposal system, bring in electricity and plumbing, renovate all the old buildings and install a certifiable commercial kitchen. And then we needed to develop a marketing plan and train a cadre of hospitality professionals, an overwhelming project requiring years to launch.

Two months later we opened.

Few of the aforementioned amenities were complete by then… well, actually none of them were. Guests had to backpack in with their suitcases, for instance; and I had to lug water cans from a distant farm well. Kerosene lanterns and gaslights were all we had for lighting. Guests stood in mud in a makeshift shower in the woods, with a tattered sail cloth to screen their bodies, and a trickle of tepid water from a hanging shower bag to wash away the wood smoke and mosquito repellent. And all of us—regardless of gender, economic status, national origin, or sexual preference—pooped in a common bucket. But with the frontier ambience, from the day we opened for business, night after night after night, those three guest beds were full.

By the end of the summer (this was 1986) we had finished remodeling the attic—or "The Garret," as it became known. We now had four rooms. The following summer the oil storage shed became our fifth accommodation (The Oil House). A year later, "The Woodshed" appeared for rent in our brochure (previously a creaky barn). Six rooms filled every night!

From there on out, a marvelous progression of stories unfolded.

Why, I could write a book on the events that followed! In fact, I already have: It's called *Island Lighthouse Inn: A Chronicle*, published in 1997 by Pilgrim Press. After three hardcover printings, the publisher toyed with the possibility of going to paperback, but that never happened. Now it's out of print, so if you'd like to read that account, you'll have to search for a used one on Amazon.com or find a dog-eared copy on your local rummage sale table.

Here's what I *can* do to describe the era Judi and I ran the lighthouse inn: I'll recount three selected vignettes. I realize that's an inadequate representation of the ten thousand warm bodies that tumbled across our lumpy mattresses and wore trenches in the island's trails, the myriad chefs who filled our kitchen with their culinary fireworks and personality defects. And it's impossible to do justice to all the local folk who worked here and made the ambience sweet or bitter depending on the drama driving their own lives. The point of this chapter will be to give a backwards glimpse at all the years we spent here—like flashes in time.

Flash in Time #1
The Night We Lost Our Guests

I could tell from the moment they stepped off the mail boat that I'd be dealing with trouble.

She seemed okay, the lady who had booked the reservation (let's call her "Dagmar"). She alit on the dock like a butterfly, her floppy hat fluttering in the October breeze so hard she had to clutch it with one hand or lose it overboard. With the other hand, encrusted with thick rings and spangled bracelets, she dragged an overnight bag festooned with lighthouse images. She dropped her burden on the float and stretched her arms to the skies, her orange muumuu wafting so wildly from sea gusts that I feared she might be blown away.

"Oh, Gawd," she said. "We're finally here at the lighthouse—a dream come true."

When she realized I was her host, she seized me in an impassioned hug. "When I read about the lighthouse inn, I knew it was calling me. We've come all the way from Idaho, you know. This is just what we need: peace and quiet, gorgeous scenery, a place to rest and recuperate, the perfect salve for me and the boys—Gawd only knows we need it!" she said, turning back toward the boat to make sure her charges had followed her onto the dock.

Two young men swaggered off the boat. They stood side by side like a tag team of wrestlers waiting to be introduced, glowering, threatening, letting the whole world know they were unaffected by pretty seaside lodges and sweet ocean breezes.

"This is my son, Terrance (not his true name)," she said, beckoning the fiercer one to come forward. He sauntered over.

"Welcome to the lighthouse, Terrance," I said, offering a hand.

He locked on to me with a fist of fingers thick as bratwurst. His sleeveless T-shirt left exposed biceps bulging with tattooed chains and spiders that seemed to crawl when he pumped my hand with a grasp so fierce I feared my digits might be pureed into soup. Still as marbles, his narrow eyes never flinched. An unintelligible salutation grunted from his belly.

"And this is my little Hermie (also a borrowed name, of course)," said Dagmar. "Hermie and Terrance are lifelong friends."

"Little Hermie" collected his gear and pushed past me: no offer of a handshake, no indication that I existed. He trailed after Terrance up the ramp, a miniature copy of his crony: shaved head, angry aura, muscled, and ready for war. But instead of the looming, ogre size of his pal, Hermie was short and squat, shaped like a pit bull with a personality to match.

While "the boys" tramped off toward the Keeper's House, Dagmar lingered on the dock fussing with her things—cueing me that she wanted to talk.

"Don't worry about the boys," she said, her bubbly words pouring like champagne from her crimson lips. "I promised Mr. Durkee, their probation officer, that I'd keep a tight leash on them. At heart, they're really sweet kids, you know, just had a bit of bad luck." She scrunched her shoulders in a certain knowing way that conveyed the message that I, too, should understand their situation. All the two darlings needed, Dagmar explained, was a little "lighthouse magic" to straighten out their lives, a break from an unfair life. That's why she had brought them here, she said, to "show them the light," she summarized, and she hoped I'd empathize.

Another guest searching for the magic tonic, I thought to myself, realizing once more I was not the only one to fall under the spell of sea-sprayed towers and flashing beacons. Here we go again!

* * * *

Judi got our new arrivals settled into the Horizon Room. All other guests had gathered downstairs for hors d'oeuvres and sparkling cider. Judi invited the trio to join. Apparently the prospect of sipping alcohol-free apple juice and nibbling dry sesame crackers didn't have much appeal. They never showed up. Nor did they wander outside to watch the sunset, the way guests usually do. Probably exhausted from their journey, we thought, or simply uncomfortable around inn-going folk. Judi was certain Dagmar would have enjoyed her baba ghanoush.

* * * *

The frightening weather that night is recorded in my memory as permanently as my first Halloween. The barren hardwoods had passed beyond their autumn glory. Leaves the color of children's finger paint piled up in low spots all across the island. When the mail boat delivered this trio, the sun was already sinking behind the Camden Hills, while minute by minute you could feel the temperature dropping. Winds picked up and drove our guests inside to wait for the dinner bell. By the time the first course was served, it was black as tar outside and blustery gusts rattled the old wood windows so hard that diners paused their nibbling to worry.

Three chairs remained empty. Were the new guests still fatigued from their journey? Cloistered in the Horizon Room, primping for dinner conversation? I'd rung the bell several times, but Judi prodded me to go upstairs and knock on their door.

I rapped—two or three times. No answer. I called, "Suppertime—come and get it!" Still, nothing. I waited a moment longer, then built up my courage and twisted the doorknob, expecting to find the door secured. But it folded open easily. The room was quiet, dark...and empty. Unopened bags, jackets, Dagmar's purse, all lay around the room untouched.

Downstairs the mood in the dining room signaled good cheer. Aromas from the kitchen promised tasty fare. But as I descended the steps to the foyer, I felt only worry. When I announced the results of my search to the kitchen crew, a hush replaced the jovial banter. Everyone knew: This was no night for guests to go missing!

"Did you check the boathouse?" said Judi.

"What about the Adirondack chairs?" asked Heather. "Maybe they dozed off out there."

I had checked everywhere. As the terrifying reality of their absence sunk in, our dishwasher, Brian, arrived. Everyone turned to him and blurted out the situation: Had he seen them on the path somewhere? Had there been any reports to the park rangers about hikers with twisted ankles? Any muggings? Any murders?

"Oh, yeah," said Brian. "I just came by Frank Blasdell's place. He said he saw a couple of skinheads and an old lady wandering around late in the afternoon—he remembered clearly, he said, 'cause they were lookin' so nasty. Those dudes wore nothing but T-shirts and muscle."

Heather clicked on the marine radio and switched to the NORAD station. "...and for eastern Penobscot Bay tonight, expect gale force winds with temperatures dropping into the twenties."

* * * *

Thirty minutes later we assembled at the ranger station.

Stormy, Brad, and Nicole were there in uniform; packing their portable radios and all the flashlights they could muster. A steady stream of islanders arrived in pickup trucks or on foot, all wearing heavy outer gear and rugged boots. Someone reported that others were at the town hall brewing coffee and heating up food. Inside the ranger shack, the increasing winds blew through cracks in the frail siding and underneath the door. Even inside the cabin, the wind's wailing madness made it hard to hear.

Stormy took charge. He was the head ranger, and knew the park trails best. Plus, he was a half foot taller than any of us, and knew how to take command.

"All right, now. We need to split into teams. No one goes alone. There are enough of us to cover the most likely trails. Brucie and Boogers can circle the island road by truck."

But I'm thinking: This is insane. The trails crisscross twelve square miles of wilderness and there is no moon tonight. With the thunderous crashing surf, the creaking tall spruce straining to hold onto the earth, the wind howling so fiercely, how could we even hear a cry for help? And they could have wandered off the trail. And with the windchill taken into consideration, the temperature could plunge down to zero!

Stormy asked me to describe the trio (as if there might be some other threesome wandering around out there). While I painted a picture of the tattoos and muscles and the bad attitudes, Dagmar's dance-hall tresses and her day-glo wardrobe, the assembled searchers stiffened into silence, their mouths agape, perhaps considering a change of mind and beating a quick retreat to a warm hearth and a steaming toddy. But in the end, of course, duty called; in situations like this, island folks rise to the occasion.

Brad and I chose to search the shore trail from the lighthouse to Seal Trap, and then back to the road by the Trial Point Trail. He was a hardened hiker and I probably knew that stretch of shore better than most. Bundled-up volunteers surged into the night in teams of two or three, each assigned to a separate path: The Ridge Trail, the Nat Merchant Trail, Black Dinah, the Duck Harbor trail, Eli's Creek Loop. This was 1989, back when cell phones were still heavy clunky monsters that required hours to charge—and islands were void of cellular towers. And global positioning devices had only appeared on guided missiles.

Judi remained at the Keeper's House, stoking the wood stoves and keeping the tea kettle steaming, with the ship-to-shore radio crackling on Channel 16. Nicole took up her post at the ranger station, reporting every few minutes by radio to the park headquarters on Mount Desert Island. Brucie and Boogers kept circling the fourteen-mile rutted path around the island, stopping now and then to holler into the woods, their voices feeble and ineffective against the screaming winds. Back at the town hall, less nimble citizens assembled to brew coffee and gather first aid equipment. Someone radioed Buster to have the mail boat ready.

By three o'clock in the morning, search teams had started arriving back at the ranger station. Like Brad and me, others returned with nothing but disappointing reports, aching feet and bruised knees from stumbles in the dark, runny noses, and frosted fingers. Worst of all, each disturbing account heightened the sense of dread. And the weather continued to worsen.

"*...skreep...skreep...skreep...This is a winter weather warning,*" blurted the mechanical voice on NORAD. "*Gale force winds expected over east Penobscot Bay until six o'clock a.m.... temperatures falling into the low twenties...windchill factor nearing zero.*"

Things couldn't get any graver.

But they did: Greg Runge staggered in, the last to report—he had taken the Long Pond Trail from beginning to end. The most skilled of the island's woods-wise folk, if anyone could track down prey, it would be Greg. He pulled off his gloves and accepted a cup of coffee, while we all gathered around in anticipation. Did he find anything, see anything, sight any flickering campfire, hear any desperate calling?

"Gunshots," he said. "Up on the Long Pond Trail. Must have been three or four or more. With the wind howling, I couldn't tell from what direction."

"We need reinforcements," said Stormy.

He depressed the radio broadcast button and spoke to whoever sat across the bay at the park headquarters, our connection to "America," a link to the outside world, where help might arrive from the search and rescue people, or the sheriff's office, or the U.S. Marines. By this time, we were horribly exhausted, cold, and scared. Paranoia began to take hold.

"We have a situation here that's getting out of hand," continued Stormy's radio report, slick with practiced professionalism, despite his obvious panic. "Three missing subjects in the Park. Survivalist types—possibly dangerous. Gunshots reported on the ridge. Send whatever reinforcements you've got, *post haste*—and make sure to bring your weapons!"

Acadia National Park Headquarters requested infrared heat-seeking airplanes be sent, but the National Guard declined, citing weather conditions rendering them useless—any human heat would be instantly dissipated by the screeching frigid wind.

Search dogs, on the other hand, were a prudent option. Park headquarters would send an emergency team right over, but the situation on the water was too nasty for *Miss Annie*, the park's prim little cruiser. The canine team would have to drive to Stonington and have Buster ferry them over on *Mink*, the 48-foot mail boat, built beefy and strong enough to barge her way through almost any winter weather.

I wondered what breed of dogs they would bring. Hunting-type hounds are used for tracking, relying on scents to locate their quarry. Other dogs boast aptitudes for locating narcotics, bombs, truffles, or unfortunate folks trapped in the rubble of tumbled buildings. Then too, there are the unlucky critters that specialize in locating cadavers, featured on TV dramas, sniffing out victims of mass murderers or Mafia hit squads.

Meanwhile, there's the innkeeper to consider: Imagine how I felt! This was all unfolding on my watch. I was the guy who masterminded this lighthouse inn experience, the host who coaxed naïve folk to pay hundreds of dollars to put themselves at risk. Would I be the target of opportunist lawyers if some sorry bloke tripped and broke his neck, if Dagmar got nipped by a rabid squirrel or if she clawed out her own eyes in an emotional fit? But most of all, I worried about my legacy: Would this disaster diminish the glory of my creation into a front-page story in the Island Advantages*: "Three Perfectly Nice People Frozen to Death Due to Innkeeper's Negligence."*

When the mail boat finally arrived, we were all relieved to see six extra rangers disembark with the dogs. We hustled them up to the ranger shack and summarized the situation. Soon we headed out anew, with fresh searchers and eager hounds. But in spite of the reinforcements, a pervasive dismal atmosphere reigned that dampened spirits. Was it too late? Still, no one even knew who these missing people were, or why they had plunged into the woods under such mysterious conditions. Some of us were half convinced that these missing guests were foreign terrorists, sent here to infiltrate our national defenses, or smuggling cartel types setting up a reception zone for landing a flotilla of narcotics.

That's when Brucie's pickup sputtered up to the town hall. The missing trio limped inside, their skimpy clothing torn and tattered, their arms and faces crisscrossed with scratches. Little Hermie struggled with a sprained ankle, and Terrance sported a nasty bruise that ran from his chin to his temple, and Dagmar's gorgeous tresses were snarled and speckled with pine needles. Villagers wrapped the three in woolen blankets and plied them with hot coffee and cornbread slathered in beach plum jelly. The EMTs clambered over them like a swarm of greenhead flies on a dung pile, checking their vital signs, looking for indications of hypothermia, hysteria, slashed wrists, or bullet holes.

Dagmar was sobbing.

"Everything will be all right. The boys are as strong as ever," I told her, hoping to assuage her anguish.

"Oh, I'm sure we'll be okay," she said. "That's not why I'm crying."

"Really?"

"No. It's...it's that I'm so *happy!* I can't believe what these folks have done for us! Your entire town! I've never felt so...so overwhelmed with gratitude."

* * * *

Five years later Dagmar returned alone to the Keeper's House.

"It's great to have you back," I said when I met her on the dock.

Gone were the gaudy clothing and fire engine lipstick colors. Her hair had been neatly cropped in a simpler style. Her transformed appearance was matched by a more sedate presence, too. Unlike her first visit, when she was obsessed with protecting "the boys" from an unfair world, this time our stroll up the path to the inn was leisurely and peaceful, as if she no longer worried.

My intuition tugged. Wondrous things must have happened. As we paused on the porch, I couldn't resist popping the question. "How have you been?" I asked.

"Thanks to that terrifying night on the mountain, *I changed*!" Her words gushed in a wave of happiness.

"Really?" I said. "Tell me what happened, once you guys disappeared from the inn."

She settled back in her chair, took another sip of tea and placed the cup squarely on the lobster crate that served as our front yard coffee table.

"As usual, the boys were uptight and angry, about this and that, everything. It was getting dark by then, and turning colder, too. Terrance thought a little jogging might help us stay warm. Off we went. We never thought about jackets, water bottles or where we could go."

I sat still and listened.

"A pretty path toward the woods caught our eye. Then, a fork—or so it seemed, or was it a wisp of deer trail—I really can't remember! Soon, though, the trail fizzled out. We tried one direction, then another, each boy sure he had a better idea. Arguments broke out. Then we finally tried to turn back, but…we were lost!"

"You must have been terrified," I said.

"We crashed through the woods, first this way,…then that. The wind picked up. Darkness closed in so quickly. Felt as if God had switched off the lights—do you remember, Jeff, how there was no moon that night?"

"Yes, of course," I said.

By now, she was steaming along, recounting the experience as if it were just last night. "The chill—that was the worst of all—a numbing coldness that set us chattering. We scrubbed our arms and tramped our feet trying to stay warm."

She went on to explain how they foundered through the abyss, branches raking at their eyes, snarly roots catching the toes of their shoes. Winds ravaged the tall spruce so viciously, their roots roiled beneath the shallow crust of soil, their trunks flexing, bending, under so much strain that every minute one would snap, sending sharp concussions shooting through the darkness. "**Crack. Crack, crack**," she mimicked the snapping branches.

I said, "Did it sound like...like, gunshots?"

"Yes, like gunshots," she said.

She told me how, amid the din of the storm, she broke into wailing, her shrieks and sobs absorbed by winds tearing through the forest canopy at sixty miles an hour. Hermie was sobbing too. Even giant Terrance stood incapacitated, shaking like the trembling trees around them, helpless, scared, shuddering uncontrollably in the frigid air, lost in the Wilderness Annex Area of Acadia National Park.

"Then," she explained, "we collapsed on the ground. Scrubbed about in the undergrowth—I remember how numb my fingers were—trying to rake together leaves, twigs, pinecones, anything...anything to make a heap of litter. We buried ourselves and shuddered. Rubbing each other—that's all we could do, to keep the circulation flowing."

How many hours were they there? Six? Eight? Ten? She couldn't say. In chattering phrases they prayed together, "Our Father who art in Heaven..." while morbid images thickened in their minds, like the ice solidifying in the low spots around them: "We will die here," she remembered thinking.

But the sun *did* rise, she recalled.

And they *did* survive...

At daybreak they staggered half-crazed to their feet. The wind had abated. They could see again.

"Downhill," she remembered barking at the boys, thinking as long as they descended, sooner or later they would find a path, a road, or at least the shore, someplace where they might be found.

Their legs barely functioned. Step by labored step, they struggled downward, with hands numb, jaws chattering. But with each step their muscles loosened. Thankfully, those first cautious paces turned to unrestrained hurry. Downhill they plunged like reckless slalom racers, careening around trees and boulders in a panicked race to find warmth, shelter, a cup of tea, a human face, a blessed chance to live again. Within minutes they sighted a patch of blacktop through the trees and heard the glorious rumble of Brucie's pickup truck. Ten minutes later they were in the Town Hall, wrapped in blankets and weeping.

Here's how it ended: Terrance was meaner than ever, and demanded that I buzz back to the lighthouse and retrieve their stuff. I fetched their things and delivered them to the mail boat. Townspeople who had been up all night lined the road to see them off, feeling sad about the trauma suffered, but wearily content the trio survived. When the three shunted down the hill to the boat landing, there was Gordon Chapin preparing to load a batch of lobster traps on *Mabelle Louise.* As the boys stomped down to board *Mink*, Gordy shouted out.

"So what do you fellows think of our island?"

Terrance sneered. "It sucks," he said.

* * * *

Dagmar slumped in her chair, re-living the experience that had drained her emotionally. But a sweet smile creased her tired face.

"I remember at the time you said you felt an immense feeling of gratitude," I said.

She said, "All that night on the mountain, I kept thinking, 'if we manage to see the light of day, I can't go on bogged down forever in my personal life.' Then, when we found our way down the mountain, and saw a whole town unified to help us, I realized I, too, needed to find a new path, some place where I could serve a cause more worthy than country club teas, and self-recrimination over situations I couldn't control."

"A *way out*?" I said.

"Yes."

"And...did you?"

"I quit my job at the brokerage firm. And I stopped frosting my hair...actually got most of it sheared right off," he giggled, remembering.

"It's very fetching," I said.

"And I went back to graduate school...got my Masters Degree in Social Work...adoptions—that's my thing, you know, home evaluations, placing little ones with families where they'll have a better chance. I love it. Most of all, it lets me know I'm serving a cause greater than my own private life."

"That's wonderful, Dagmar," I said.

"And it all came about because of the lighthouse. It called me, somehow. Mysterious...the way I read about it, felt magnetically pulled to it. That night on the mountain, amid the terror and confusion, it was the image of the lighthouse that kept me going...and ultimately gave new direction to my life. I was lost. Like a ship tossing at sea—the lighthouse saved my life. Can you imagine, Jeff, how powerful a force that can be?"

"Yes, I can," I said.

Flash in Time #2
The Chocolate Cake Contest

Every year at the end of the season, Judi and I would organize a special celebration for everyone at the lighthouse. For instance, several times we turned the inn into a haunted house for Halloween, with the staff and our friends participating as chainsaw-wielding maniacs or witches chanting over boiling cauldrons, scaring the bejesus out of the island kids and anyone else with the nerve to hike in. Other years we organized a hootenanny, a fancy sit-down dinner, a murder mystery night, and a silly awards gala. Of all those autumn closings, perhaps the most memorable was the chocolate cake contest.

Its origins are legendary. For years, the inn's cooks and helpers had been feuding over who made the best chocolate cake.

Deborah claimed hers was the tastiest. "Flavor is everything," she insisted. "When it comes to chocolate cake, you can't fiddle around worrying about calories or costs. You gotta' knock 'em dead with the eggs and butter—that's the only way to do it."

Judi was more conscientious. "We need to care about the ingredients," she liked to say. "Organic is key, so we don't poison the earth or the body. Think about your *karma*—the soul knows the difference between what's right and wrong."

Laurie Barter claimed she had a "secret ingredient" that made all diners swoon, hinting that once her cake was tasted, no dessert aficionado would ever eat anything else.

Lisa argued for tradition. As the inn's sole native island cook, she was sure that only hands coursing with island blood could bake the perfect cake. When she topped off a creation with her creamy dark frosting, there was something authoritative in the way that final swipe christened the swirly surface, declaring, "This is the way we do it, the way we always have, the *proper* way to frost a cake!"

Normally, the lighthouse kitchen was a congenial place, with folks working together to create the perfect ambience. Heaven only knows what horrid force fostered the malaise that spread that summer. It all started with harmless joisting and good-natured bragging.

"My cake has the perfect texture."

"Well, maybe a little too grainy. Mine is more sophisticated."

"Hers is a little rich for my taste. I prefer my frosting."

"She ruins her presentation with those awful decorations."

"I use only home-grown eggs, not that store-bought poison."

"Hers comes back to the kitchen only partially eaten."

"I get the most compliments."

"I get the most requests for my recipe."

"She makes some pretty crappy ones."

"Hers *really* sucks."

By Labor Day things were getting out of hand. You could feel tension thicken with each dessert presentation, the cook taking extra care to arrange each slice perfectly, polished as a magazine cover, garnished with the freshest glimmering strawberries, a drizzle of mouth-watering syrup, not a spatter or crumb out of place. It was expected that the server would present the masterpiece with an elegant flourish and a glowing acknowledgment to the baker, who listened from behind the dining room door. But it was getting to the point that whichever competitor was serving would simply deal out the fifth course with no credit to the cook.

Open warfare threatened. Fortunately, just in the nick of time, the kitchen combatants realized that the inn would suffer if things weren't mollified. That's when the idea of the contest materialized—the only way to settle the issue, once and for all. Begrudgingly, all parties consented.

Together, they decided the cake duel should take place on the last night of the season, with the decks cleared for action. It would be a "blind test," where a numbered slice of each cake would be served, with no hint of the identity of the baker. The public would be invited to judge. It's my opinion that the cooks became so worried about the consequences of losing that they decided to minimize their ego investments by spreading the liability. Anyone with an oven and eggbeater could join the fray. By the time Columbus Day rolled around, there were a dozen island bakers signed up to do battle in the First Annual Keeper's House Chocolate Cake Bake-Off Contest.

All parties consented to Ruth Van Doren serving as referee, since she is allergic to chocolate and wouldn't be tasting. However, there were still concerns that Ruthie had a "conflict of interest" because Harold, her husband, was one of the entrants.

On the night of the contest, Ruthie used a magic marker to section-off large paper plates into pie-shaped areas, each section numbered 1 through 12 (only she knew the assignment of number to baker). Twenty-five judging citizens of Isle au Haut gathered with forks and salivary glands at the ready, with only water to cleanse the pallet. Pillars of island tradition were there, like Billy and Bernadine Barter—she dressed for the occasion in flashing sparkles, he slouched on the couch telling jokes and slapping his knee, despite the seriousness of the event. Each taster would note down his or her top three choices by number. Ruth would do the tally, adding up the votes awarded each sample. Whichever number received the most first place votes would be declared the winner. Only then would Ruthie reveal the baker represented by that number.

While the general atmosphere was bubbly that night, beneath the surface, tension ran deep. I could see it in Laurie's eyes as she stood fretting at the kitchen door, in the nervous boasting of cooks whose culinary reputations were on the line, in the way Harold (the peacemaker) sermonized on the merits of good-natured rivalry, as if a lack of moral principles could result in an ugly riot, a slugfest of culinary egos and gooey barrages of hurled chocolate cake.

The dining room was packed solid, the crowd overflowing into the living room, where tasters sat with plates in their laps and dabbed at the corners of their mouths with paper napkins. "Ahs" and "Ohs" rippled through the inn, sounding like a covey of doves at the feeder. The bakers had planted themselves amid the crowd, trying to determine which sample was their own, so they could lobby those sitting around them. But Ruthie had done her job well. Even those chefs with the keenest noses and most discerning eyes were helpless to identify their own creations.

I can still remember struggling to cram down the dozen slices. Even with water to lubricate the passage, each additional sample backed up to the point I almost choked.

"Jeffrey!" Judi prompted from her chair beside me. "Slow down! That's no way to judge a cake! Take only little bites that you can savor."

"Yes, dear," I responded.

But this contest was crucial. The rivalry between the staff had to be quelled, or my business would suffer. How better to cast an honest vote than by stuffing down every crumb. I noted down number 9 as my first choice, followed by two other also-rans that hardly mattered.

Others marked their preferences, too, and Heather collected the slips of paper. Ruthie cleared the kitchen counter so she'd have a space free of frosting smears to tabulate the results. All tasters were barred from the kitchen, to avoid distracting the judge or the temptation to slip in additional ballots. Relegated to the other rooms, cooks and participants alike waited for the results: Laurie stood alone, twisting the corner of her apron. Lisa sat with her Mom, Geri, with a look of satisfaction. Deborah chatted away merrily, as if she didn't really care. Harold sat quietly with his hands in his lap, wondering if there would be space on his shelf for one more historic trophy.

Chatter ceased when Ruthie appeared in the kitchen doorway, a sheet of paper in hand.

"Okay, folks. We have the results."

Silence. The people's tribunal sat straight-backed and serious. The cooks fidgeted nervously, with hands clenched, smiles forced.

I can't recall who won third place or second. I'd venture to guess no one else can either, except for the two unfortunates who garnered those places. They probably smiled and nodded, accepting with practiced grace the humiliation of knowing they hadn't won gold. The drama only heightened for the remaining contestants: Two erstwhile competitors had been eliminated.

This was it. The moment had finally arrived. The suspense and tension would be resolved. Ruthie cleared her voice, glanced at the slip of paper.

"And the winner by a huge margin—sixteen votes cast out of twenty-five—judged by all of you present here, for the best chocolate cake ever baked on Isle au Haut, is…ta-dah…number nine—our dear friend, Geri Turner!"

The outbreak of applause and shouted plaudits was genuine enough, I guess, but beneath the clapping and hooting ran sublime little currents of rebellion, a little resentment eddied in corners of the dining room, a pocket of disbelief here and there. Even while cheering, subtle moods rippled beneath the surface: heartbreak, shock, a bit of anger. Others reached out with embraces for Geri.

The most surprised of all was Geri Turner. Wide-eyed and humbled, she sat glued in her chair, visibly shocked. Then, little by little, her mood, the expression on her face, her posture, all transformed in a slow-motion metamorphosis. Her face turned cherry red. And she slumped forward, head bowed with hands shielding her face, shoulders trembling. The celebratory mood suddenly paused. Was she simply embarrassed by all the fuss or was it something else?

Geri began to giggle. Then erupted to laughter. That morphed into tears, then back to giggles again. What on Earth? we all wondered! She finally regained enough composure to explain.

"I'm so embarrassed," she said. "I have to apologize. You see, I have to tell the truth. I never expected this. My entry, you see…well, I just threw together a Betty Crocker box cake, canned frosting and all."

* * * *

Later, folks trailed away into the blackened woods, the lighthouse illuminating the path with her pulsing flashes. Sated with chocolate and happiness, every bloated participant and every joyous cook had come to grips with what had happened that night. This had been a war of ego and skill. But, in the end, it wasn't the individual superstar who won—the blue ribbon went to the collective effort. The Chocolate Cake Contest had been a smashing success because, ultimately, everybody united in celebrating together.

Flash in Time #3
When Broadway Came to the Lighthouse

I never knew what to expect when I greeted guests arriving on the mail boat. Once we hosted a news anchor from a network TV corporation. There was a State Supreme Court Judge, the requisite movie starlet, and the archeologist who had dredged up millions in doubloons from the hulks of Spanish treasure ships. More common people included future cherished friends—lovers of the island who later built homes here and became key figures in the history of the Island. But of them all, there's one guest who stands out as emblematic of the wondrous people attracted to the Keeper's House.

Peter Valentyne and his partner, Mark, came to stay one summer in the mid-1990s. They had a fabulous time chattering with other guests, exploring the island's trails, and discovering the hidden secrets that make the island special. But when they checked out and returned to New York City, I never expected what followed.

Inspired by his time here, Peter, a playwright, had gotten right to work and written a script titled, *The Logic of Solids*. His play was based on what he had experienced at the inn, the chemistry between the odd collection of guests, the innkeeper and his wife, the lighthouse itself, and the magical baton effect it had in conducting events. We were pleased of course, but this recognition was nothing uncommon for this blessed two acres. Already, the Keeper's House had inspired poetry, paintings, and essays in dozens of publications all across the nation. But Peter's play was destined to become more than a scrapbook clipping and a few lines of verse Scotch-taped to the refrigerator.

It opened Off-Broadway in 1996. Some good reviews were written. It wasn't like *Cats*, of course, didn't hit that broad common denominator, or earn millions for the playwright. Personally, though, when I read the script, I was profoundly moved by the lyrical message and the way Peter portrayed the mystery of the lighthouse and its power to alter people's lives. This is potent stuff, I felt. The life of *The Logic of Solids* didn't die when the theater marquee announced a new production, Peter's play was to be reborn on a grander stage than any New York venue.

"All proceeds will go toward the lighthouse restoration," said Peter. "The entire cast will perform at the lighthouse for free. The soundman, too, and the clarinetist, the director, and the stage prop people. Everybody wants to come to Isle au Haut just to help the lighthouse."

"But Peter," I said, "how could we pull it off? We have no sound system here, no Broadway technical stuff."

"Body mikes, that's the trick," Peter explained how they planned to use them with hidden speakers buried in the raspberry bushes. The actors would speak their lines from the upstairs bedroom windows, when they crawled up through the rocks, or cast ashes from the lighthouse catwalk.

I started to get the picture. "Yeah, like theater-in-the-round, with the assembled masses seated in the yard, on the rocks, lounging on the boardwalk..." I said.

"...the actors passing through the audience as the action progresses," Peter replied, finishing my thought.

The concept jibed perfectly with the location. After all, Peter's play was set at the lighthouse station. This was a dream-come-true for any theatrical production, the real-life site where the action actually unfolds, the opportunity for viewers to sit amid the developing drama of other people's lives.

The island became infected with Broadway fever. The mail boat company volunteered to provide a free special trip to transport off-island theater buffs, while the *Island Advantages* printed alluring public invitations. The Town's Board of Selectmen authorized use of the lighthouse tower for the performance, and the chairs from the library and Town Hall were at our disposal. Summer folk came forward to offer housing and meals for the visiting cast.

There was only one problem. In the middle of the trail, right where it arrives at the lighthouse station, Scene I in the First Act called for fornication.

I broached the subject with Peter.

"Geez, Peter, I love your play, you know, but having sex acted out seems a bit much. We need to tone it down a bit. This is Isle au Haut, where we could really ruffle feathers among our donor base."

"It's only acting," he said. "Besides, being true to the script is a matter of principle. We did it in New York without fail, every night, for the entire eleven day run and never got raided."

"I'm concerned, Peter. I'm the guy on watch here. If dire consequences emerge, if the lighthouse campaign suffers, if the Knox County Vice Squad gets alerted, or the Point Lookout people start carping, I'll be the one who gets fingered."

"But its stifling free expression," said Peter.

I glowered.

"Well, I suppose I can talk to the actors and director," he said.

Visions swarmed in my mind of vice squads landing by amphibious craft, phalanxes of TV reporters arriving by helicopter, all our hard work ruined by unsavory action. I needed to pound this home.

"Let's be clear," I said to my friend, "We'll go ahead with the production, but under no circumstances will there be any front yard humping."

* * * *

On the evening before the performance, it seemed everything had been resolved. The director and the pair of gorgeous actors billed to engage in the turf-tumbling exercise had begrudgingly consented to omit the carnal stuff.

Pat and Dick Marks had organized a pre-performance dinner party for the entire cast over on the east side of the Island at their oceanfront home. We organized a fleet of island junkers to drive the New Yorkers over to feast on Portobellos and pinot noir.

I loaded a bunch of actors into Nellie Belle (my 1950s Willys) and bumped off to the Marks' soiree. Squished in next to me was the precocious young woman who played Rosemary, the sex-addicted character who, on the following afternoon, would be entrusted to keep her panties on. While most people reflected the excitement and anticipation of the next day's event, she seemed reserved and sulky.

After a few minutes of bumping along she spoke. "I didn't really agree to the censorship, you know," she said. "It violates my beliefs, my rights..."

"Huh," I said, trying to ignore the swaying body next to me that lurched against my steering arm with every pothole we hit.

"Rosemary" went on to pontificate about the critical need for nudity and sex on stage. I was aware that during that era nudity was de rigueur on Broadway, but never in my imagination did I expect to be confronted with the issue, here on Isle au Haut, here in *my* life, threatening *my* future.

"My body is my temple," she said. "If I truly act, if I am to be the *real* Rosemary, my body must be true as well, my juices flowing, my lust seething..."

I was so distracted by "Rosemary's" impassioned monologue that my driver's focus failed. Nellie Belle hit a nasty rut in front of Wayne's house and my passengers went flying, "Rosemary's" resources squishing against my steering arm.

"Holy shit," I thought, "What have I got myself into?"

All during the feast at the Marks's, all during my sleepless night, I worried constantly. Would the cast stay on the censored script during the next day's performance?

* * * *

In the morning, things progressed so perfectly that my fears almost disappeared. The weather was perfect. Spirits were high. Volunteers arrived in pickups stacked with folding chairs. A dazzling display of breakfast goodies and urns of coffee sated the busy cast and crew. Squawks and whistles from testing speakers attracted passing seagulls. A sense of possibility, of grandeur permeated the atmosphere. You could feel it. This would be the most stellar moment in the history of the lighthouse.

Right on schedule, the mail boat arrived, packed to the gunwales with a festive crowd of theatergoers. Up the path from the town road, locals and summer residents appeared two by two, toting picnic lunches and plastic chairs. Meanwhile, the stage crew checked props and the soundman adjusted the tiny hidden microphones snuggled into the cleavages and collars of all the actors. Soon, all were settled and the hubbub diminished, as if cued by a dimming dome of celestial light. Unseen, lilting loon-like sounds of a clarinet drifted up from the shore. One could *feel* the curtain rising.

The Logic of Solids

ACT 1, Scene 1

A bluff along a path by the ocean winding towards the lighthouse. Enter MRS. MALARKEY and ROBERT STONE.

MRS. MALARKEY
(looking at her brochure)

The brochure does say keep to the right…

As if on cue, seagulls swooped overhead and the gentle gush of summer surf played in the rocks below, so perfectly timed one would think these sounds were controlled by the soundboard nestled in the flowerbed. Mrs. Malarkey and Robert Stone make their entrance just as prescribed in the script. They engage in banter meant to develop their characters and introduce subsequent players: She is a babbling lighthouse fanatic who recently tried to murder her ex-husband by braining him with a lighthouse snow globe. He is a shy, handsome young fellow, recently ordained as a minister, still looking to wet his feet in real-life situations.

Malarkey and Stone drift toward the Keeper's House.

Then Rosemary and Clyde enter the clearing. This is the scary part for me, the scene in the script where they banter a bit before stripping off everything and tumbling in the grass.

"Don't do it! Please, oh, please, oh, please, don't do it," I breathe to myself.

Their pace slows. They come to a stop. They turn toward each other. Rosemary emits an audible giggle. Clyde's hand slips slowly, seductively, to the small of her back.

All across the lighthouse grounds, the crowd tenses with anticipation, their senses heightened by the sensuous acting, feeling the rush of hormones, the heat of the actors passion.

"Please, oh, please, oh please…" I secretly anguish.

Then, in a torrent of unbridled desire, she tears off her flimsy tee shirt, exposing her beauties for all to see.

"Oh, my God," I say under my breath, cringing. "This is it. I'm destroyed."

In panic, I survey the crowd, looking to see who stalks out, who organizes the vigilante gang, who sets fire to my dreams. *I imagine hearing responses from familiar gaping faces.*

"Gawd almighty!" gasps Gordon Chapin.

"Good gorry!" whispers Harold Van Doren.

"Our father who art in Heaven!" intones the Reverend Theodore H. Hoskins.

Having flung her top into the bayberry bushes, Rosemary then leaps on Clyde and implants a slobbery kiss. Then, their moment of passion is thankfully interrupted by the emergence of ESTHER and NICK, the next characters to wander into the clearing. Rosemary struggles to untangle her top from the undergrowth and wiggles back into it. And the play goes on.

Whew! That was it, a major surprise and a compromise on "Rosemary's" part: We avoided the messy stuff; she got her flash of glory.

Now fully dressed, the actors carried on with their lines. No ticket-buying donor stalked out. No screams of outrage or recrimination. In fact, a certain levity reigned, as if the audience was satisfied that they were getting their money's worth. After all, if the starlet strips off her top, this must be real Broadway stuff!

I relaxed and enjoyed the show.

Here's the way the play went: A strange and varied consortium of guests come into conflict with each other and their own individual values. Beneath the flickering power of the lighthouse and the grounding influence of the keeper's wife, things come to a climax when a grieving woman hurls her lover's ashes from the top of the tower, bathing the others in snowy recognition of what really matters in life. Interestingly, the keeper himself never appears in the play until the very last scene. With the permission of Peter Valentyne, my friend the author, we reprint here the final scene from *The Logic of Solids*.

ACT 11, Scene 8

The Lighthouse Inn kitchen late at night. The KEEPER enters to find his WIFE writing at the kitchen table, bent like a question mark over paper and pen. Sitting in front of her is the murder weapon: the lighthouse snow globe.

KEEPER
Still up? Can't sleep?

KEEPER'S WIFE
I wanted to finish this.

KEEPER
Another story?

KEEPER'S WIFE
Actually, I'm trying out another form.

KEEPER
Oh.

KEEPER'S WIFE
A play this time.

KEEPER
What's it about?

KEEPER'S WIFE
This place. A lighthouse inn on an island in Maine. About the different combinations of people who pass through here...why they come. How some are going away from things and others are coming towards. (BEAT) All kinds of people. Some of them barely bother to learn our names. I'm just a cook, maid, and bottle washer to a few of them, while to others I'm the wife of a lighthouse keeper, while still to others I'm a writer who happens to be all the other things combined. (BEAT) So much happens here...yet we somehow remain on the periphery, you and I.

KEEPER
Oh, I don't know. Our lives are rich enough. I often feel we're at the center of the storm.

KEEPER'S WIFE
I'm not saying our lives aren't rich. I wouldn't want to be anywhere else.

KEEPER
So, is there a story? A plot?

KEEPER'S WIFE
It's about the lighthouse.

KEEPER
I know that. But what about the lighthouse? Its history?

KEEPER'S WIFE
I'm not as literal minded as you are.

KEEPER
So what then?

KEEPER'S WIFE
It's about a lighthouse that needs people to express the things it can't say.

KEEPER
Okay.

KEEPER'S WIFE
Remember that couple from Connecticut…the Thorndykes?

KEEPER
The snooty ones…back in July.

KEEPER'S WIFE
Well, in my play they're called the Thicks. And remember those two young women from Piscataway, Ellen and Diane?

KEEPER
The…oh, the couple?

KEEPER'S WIFE
I knew you'd remember them. I changed their names to Lois and Elaine….to protect the innocent…or the guilty…whichever way you want to look at it.

KEEPER
So you're putting all our strangest characters together in one play.

KEEPER'S WIFE
I wouldn't say strange. I find them the most inspiring. It's curious who stands out in memory and why. It seems to me it's people's peculiarities, their odd habits or unlikely aspirations that linger on. I see them as their virtues.

KEEPER
And yours is the lighthouse's point of view.

KEEPER'S WIFE
It is rather up to me, isn't it? Let's just say it's the point of view of two not so innocent bystanders.

KEEPER
Write what you know, that's what I say.

KEEPERS WIFE
It's just that I'm having trouble with the ending.

KEEPER
How long have you been working on this?

KEEPER'S WIFE
Months now. (BEAT) It seems vaguely distasteful. And it was such a sweet story up to there. A kind of equation. Lovers uniting, liars daring to tell the truth, dragons being slayed.

KEEPER
If it's an equation…then do the math. It's a matter of finding the logical conclusion.

KEEPER'S WIFE
You're a big help.

KEEPER
(slightly edgy)
If you don't want my advice, then leave me out of it.

KEEPER'S WIFE
Yes, dear.

KEEPER
I'm sure you'll work it out. (BEAT) I'm going to bed.

KEEPER'S WIFE
I won't be long.

KEEPER
Guests tomorrow, remember.

KEEPER'S WIFE
How could I forget?

The KEEPER exits, presumably for bed. The KEEPER'S WIFE takes out a lighter, looks at it briefly, lights a cigarette, and continues her work.

LIGHTS DIM OUT.

THE END

* * * *

Like single cropped scenes from miles of moving picture film, these three "flashes in time" are examples of the sweet and crazy events that tumbled by during the decades Judi and I rented rooms at the Isle au Haut Lighthouse Station. So much of our past is left untold, the helicopter landing, the day the whale swam by, the weddings of our children, the infamous croquet tournament in the woods, our own fiftieth wedding anniversary. Of course not all events turned out so enchanting. Most notably, starting in 1996, the island became a battleground for who would own the lighthouse tower.

This question of ownership threatened to drive Judi and me off the Island.

Waiting for the mailboat, circa 2004. Photograph by Bob Walker.

Jeff and Judi at the Keepers House. Circa 1992. Photograph courtesy of Bob Walker.

Chapter 13

The Heron Neck Fire and the Lighthouse War

If you stand here at the tip of Robinson Point on a fogless night and look westerly, just a degree south of Vinalhaven, you'll see a speck of fixed red light on Green Island. That's the Heron Neck Lighthouse Station. If you had been here on April 19, 1989, it would have been dramatically easier to notice—the Heron Neck keeper's house was on fire.

An electrical malfunction had occurred in the closed-down building, empty since the tower's automation in 1982. Soon the roof was aflame. Volunteer firemen from Vinalhaven responded quickly, but they were slowed by the channel separating the two islands. Eventually they did get two seawater pumps up to the station and began hosing down the house. A Coast Guard ship arrived and the fire was finally extinguished, but not before the roof was destroyed and the entire house damaged by smoke and water.

Four long years passed while the Coast Guard foundered in indecision on what to do with the crippled building. The citizens of Vinalhaven and surrounding communities stewed angrily, witnessing the ongoing deterioration of their lighthouse station. The Coast Guard was neither financially prepared nor organizationally mandated to expend tens of thousands to repair obsolete, unused buildings. Nor was the small struggling Town of Vinalhaven able to help. Nor the State of Maine. Complicating matters, Heron Neck was isolated on a small knob of rock, far from the nation's population centers, off the beaten track for tourists and cruise ships, visited only by a few wandering yachtsmen and the local fishermen who found the waters there perfect for lobstering.

But not everyone was idle.

The Island Institute, based in Rockland, Maine, had been founded in 1983. Its mission: *to sustain Maine's island and coastal communities, and exchange ideas and experiences to further the sustainability of communities here and elsewhere.* While the Coast Guard waffled in dealing with the situation, the Island Institute saw an opportunity to put their mission into action. Led by Peter Ralston, one of its founders, the Institute evaluated options for how to save the Heron Neck keeper's house.

Ralston had a vision. What if he could convince the Coast Guard to license the Institute to be responsible for the damaged station? That would relieve the government of the burden and open up possibilities for more imaginative thinking, involving local folks who had personal attachments to the lighthouse. By this time the Coast Guard was taking a beating in the press and all across the nation because of its inability to save the station. Over the past thirty years, as lighthouses became automated and the keepers' families removed, maintenance costs for these empty buildings couldn't be justified in the Coast Guard's budget. Initially, many were auctioned to the highest bidder, an action that caused resentments within coastal communities that regarded these stations as part of their heritage. Blowing up keepers' houses or burning them down were the usual methods for dealing with troublesome unused buildings. But in the face of the "Lighthouse Renaissance" in the early 1980s, those traditions now ran counter to a public that no longer tolerated matches and dynamite as appropriate solutions. The existing system was no longer acceptable. The Coast Guard consented to Ralston's offer.

By the time the Institute's arrangement with the Coast Guard was consummated, Ralston had found a private party to finance the restoration. Eventually, with the restoration complete, the deed to Heron Neck

Lighthouse was transferred in full to the individual who had paid for its salvation. In return, the new owner signed an easement that allowed limited public access to the station in perpetuity. Most importantly, instead of being destroyed, this beautifully restored station lives on. The Institute's accomplishment provided a model that worked.

Ralston realized that the success at Heron Neck might be repeated elsewhere. Instead of distant bureaucratic entities calling the shots, why not turn to the local communities, who care deeply about their lighthouses and have vested historic, cultural, and economic interests in their survival. Ralston and the Island Institute plunged ahead with this new idea. Within the year he had researched the entire chain of beacons along the Maine coast and edited the list down to several dozen that faced challenges similar to Heron Neck: isolation, nonessential ancillary buildings not maintained by the Coast Guard, and small local populations with limited resources. By 1993 Ralston and the Island Institute were on the brink of introducing new legislation to the U.S. Congress: a plan to save Maine's lighthouses. Only a few courtesy calls were needed to finish preparations.

* * * *

When Judi and I first arrived at the Isle au Haut Lighthouse Station in 1986, the deteriorating tower was barricaded to the public. A high chain-link fence barred off the area, with intimidating signage to scare away curious day hikers or lurking looters.

The following year, we were able to negotiate with the Coast Guard Headquarters in Southwest Harbor: they would allow me to remove the barrier and signage if we provided an architecturally appropriate locking gate with a simple notice identifying the tower as off-limits. At the same time, we referenced old photographs to design and rebuild the long-ago destroyed boardwalk that united the front porch of the keeper's house with the bridge into the tower. This visually returned the station to the way it was designed.

Although we owned only the ancillary buildings at the station, I had become obsessed with the ragged tower looming in my front yard, the icon that had made our inn so attractive. In the first years after we opened, the news stories and television coverage never ceased. Almost weekly, new accounts glowed across the nation about the adventurous young couple with the lighthouse inn. It was hard to face a reporter and admit the tower wasn't really mine.

"Historically, visually, culturally, the lighthouse is part of the Keeper's House Inn," I'd say. "It's all one big fat unit, in every conceivable way."

"You mean the *actual* lighthouse tower isn't really yours?" the reporter would say.

I'd hem and haw. "Well, not *legally*. But I'm the one who keeps an eye on her, the one who cares the most, and, besides,…"

I must say, I was pretty proud of myself. I had felt the same way about working out the purchase of the property when we had no money. With sheer willpower and persistence, I had managed to move things forward to realize my fantasy. But little by little my mistaken sense of ownership had increased—the lighthouse was becoming *my* lighthouse (at least, to me, it felt that way).

As the Heron Neck Lighthouse story developed, I watched with nervous interest. Would *my* tower ever be affected by the actions of the Island Institute? In the midst of this period of angst, I unexpectedly received a note to call Peter Ralston.

We had no telephone at the lighthouse, so I rode my bike to the Town Hall where a microwave phone served the island population (in 1987 Isle au Haut had been the last town in the United States to install telephone service). As I punched in the numbers, I was nervous, excited, unsure of what to expect.

"Hello. Island Institute. How may I direct your call?" a voice said.

"Jeff Burke here, on Isle au Haut," I choked out the words. "Yes, may I please speak to Peter Ralston?"

"Just a moment," she said, shunting me onto "hold."

I waited for an eternity, it seemed. I remembered how a few years ago I had met Philip Conkling, the Institute's Executive Director, at a lighthouse conference in Washington. Mr. Conkling criticized me for not having worked with the Institute when Judi and I were acquiring the lighthouse station in 1986 (I had never even heard of the Island Institute in 1986—perhaps the Institute expected a repeat of the

Heron Neck process?). Now, I was worried that this call might be another occasion for the Institute to find fault with my dreams. They had recently published a booklet—I found out later—that made a compelling argument for why these historic properties should remain in the public domain and never fall prey to the plunder of private ownership. (That meant me!)

"Jeff?" The voice jarred me back to the present. "This is Peter Ralston. Thanks for your call-back."

Peter proceeded to give me a rundown on the Institute's plan to use legislation to transfer ownership of 22 Maine lighthouses to selected nonprofits, ones like Heron Neck. These lights needed stewards to protect them, enhance them, and bring them back to the status they deserved. Of the entire list chosen by the Institute to receive deeds, all were nonprofits, he explained, with one exception.

"We would like you and Judi to be the new owners of the Isle au Haut lighthouse tower," he said. "You've demonstrated by your success with the Keeper's House Inn that you're committed to historic preservation. We're impressed with how you opened up the site to the public, so the broader masses have access. What do you say?"

I could barely speak. The ramifications were overwhelming. I can't even remember the rest of the conversation, only the very ending.

"Well," I stammered. "Well, I guess.... well, okay. Yes."

The Island Institute had made me the happiest man on the planet.

* * * *

In the weeks that followed, The Island Institute polished its appropriations bill to be submitted to the U.S. Congress. On July 12, 1994, I was thrilled to read how the *Portland Press Herald* had picked up the story and broke the news. Included in the article was the list of selected lighthouses, each coupled with the intended recipient for the deed: state parks, colleges, municipalities, conservation groups, and lighthouse associations. Right there, along with all those nonprofits it also listed: "Isle au Haut Light would be given to a bed and breakfast called The Keeper's House," according to the Island Institute's proposal. The following month, the same story was echoed in the August *Lighthouse Digest*, noting, "This [Isle au Haut lighthouse] would be the only transfer to a private individual."

Can you imagine being offered the ownership of a gorgeous lighthouse, absolutely free! I found myself roaming the station grounds, a tape measure in my hand, dreaming of future expansions, additions, and a room for rent in the tower, all sorts of bizarre shenanigans to take advantage of my good fortune. Just think, I fantasized, the charm the tower could offer with a Murphy bed that unfolds from the wall, a hidden stereo system whispering Nat King Cole tunes, an ice-filled bucket of imported champagne that descends from the lantern vent. Wouldn't that be romantic? And think of the outrageous fee it would garner, a gazillion dollars to finally push us into the black and sweep us into a future of economic bliss.

At the same time, a wary malaise haunted me; something wasn't right with my scheming. I noticed that folks in the village never extended congratulations or queried me about the Institute's plan.

Ed White, the island's renegade hippy philosopher, the only one (besides my wife) who could look me in the eye and say what he honestly thought, delivered his opinion.

"Don't screw up the tower," he said.

"But..." I started to say. But already I knew where he was going.

"They picked you guys because they trust you to do the right thing, not screw it up with cutesy décor, flower pots, and signs that demand, 'DO NOT DISTURB.' What are you thinking anyway?"

The truth unveiled.

As it turned out, it didn't matter; the appropriations bill offered by the Island Institute never got through Congress. It died in the bowels of the Capitol on the desk of some disappointed intern.

What a sad loss for Peter Ralston and the Island Institute! And for Isle au Haut, as well. As for me, after the deal fell through, I could more clearly see, that despite my romance with the tower, Judi and I didn't have the resources to give it the care it required. We had been fortunate to have the ancillary buildings fall in our laps, and we were doing fine with the inn, but considering our college-bound children and our own advancing ages, our tiny inn could never generate the income needed to restore and care for a massive crumbling lighthouse tower. It was better —I tried to assure myself—that it would never be mine.

* * * *

Then, the strangest thing happened.

Shortly after the Institute's plan went awry, a young design engineer from the Coast Guard, Lieutenant Brenda Kerr, contacted me. The Coast Guard was preparing to do a major restoration of the Isle au Haut Lighthouse tower. She herself was drawing up the work plans, in conjunction with the State Office of Historic Preservation. 1996 would be the target year.

Imagine, after all the hand-wringing and worry, after all the self-recrimination, the congressional derailment of the Institute's proposal, the worry for the tower's future, now, all of a sudden, totally unexpected, the "bad guys," the unenlightened United States Coast Guard, were jumping into the fray to rescue our beloved lighthouse! Although the Coast Guard was simply following their mandate, it was my inclination to believe that all the national press the inn had generated had been the force that led to our shoddy tower being selected for renovation.

Then, if you can believe it, an even stranger thing happened! Out of nowhere—it seemed—a revamped appropriations bill was introduced in Congress (It turns out, after all, that Peter Ralston had never given up). This was The Maine Lights Bill of 1996, and even stranger yet, the bill, sponsored by Maine's Senator Olympia Snowe, passed the U.S. Senate and was signed into law by President Clinton. Twenty-two Maine lighthouse stations were listed, including Isle au Haut. This bill, however, identified no preordained recipients to receive the deeds. That may have been one reason why it sailed so smoothly through the process.

I rejoiced for the lighthouse. On the other hand, I was disappointed. Why hadn't Jeff and Judi been selected to get the lighthouse this second time around? It never occurred to me that the first bill failed because of inherent weaknesses. The second one passed because it was so much better planned—it included crucial provisions the original bill lacked. For instance, recipients of deeds would be chosen by a Maine Lighthouse Selection Committee made up of Coast Guard brass, State Historic Preservation officials, lighthouse experts, and planners and experts of various shades and stripes. Qualified parties (nonprofits, state and local municipalities, parks, and the like) were all welcome to apply for ownership. Selection would be based on specific criteria, including long-range ability to take on the project. Also, strict covenants would be written into the deeds. No commercial use would be allowed, historic preservation standards must be upheld, and plans for use must include environmental protection, education, and public access. Each of the 22 lights would be under the watchful eye of the State Office of Historic Preservation, which could declare a deed null and void if any acquiring party failed in their obligations.

Bingo! Since I was out of the running, the Town of Isle au Haut should apply—wouldn't that be a workable solution? That way everything would be local, and the people here could gain the access they had never had before.

I must have chatted with every citizen on the island that summer—in their homes, on the Town Landing, standing in line at the island store, waiting at the Post Office while the mail was being sorted. Lots of folks felt the same as I. So we got to work and started a municipal lighthouse committee. What a blast this would be, fun and simple, a cakewalk to claiming the lighthouse!

The reality turned out to be otherwise. This seemingly innocent campaign led to a two-year island civil war, an earthquake of ugliness that pitted neighbor against neighbor.

I was at the epicenter.

* * * *

Let's meet the members of that original Isle au Haut Lighthouse Committee.

1. Me, Jeffrey Burke, transplant from Ohio, founder and owner of the inn at the lighthouse station, with an understandably high level of interest in the future of the tower.

2. Linda Greenlaw, descendent of the island's Robinson/Greenlaw lineage, who grew up summers living in the keeper's house. She was the renowned swordfish boat captain made famous in Sebastian Junger's *The Perfect Storm*. Linda was soon to begin her own writing career with her breakout *New York Times* Best Seller, *The Hungry Ocean*.
3. Barbara Brown, genteel summer resident, dedicated member of the Library Committee and the Isle au Haut Historical Society. She was the hiker who shared the warm months sipping tea and bird-watching with other summer ladies.
4. Wayne Barter, Head Ranger for the island's division of Acadia National Park. He was quiet and reclusive, a direct descendent of the island's first permanent settler, a history buff and collector of large-caliber rifles and Indian artifacts.
5. Laurie Barter, employee at the inn from the age of seventeen.
6. Dave Hiltz, lobsterman, hunter, outdoorsman extraordinaire, with a boat loud enough to warn folks in Kazakhstan to get out of the way. Sweet or sour depending on the day, Dave had the energy to get things moving.

As usual, as soon as any group on the island rallies together to wage a campaign for any purpose—except for house fires, missing people, or dire medical emergencies—opposition instantly emerges. So, here's the most important thing to remember: The "Lighthouse War" didn't have anything to do with the lighthouse! Like every other island in Maine, maybe every other small town in America—in the entire world, perhaps—the *war* was driven by longtime feuds, internecine hostilities that had brewed for decades, and spats and spurns and misunderstandings that hobbled the town with ever-shifting alliances of folks who wouldn't speak to each other.

The lighthouse had become the latest battleground.

Overnight our seemingly uncontroversial plan to have the town become the owner of its historic icon became the target of unrelenting assault. A fast-emerging band of naysayers proposed leaving the fate of our lighthouse in the hands of some undesignated outside nonprofit organization. They did not want the town to take title. On the face of it, it seemed a logical alternative, but this seemingly trivial disagreement became a nasty slugfest between "them and us."

"Our side" worked with the Maine Lighthouse Selection Committee to implement the step-by-step procedures outlined in the Maine Lighthouse Program, while "their side" cornered every likely listener to hear their litany of reasons why our plan was evil. These opponents focused on two central issues: First and foremost, town-owned buildings are maintained by municipal taxes, so the cost of restoring the lighthouse and keeping it in good repair (as required by the Maine Lighthouse Program) would cause drastic increases in property taxes, a major commitment for a tiny island population. This was a very sound argument.

Also "their side" assailed the innkeepers' reputation at every opportunity, insisting that the Burkes' goal was personal financial enrichment, that we were just two more folks "from away" here to rape the island. This was an appealing approach to some native islanders intent on keeping the island "pure," and to some summer residents who didn't know us personally and detested ever-skyrocketing property taxes.

To push forward our campaign, the Committee launched a newsletter, *Lighthouse Flashes*, which addressed these central concerns. Since the lighthouse stood out so prominently as the symbol of the island's maritime heritage, universal opinion insisted that the tower should not be entrusted to the will of any outside party, particularly the constantly dreaded force of *tourism*, the bogeyman that haunts all Maine's quaint little fishing villages. In fact, when the Keeper's House Inn first opened, there had been much ado over the impact it might have on the island's tradition of resistance to that scourge. But after a few years in operation, it became acknowledged that the jobs, additional income for the island, and activity at Robinson Point were helpful and welcome. Still, the possibility that the Burkes might somehow manipulate the lighthouse for their own benefit was a concern to many. Even more repugnant to the local imagination, was the possibility that the title might end up in the hands of some nefarious off-island force that would convert the lighthouse into a hot dog stand or outfit it with dockage for pleasure yachts. From the get-go, *Lighthouse Flashes* proclaimed that the Lighthouse Committee stood for ownership by the Town of Isle au Haut.

◆ Lighthouse Flashes ◆

August 15, 1997 | Vol. 1, No. 2 | Bob Blaisdell, Editor

Bernadine's Talent Show to Kick off Fund Raising

f the Town votes "yes"next week to apply for and accept the Lighthouse at the

"I can't imagine it not being there" said Bernie

Special Town Meeting, the first dollars towards its restoration will flow from Bernadine's Talent Show, according to the producer of the popular event. Looking out her living room window at the lighthouse across the cove, Bernie explained her desire to donate this year's proceeds towards saving Isle Au Haut Light. "I can't imagine it not being there" said Bernie. "How many fishermen has it saved over all these years?.Billy's ancestors lived there, tending the light and that gorgeous old tower flashing red in the winter seems to me that's a warning we'll always need!!! "

BEAST OR BEAUTY

Would the lighthouse be an enormous dollar-devouring albatross for the Town? A crumbling anachronism? Maybe . . . and maybe not. In fact, maybe the lighthouse could be a very valuable asset.

The Keeper's House Inn is a reflection of the magic found on Robinson Point.The inn flourished immediately; most folks would say it has benefited the island. The lighthouse shares the same point of land, the same attraction, the same place on the National Register of Historic Places. The Isle Au Haut Lighthouse Committee believes we can duplicate this process, not by renting mattress space in the lantern room, but by addressing the human need to nurture and protect what is rare and beautiful. In today's world, there are few more perfect candidates than the Isle Au Haut light.

Give us the chance to prove it.

Lighthouse Committee

Laurie Barter, Chair
Jeff Burke,Project Director, Research
Wayne Barter, Park & Boat Liaison
Linda Greenlaw, Community Liaison
Dave Hiltz,Estimates and Bids
Barbara Brown, Grants

Lighthouse Flashes is designed, edited, and produced by Bob Blaisdell

What's the "struggle" all about ???

In last week's issue of LIGHTHOUSE FLASHES, we talked about the "struggle" over cost and funding. Most people found the central idea of this article clearly stated and helpful: that the selectmen are asking all the right questions, and the Isle Au Haut Lighthouse Committee is seeking the answers. In other words, we are struggling *together* with an important community issue, not *against* each other. On with the job!

HUSKO DELIVERS ESTIMATE

A priority mail packet from New Jersey arrived at the Post Office this week. Inside we found our plans and specifications, and a solid proposal letter from Ian and Husko of Two Brothers Restorations, they are the outfit that did such a splendid job on the church. They have restored water front buildings and churches 300 feet high, are used to working with tides and weather, and they are highly respected on this island. The figure they are giving us, together with the Coast Guard's work estimate, is beginning to give an understanding of the nature of the job and its cost. We hope to have at least one more estimate by Town Meeting that should give a balanced picture.

One of our organizing newsletters, Lighthouse Flashes. 1998.
Photo restoration by William Brehm.

Lighthouse Flashes also repeatedly discussed the issue of property taxes. From its inception, the Lighthouse Committee put forward the plan that no town tax dollars be spent on the lighthouse. The Committee would be charged with raising all necessary funds from sources other than the town. In this manner, the town would be able to control the fate of the lighthouse without imposing any new taxes.

To complement the coverage of the newsletter, a series of forums and Special Town Meetings were convened over the course of 1997 and 1998. Residents and non-residents alike began to understand the advantages of ownership of the tower by the town. But "their side" was also right: Jeff and Judi Burke did, in fact, have major conflicts of interest. After all, the lighthouse station had become our life's major creation and I was the one who conceived this marvelous inn, a fresh concept rare in the commercial world. The Keeper's House had "made it," and I was proud of the success. Nevertheless, the tenacious character attacks began to take a toll on me.

When I stopped at the Island Store to grab a copy of the *Bangor Daily News*, sometimes people snapped at me. The gift shop lady glowered when I dropped by with the new issue of *Lighthouse Flashes*. "What now?" she complained. "Conflict of interest," was the refrain I kept hearing, muttered in the Post Office and on the Town Landing.

Still, there was no doubt everyone wanted to save the lighthouse, in one form or another. But why were the Burkes (it seemed to many) calling the shots and making the money? It got to the point where the occasional slight or off-handed criticism bit deep as a dagger strike, designed to drive us off—the usual fate directed at those who didn't go along with "the way we do it here."

We were devastated. I couldn't sleep at night—my vivid imagination tumbled into depression. Everywhere loomed nasty opinions and misinformed arguments. The island was split in two. Under all the pressure, our lives were crumbling, and all we had built was threatened. Maybe Isle au Haut wasn't our nirvana. Maybe the time had come to seek somewhere else to live. Things got so heated, and I was at the center of so many issues, that Judi and I decided to escape the island for a week to lick our wounds and rethink our future.

In Portland, we sat in a café and made a list of reasons to stay on the island and a list of reasons to leave. Finally, by the end of the week, because of the stress and the inability to see my way through it, I decided to resign from the Lighthouse Committee. But we also reaffirmed our commitment to the island. No way would we be driven off! By then, several other committee members had already resigned, unable to cope with the nasty climate generated by the Lighthouse War. New recruits stepped forward to fill the void. The Committee became stronger than ever.

Taking time off from his profession of diving for sea urchins, David Quinby, the Committee's Treasurer, managed the stream of donations to care for the tower. Dave Hiltz, a lobsterman, became the Chair of the Committee and later negotiated with contractors to bring to fruition the restoration of the lighthouse. Our work was strengthened immensely by the presence of Bernadine Barter and her husband, Billy, who brought two hundred years of family dedication to the island to bear, as well as the participation of Bob Turner and his daughter, Lisa, whose ancestors are the most numerous in the island's history. With all these folks and their family legacies aboard, it was futile for the naysayers to argue that the Isle au Haut Lighthouse Committee was the vile plot of "folks from away."

Other than my resignation from the Committee, little really changed for me. I continued to write articles for *Lighthouse Flashes*. And the town delegated me to craft the application submitted to the Maine Lighthouse Selection Committee. I was still representing the town at events and meetings pertaining to the lighthouse and deeply engaged in the organizing and publicity for the committee's fundraising events. No matter how hard I tried, I couldn't let go of my baby.

For two years there were a series of town meetings, consultations with lawyers, long conversations with officials in Augusta, wrangling with citizens on the Town Landing and at kitchen tables, all that sort of arm-twisting, ego-inflating, fear-mongering stuff

Bernadine and Billy Barter. Oil portrait by the author. 2011.
Photography by William Brehm.

people in conflict do. Messy as it was, things moved forward.

But one issue threatened to derail the progress: The Maine Lighthouse Selection Committee requested that Judi and I provide a deeded right-of-way to the town across our two acres. This was something we had planned on doing—but the personal attacks by town officials had made us wary. We countered by suggesting a "working partnership" between the inn and the town that would best guarantee the interests of both parties, including an easement designed to protect our rights; the two-year civil war had left us convinced that if we ever lost control over our back yard, any obstreperous element could use a future right-of-way to harass us. The town's attorney recommended the easement not be accepted. Strangely, even though our offer was officially accepted by a majority of the Board of Selectmen on September 14, 1998, the right-of-way was never filed with the Knox County Registrar.

Regardless, for the past twelve years, the inn, the Coast Guard, and the town had collaborated on numerous events: open lighthouse tours, educational programs, the play, and the alternative energy fair. We were convinced this good working relationship was the best way to honor the and fulfill public good. The Maine Lighthouse Selection Committee agreed and pointed out, in addition, that viewing the historic landmark from the water (by mail boat, yacht, fishing boat, lighthouse tours, or kayak) was a historical pattern that had always existed.

Regardless of the messy personal side issues, one thing was clear: At every step along the way, the vast majority of islanders supported seeking town ownership for the lighthouse tower. Finally, due to the deadline established by the Maine Lighthouse Selection Committee, on September 9, 1998, Isle au Haut held a final Special Town Meeting, specifically to vote on whether or not to accept title to the Isle au Haut Lighthouse tower. With a hundred nervous summer residents watching, the registered inhabitants voted. The motion carried, 41 to 2.

The following summer of 1999, the Isle au Haut Lighthouse was beautifully restored by professionals, paid for by voluntary donations to the Town of Isle au Haut Lighthouse Fund, and brought to fruition by a hardworking committee who never gave up.

* * * *

Once the restoration was completed, the lighthouse stood for the next two decades proud and precious, welcoming travelers, fishermen, and summer folk back to the island's harbor. As of today, the Town of Isle au Haut has yet to acquire a penny of tax money for the lighthouse.

We have a 501(c)3 non-profit group, Friends of the Isle au Haut Lighthouse, that supports the town's lighthouse committee with fund-raising. We have a docent-guided tour program and regular open lighthouse events every summer.

And, all the proceeds from this book, which provides a comprehensive history of the lighthouse station, will be donated to the friends of Isle au Haut Lighthouse for future maintenance and renovation.

Chapter 14

The Daily Eco-Tour

Every morning after breakfast, I'd meet our assembled guests outside on the walkway to the lighthouse.

"Okay, everybody! Are you ready for the eco-tour?"

"Lead the way!" they chorused.

Off we'd go on the circuit: to the cellar where the water maker hummed, forcing seawater through membranes that delivered drinking water; to the boat house with the windmill on top that converted breezes into electricity; to the sewage disposal system, where deep peat moss beds sanitized potty water; to the photovoltaic panels, the solar food cookers, the humanure collection station, and all the rest that caused eyebrows to arch and generated so many questions.

"What on earth led you to install all this stuff?" was the most frequent query.

Here's how it happened.

* * * *

Richard Komp came to the Keeper's House in 1988, lugging a small homemade photovoltaic panel and a couple of golf cart batteries. At my behest, this renegade ex-college professor had assembled a rig to recharge all the flashlight batteries used by the inn's guests. In 1988 this was a big departure from the accepted norm of chucking old ones in the trash and simply buying replacements.

I watched while he snugged the connectors on the panels and polished the glazing with his handkerchief.

"Yer set to go!" he said. "But what you really need here is a full-sized system to harvest the sun's energy. That would be a nifty way to teach your guests how to save the earth."

Then he used the hanky to mop his forehead and to push his thick mop of snowy hair out of his field of vision. He glowered down the path toward the boathouse where our stinky generator spewed black exhaust and peace-shattering clatter.

"Then you could turn that nasty machine into a boat mooring," he said, his toothless jaws churning, the way they always did when he pontificated about the sins of capitalism, and how the world could be saved with recycling, alternative energy systems, a ban on everything nuclear. Vegetarian diets, good wine, poetry, and music could bring us world peace, he said.

During his stay with us, we learned that he had founded the Maine Solar Energy Association. He had taught alternative energy workshops all across New England. By the mid-1990s, his efforts had expanded to Central America (and in even later years, into the heart of Africa). We were invited to join him on a trip to Nicaragua where he had established a school in Managua to teach and promote solar energy for generating electricity, for cooking, and for kiln-drying coffee and lumber—all without producing the toxic smoke that caused respiratory ailments and polluted the atmosphere.

Richard made it clear: We would join his delegation, not as lecturers on "the American Way," but as students of the Nicaraguans.

* * * *

Still suffering from the effects of the bloody civil war of the 1980s, Nicaragua remained one of the poorest countries in the Western Hemisphere when we arrived in 1999. Twenty years prior, the Somoza dictatorship had been deposed by the Sandinista movement. Dramatic improvements for the poor and landless followed. This brought on a vicious counterrevolution during the 1980s, funded by the "Iran–

Contra scandal," Oliver North's infamous secret manipulation of arms sales to wage war against the new democracy—against the wishes of Congress. Although the end of hostilities was welcomed, little had changed in living standards. Nicaraguans scratched by with little financial capital from wealthy nations.

Then came Richard Komp. Let's make do with what we have, he proffered. No electricity, *no problema*; we'll make our own. With some financial assistance from Canada, Rich and a core group of faculty and students from *La Universidad Nacional* in Managua, Komp launched a neighborhood group, *Grupo Fenix* (The Phoenix Group). The name symbolized the ancient Greek myth of the glorious bird that, after a hundred years of splendor, would burst into flames. Once the conflagration cooled, a new fledgling phoenix would be reborn from the ashes to soar again. Hence, the post-civil war Nicaraguan people would be reborn from the ashes of the conflict to prosper by working together. Unlike classic modern warfare where nations might hurl missiles and drop bombs across wide oceans, these 1980s Central American slaughters often played out in local communities, pitting neighbor against neighbor, brother against brother. *Grupo Fenix* was forged to reunite the community by bringing both Sandinista and Contra together to solve the most common problems: creating electricity, improving education and health, and putting people to work.

During our first week there, members of *Grupo Fenix* taught us how to make photovoltaic panels, soldering together shards of rejected cells commercial manufacturers couldn't use. No imported parts were used to fashion their systems. Local women joined our workshop to demonstrate how cardboard boxes, wadded newspaper, tinfoil, and homemade glue could be used to fashion solar cookers, needed since nearby land had been stripped of timber to be used for cooking. With tight lids and aluminum foil reflectors focused on the region's abundant sun, these devices worked like crock pots, using the sun's celestial fire to roast even the toughest chicken.

During our second week we headed for the countryside. Here we met with a group of landmine victims, both ex-Sandinista and ex-Contra, who had come together to serve their community. We had brought along a solar panel made in the workshop, a 12-volt battery, and a shop-made regulator. Together with the veterans, we bounced by jeep across billy-goat terrain to a secluded mountain village where no light bulb had ever shone. The schoolhouse had a single room, a hard-packed dirt floor, a willing teacher, and nothing more. We hooked up the jerry-rigged photovoltaic system.

That night people from all around the countryside trekked in for the ceremony. Speeches were delivered, of course, plaudits given, but that all paled at the magic moment the bulb was switched on. A lighthouse in the jungle! The results: life changing! The cost: almost nothing! The side benefit: ex-enemies working together! The teacher was now able to teach evening literacy classes.

Two of the main beneficiaries of this trip turned out to be Judi and me. We were transformed. If illiterate barrio ladies and civil war vets with missing limbs could accomplish such breakthroughs in alternative energy, why couldn't we as well?

* * * *

Back at the lighthouse, we got right to work. The Isle au Haut Lighthouse Station would become a living demonstration of alternative sustainable technology, all inspired by our Nicaraguan experience.

How odd it was. Originally the attraction of the lighthouse inn came from the reality that it had so little infrastructure, no power lines or plumbing. We had billed our "frontier ambience" as rarified and special, worth a couple of hundred bucks per night just to come pee in the bushes. Now, following this expedition to Nicaragua, the lighthouse station offered new opportunities. Our lives can be brightened without exploiting fossil fuels. The sun provides everything needed for health and happiness: electricity, heat, food, all without the downside of atmospheric pollution and crippling kitchen smoke. We can save trees *and* reduce fossil fuels!

Already we had a photovoltaic experiment in place. But the tiny system Richard had built a decade earlier was no longer adequate for our growing business. We asked a local solar advocate to build us a larger version, an array of panels and batteries adequate to support our flourishing inn well into the future. Realizing that summers are short (but sunny), and winters are long (but windy), we asked, "let's add a suitable windmill so power can be generated year-round."

Then, using the tanks from two 80-gallon water heaters, I built a solar hot water heater, an insulated contraption with huge glittery gaping doors that looked like the wings on a B52. During daylight hours, they were open as reflectors to soak in sunlight and heat the blackened tanks. In the late afternoon, I'd shut them tight as a cocoon, to hold in the collected heat.

Next came the solar food cookers. Instead of the cardboard and crumpled newspaper used in Nicaragua, I constructed our ovens with high-grade plywood and foam insulation, aluminumized Mylar for the reflective sides, tempered glass for the tops to retain heat (and to allow one to see inside and watch the cooking process). This baby could roast a four-pound chicken in five hours, as long as the cook kept the thing centered on the sun. Even fussier was my parabolic solar cooker. It could fry eggs at 700 degrees, but needed to be aimed as accurately as a laser, focusing its reflectors onto a focal point the size of a quarter.

And why be limited to what we learned in Nicaragua? Transportation was never addressed there, but here at the lighthouse, where everything moves by water, a more sustainable technology was needed. I built a biodiesel laboratory in the boathouse, a high-tech operation to generate fuel for my boat. The boathouse took on the atmosphere of Frankenstein's laboratory with its looping tubes and chemical tanks, the stirring motors and settling vats. Using grease collected from mainland seafood restaurants, I treated the goop with a careful mixture of Drano and racecar fuel. The finished biodiesel product went into the belly of *Pax*, our 24-foot motor launch. Every afternoon, guests would board her for an hour-long "eco-tour" through the Thorofare. We motored along like the *African Queen*, and I'd give a chat about climate change and rising sea levels. But instead of emitting a toxic cloud of black exhaust, *Pax* trailed only the scent of fryolator oil (the local fishing fellows dubbed her "the french fry boat"). The byproduct of making biodiesel was soap: skin softening, sweet smelling, and nontoxic—an eco-friendly touch to supply our shower stalls (although Judi preferred to keep buying the all-natural scented patchouli bars, hand-made by mainland hippies).

One of the main attractions of the daily eco-tour was our sewage disposal system. With no sewers on the island and without a plot of soil certified acceptable for a septic leech field, we had to pursue alternative methods to dispose of our yucky water. Unlike the old days when the ocean provided a convenient place to dump, nowadays the bay is scrutinized by the Department of Environmental Protection, the State Marine Patrol, the fisheries and wildlife people, and the Coast Guard, all on the lookout for any floating turd.

So we installed an environmentally friendly peat bog sewage system. Transported by barge from Stonington (along with tons of mandated gravel), these six huge concrete bins were buried beside the keeper's house, leaving only the tops exposed, so moisture could transpire into the atmosphere. An underground pipe delivered the inn's wicked water to the bins. Through some mysterious natural chemical phenomena, bacteria are destroyed by peat moss. Our lighthouse swill became pure as Perrier.

One problem remained. Those six ugly bins—soon encrusted with dandelions and poison ivy—became a no-man's land, unsightly and threatening. Guests found them repulsive.

Our eldest son, Peter, a landscape architect and island resident, had the answer.

"Turn it into a garden," he said.

I said, "What about the deer and bunnies? Won't they gobble up the seedlings? What about the required water—isn't that a problem? And soil rich enough to raise a crop can't be found anywhere on this mound of rock. How could flowers ever flourish?"

Peter said, "Let's build a sculpted serpentine fence. Let it rise and fall along the ledges, and provide a special hidden space for the guests, where they can meditate and laze among the blooms and conifers."

Several years later, Peter's garden matured into a veritable Eden. All six bins overflowed with flowers. Surrounding the bins, he added native species of low-water-consumption trees, blueberry bushes, Scotch pine, blooming vines, and flowering mountain ash. For my fiftieth birthday, he added a dawn redwood tree (today it scrapes the sky at thirty feet or more). All this glorious growth is watered beneath the surface by thousands of gallons of pure water flowing through the broken rock—it's the effluent from toilets, sinks, showers, washing machines, and dental water picks. And every drop is pure. No pumps. No water bill. No summer-scorched vegetation.

The lighthouse inn was also blessed with the ingredients for perfect compost. I built a triple-bin compost system inside Peter's garden, a collection center for all things organic. We had unlimited seaweed at our doorstep. Twenty-six adopted chickens of nebulous heritage cooed and cackled beneath our bedroom window, converting poultry feed and garden slugs into rainbow-colored eggs and a never-ending splatter of phosphorus-rich poop. There were the daily scraps from the kitchen to add: a rich bounty of organic carrot tops, coffee grounds, unfinished dinner orts, and all the healthy garbage from feeding hikers. Add to that the garden trimmings and the wilting flowers that graced the dining room tables, and the gobs of boiled kelp left after every lobster bake.

And to top off the compost bins, I'd slop in the daily bucket from the "humanure" station (the original 1906 Victorian outhouse). Instead of a bench with an oval hole descending into the "nether world," I had retrofitted the interior with a five-gallon bucket graced with a cheapo Home Depot toilet seat. Alongside the bucket, we provided a ready supply of aromatic woodchips for covering fresh deposits. Judi's helpful horse, Thunder, also contributed recycled hay and oats to the compost bins. I did the lugging.

A layer of dry straw crowned the quagmire. Protruding from the muck, a temperature gauge reported on the slow, flameless heat that festered below, generated by the decomposing organic matter. One hundred thirty-five degrees can annihilate any lurking pathogens capable of harming humans. Black gold was the product. Mixing this magic into the garden soil guaranteed posies and herbs of the highest distinction, squash and tomatoes, radishes, peas, and tender arugula lettuce.

The inn had bicycles for guests to peddle. Every flashlight sported rechargeable batteries. No showerhead wasted water waiting for the "hot" to arrive; each hot water outlet recycled water until it was sufficiently warm. With our new solar power in place, all appliances and electrical devices hummed along on solar and wind power. The lighthouse had its own Coast Guard solar system to keep its beacon flashing. And on cooler nights when the temperature dropped, the woodstove warmed the living room with air circulated by a fan powered by a heat-generated electric motor.

As the gizmos and gadgets multiplied, so also did the appreciation by the guests. Every morning after breakfast, we'd take our guests on a walk around the station. We'd visit the cellar to show off our solar power command center, do backyard demonstrations on how to cook and heat water with the sun, traipse down to the boat house for a class on how to make biodiesel, and wander through the gardens to learn about organic growing, composting, and recycling the inn's waste back to energy, pure air, water, and food.

* * * *

Soon passenger groups on schooners appeared at the lighthouse, requesting tours. Our schoolteacher arranged for a session for the island students. We got the junior class from Rutland High School in Vermont, Audubon people, lighthouse aficionados, and the usual stream of reporters. We scheduled a "Solar Sunday" open house, complete with acoustic music, solar-baked goodies, and sweet-smelling tours on *Pax*.

My gosh! Here we were, secluded on this little island in the middle of the ocean, where the station had become a Mecca for folks curious to learn about living more sanely.

We still get calls and letters.

"Dear Jeff and Judi...when Agnes and I got home to St. Louis, we immediately converted our kitchen lighting from incandescent to compact florescent..."

"Hey, Jeff. Howie Komives here. I'm considering solar for my new house..."

"Dear Burkes: Can you send us the contact info on sewage peat moss beds...and thanks so much for the experience—the lighthouse transformed our lives!"

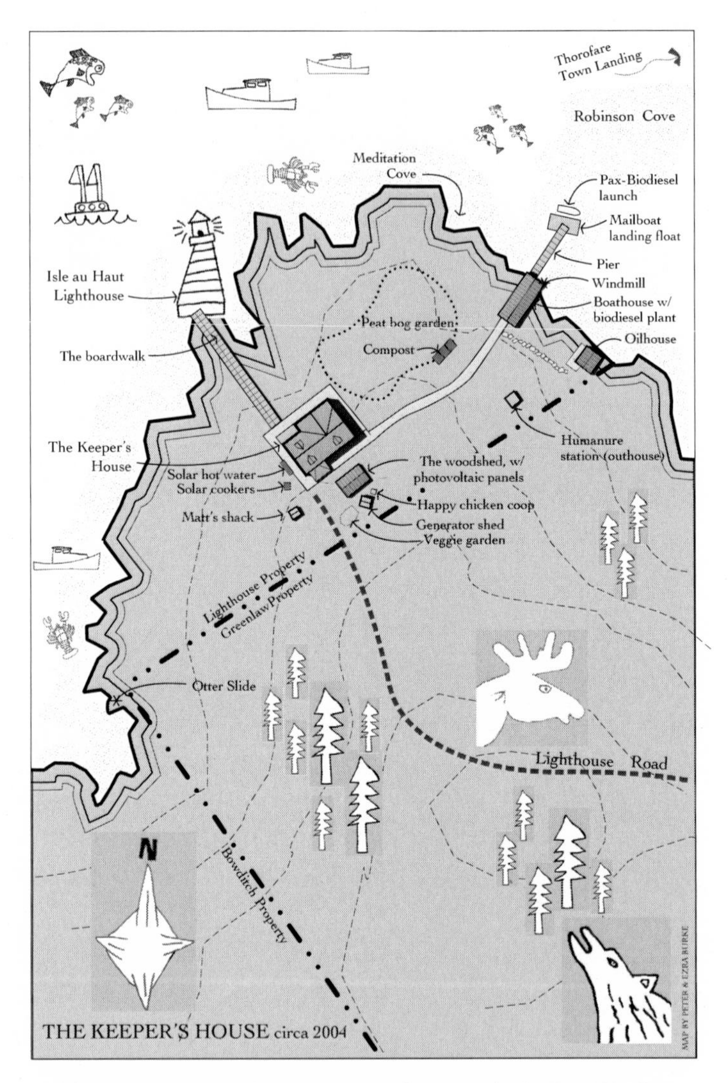

The Keepers House Inn circa 2004. Cartography by Peter Burke, Landscape Architect. Artwork by Ezra Burke.

Chapter 15

A Lesson from Jamie

After the keeper's house kitchen walls were papered with yellow toy soldier wallpaper, I surmised there must have been yet another tumultuous gathering of the Greenlaw Family Ad-Hoc Lighthouse Redecorating Committee, perhaps sometime during the 1960s. What resulted was a radical departure from the traditional white exterior of all lighthouse stations: The Greenlaws had the audacity to slather blue paint across the gable ends of the keeper's house.

It was no ordinary blue. Almost cerulean, a little darker perhaps, with a gentle nudge toward aquamarine. *Can you imagine the Greenlaw family hunkered on the shore with scores of color chips spread out on the ledges, the excitement of seeking the perfect color and the excruciating process of reaching a grudging consensus? Feelings must have been hurt, egos bruised. But regardless of the repercussions, eventually a choice was made by majority vote; the exact color, temperature, hue, intensity and sheen mandated by the winning party.* Whatever the consequences, one thing was certain—the selection was gorgeous.

As innkeeper and custodian, I was keenly aware of how beautiful it was. Not a day went by without some guest or wandering day hikers arriving in the yard and pausing, transfixed by the scene. Surrounding them on three sides was the ocean, crested with waves, a scattering of white sails cutting across the surface, a fringe of forest here and there softening the margins of the composition. Overhead, a never-ending drama of clouds tumbled along. An eagle might soar above. The aroma of baking bread, the cry of a loon, and the allure of a hammock waiting on the shore beneath a spreading spruce, all conspired to create the perfect image. But, regardless of this panoramic scenery, it was *the paint* that grabbed people's attention.

"That's the most incredibly beautiful blue I've ever seen!" they would say, gawking at the gables.

"Thank you," I'd say, as if I had some role in its provenance.

I had to admit it was alluring. When we first trudged through the overgrown woods to visit the shut-down dwelling in 1985, I was surprised by the unexpected burst of color. Then, after a few years, I became accustomed to it, fond of its warmth. In fact, the truth is I became a bit obsessed with its perpetuation. Urgently needed applications of blue became apparent. When we remodeled the oil house, I argued for the same happy hue to be applied to the trim and the entry door, much to the chagrin of Judi, who felt the original white was perfectly acceptable.

"But Judith, don't you understand, we need continuity here. We can't have the blue only on the gables, it's gotta' bring unity to the entire station."

She shrugged. "Don't go overboard, Jeffrey," she said.

"But it reflects the sky," I said. "Lets the cosmos flood in across the lighthouse station. That's what makes the folks ogle with awe."

"If you say so," said Judi, the way she does when she knows she's right, robbing me of any ammo to continue my nagging.

Then, of course, other corners of the lighthouse station called out for inclusion. The trim around the cellar sash needed a little blue as well. So did the interior walls of the kitchen and the Horizon Room. Matching accessories had to be purchased as well, ewers and shower curtains, that sort of paraphernalia. After all, how can you run a proper bed and breakfast joint unless your décor is uniform and trendy?

Some claimed I was carried away by this manic wave of blue. The purists in the lighthouse world, for instance, who preached tradition and wore replicas of lighthouse keeper's caps, like the aristocratic old gal from Glen Bernie who offered to dress our staff in starched sailor suits. Then there were the bureaucrats from the Maine State Historic Preservation Commission, who told us that **lighthouse stations are painted white!**

After a year or two of furious brushwork and rolling, the whole of Robinson Point became bathed in cerulean haze. Occasionally, it did occur to me that things might be getting a bit out of control, but the Greenlaw tradition was at stake here, as well as my own reputation. Besides, think of the flood of recent photographers that recorded this color scheme for publications that splashed our image from coast to coast, and all the pretty postcards and calendars, the TV specials, too, all displaying our snazzy lighthouse donned in robin's egg blue. I found myself defending the motif against the phalanxes of critics who harped about the color, and a certain innkeeper who came up short in the historically authentic category.

In spite of my determination—and the proscribed regulations stipulated by *The Secretary of the Interior's Guidelines for Historic Preservation*, there were other indications that I better be careful. But pride and hubris are powerful, and I had invested in many painting sessions, so I chose to pay no attention.

Already I had twice recoated the three gables with "Greenlaw blue," careful to take samples into Barter Lumber to have the color perfectly matched. I got the good stuff, too, happily paying extra to know that the paint would endure the sun and salt and stiff winter winds, rebuff mildew, and have its soft sheen endure. But now, with my color commitment under fire and the blue sea rising all around, my commitment to the color began to sag a little. Maybe something wasn't right. Maybe the buried white craved to be resurrected, wanted reinstatement to its rightful place along the coastal crown of white keepers houses. But sticking with my color habit still seemed the honorable course. Time and again, I returned to Barter's to fetch a few more gallons.

I picked a perfect morning to add the next coat—good and dry, with just enough cloud cover to moderate the surface temperature. Up went my forty-foot extension ladder, every inch needed to reach the highest peak. Always safety conscious, I placed shims beneath the ladder's feet to get her nice and straight. And, for these extra-high ascensions, I routinely used a rope to guy the ladder sideways, in case of an unexpected ocean gust or a nasty bit of earthquake.

Up I went. At the top, the can nested nicely on the second rung, propped against the siding. With one hand clutched to the top rung, I could reach all the way to the peak, layering the paint thickly against the trim boards and drip edges. Wet, fresh, glimmering rich, the blue paint once again renewed the wall, as well as my allegiance to stand behind my color choice. With my painting gear safely in place and everything organized, this was the perfect time to fetch a cup of coffee and visit the head. I backed my way back down the ladder to take a break.

When I returned, I found a group of hikers had taken over the arc of Adirondack chairs in the front yard. As usual, I indulged in the requisite welcoming banter and answered their barrage of questions. They repositioned their chairs to watch, while I prepared to rescale the ladder.

With the ladder positioned where it was, I had reached as far as I could with the brush. I'd need to scoot it sideways now, drop it a couple of rungs and reposition the ropes and shims. With the hikers still occupying me with questions, I loosed the ropes, grabbed hold and heaved sideways, while describing to the folks how lobsters are caught.

I had forgotten the paint can.

The onlookers were all shrieking by the time the blue wave hit me. It was a deluge, an entire gallon. Fortunately, the can had emptied on its way down and harmlessly bounced off sideways, ending up in a goopy mess at the foot of the ladder. The contents, however, left me awash in a tsunami of cerulean slime.

Several days later, after I had finally gotten the stuff washed out of my hair and the yard restored to somewhat near normal, I resumed my painting and finished up the gable ends. But I had had it with cerulean! What had once been a joy and a point of pride, the blue paint was beginning to be a burden.

But how could I get rid of it? Everyone in town had become fond of the bastard color. After four decades, the blue had become tradition, taken root as fiercely as kudzu. Now, something had to change. I tried to explain to folks that historically the house had always been white, planned that way by the U.S. Lighthouse Board to guide in ships at night. But to no avail; islanders and summer folk alike had grown accustomed to the blue.

Painting over the pigment became a challenge. During our first years here, the blue paint had been a handsome color that attracted journalists and photographers to emblazon the covers of magazines with the story of the Isle au Haut Lighthouse Station. National TV stations arrived as well, and radio stations aired verbal descriptions about the new lighthouse inn on Penobscot Bay that beckoned guests with Victorian gables as pristine as Disney's skies.

The locals' feelings and the journalists' accounts weren't the only problems. In 1988, the entire lighthouse station—the tower, the keeper's house, the whole works—had been placed on the National Register of Historic Places. When Earl Shuttlesworth, the Director of the State Office of Historic Preservation, came to visit and evaluate the property for inclusion, I saw him wince on noting the color. Inclusion on the Register requires strict adherence to exterior historic characteristics. The blue paint would never pass muster. At the time, the State Office was anxious to simultaneously add all 58 Maine lighthouses to the Register, so ours was provisionally included "as is," but Mr. Shuttlesworth's disapproving glare left me marked as the guy responsible for maintaining the outlaw gables on Isle au Haut.

I lay awake nights cursing the dastardly hue. I had become a convert, a turncoat, and a traitor against my own color. I wanted more than anything to return the walls to white, but all the hometown forces were aligned against me. Even my dear wife reversed her previous position.

"But Jeffrey," she said, " It really is an adorable color. Why not leave it that way?"

"You don't understand," I pleaded. "Every lighthouse in Maine is white. It's the historically accurate thing. Blue simply isn't right."

No matter how hard I tried, no words came forth to convince my wife, the town, and the visiting throngs of guests and hikers that the gables of the keeper's house should revert to their original color. The combined opinions and cultural demands of all these critics had become a tyrant, like the Queen of Hearts who ordered her knaves to paint the roses red, with any failure leading to, "Off with their heads!"

In the face of this opposition, I feared for *my* neck. Where would I find the strength to restore the gables to white?

* * * *

Meanwhile, during the time I battled the blue paint demons, the work of the Lighthouse Committee moved forward.

In August of 1998, the Maine Lighthouse Selection Committee organized a grand gathering at the Samoset Resort in Rockland to announce the selected new owners of the twenty-two lighthouse stations. Our town was represented by Selectman John Barter, Laurie Barter, the treasurer of the Lighthouse Committee, and myself, ex-officio Program Director of the campaign to obtain ownership of the lighthouse for the town of Isle au Haut. I had recently resigned as a voting member of the Lighthouse Committee because of my very real conflict of interest as owner of the abutting lighthouse station.

The conference featured music by the Camden-Rockport High School Band, succinct and appropriate speeches, and fabulous catered goodies. The highlight of the afternoon was the presentation of an original oil painting by Jamie Wyeth, *Iris at Sea*. The artist gifted his work to be used as a fund-raising tool for the Maine Lights Program. The painting was showcased on an easel at the center of the day's activities. I found an opportunity to mosey over for a look.

Iris at Sea almost knocked me off my feet.

Wyeth had painted Southern Lighthouse (where he lives) from a low angle, as if he were down in the rocks at the sea's edge, looking up at the building. I could almost feel the texture of the painted brick and smell the brine around me, the modeled detail of the keeper's house accented against a broad azure sky. In the foreground, a pair of serpentine wild irises climbed skyward, the sinewy plant juxtaposed against the hard, linear geometrical forms of the lighthouse.

The house is white. The sky is blue. The iris is the focal point. It's a masterpiece and a lesson in what makes art beautiful: Every element on the canvas must work together in a unified composition, with no single object demanding attention. More importantly for me, Wyeth's portrayal exemplifies an understanding of the relationship of architecture (and the color of the paint that coats it) to nature. Nature is fundamental; we toss in the buildings. Don't screw up the balance. Just because you like a color, don't slather it all over the composition: Let the blue sky and the iris blossoms provide the color. We are only transient observers passing through Eden's gallery, sometime-architects, builders, and garden buffs who might lend a modest hand to compliment it.

* * * *

After the conference, on the return trip to Isle au Haut, I stopped at Barter Lumber and bought a five-gallon bucket of Benjamin Moore Exterior Satin Sheen One Hundred Percent Acrylic Latex House Paint—**Pure White**.

I was mostly able to restore the original color with repeated layers of opaque pigment. Even so, these days try standing below those gables and squinting. No matter how hard you try, there exists still a subliminal trace of its past. Neither the physics of paint composition nor my desire to blot it out were able to eradicate Greenlaw blue.

Chapter 13

The Lighthouse Keeper's Daughter

Even after spending decades on Isle au Haut, sometimes Judi still felt out of place. She was intimidated by the long legacy of others who had occupied keepers' houses.

She often fretted. "How can I match up with the likes of Abbie Burgess, the Esther Robinsons, the Helen Smiths, and all the Greenlaw kin? I can't even row a boat!"

"Don't worry, dear," I told her. "You're a Cape Cod girl. You grew up with fishermen, spent your youth frolicking in the salty brine, and picking blueberries all summer long."

I wasn't able to assuage her worries.

"Yeah, but the water is colder here. And deeper, too. I feel like I'm in over my head, with all these island people tied together with centuries of maritime tradition, their intermarriages, their personal family triumphs and tragic pasts, living this 'lighthouse thing.' I'll never measure up to that."

"But remember, Judith, you have a history, too," I said.

Here is her story.

* * * *

Following the slaughters of the Spanish Civil War, World War II got under way in earnest in September 1939, when Germany invaded Poland. Things were tense along the strategic outer shore of Cape Cod, Massachusetts. The U.S. Lighthouse Service had been consolidated that year into the Coast Guard, and many lighthouse keepers had been enlisted to continue their work under the military reorganization.

At the farthest reaches of the sandy arm of the Cape, the Race Point Lighthouse near Provincetown was under the command of Addison N. Ormsby, grandfather of my wife, Judi Ormsby Burke. First serving with the U.S. Lifesaving Service, Addison had been stationed at the Calhoon Hollow station in North Truro during the early 1930s, and then transferred to the U.S. Lighthouse Service at nearby Wood End Lighthouse in 1935. Then, in 1939, the year so many lighthouse keepers traded their utilitarian togs for military uniforms, he became the last USLHS keeper at Race Point Lighthouse Station. He wasn't the only Ormsby who went through that transition. At the onset of the war, just about every Coast Guard post on the Lower Cape included at least one member of the Ormsby clan.

Addison's brother-in-law, William Joseph, headed the Coast Guard crew at the crown jewel of Cape Cod lights, Highland Lighthouse Station in North Truro (also known as Cape Cod Light). Between Race Point and North Truro, Calhoon Hollow was manned by one of Addison's sons, Donald Orsmby, Judi's father. Another son, Ralph Ormsby, was posted a bit farther south at Nauset Coast Guard Station in Orleans.

Historically, the outer shoals and shores of Cape Cod had been the graveyard for hundreds of ships. Over the decades, the Lighthouse Board and the Lighthouse Service had developed a tight network of stations all along the sandy arc, spaced no more than five to ten miles apart, with log shacks built in between each station. From sunset to sunrise, a "coastie" would walk the distance from one post to the next, equipped with flares to ward off any ship too close to shore, firing off a double salvo to bring help whenever they found a vessel in distress. In 1914 the Cape Cod Canal was opened and many ships no longer had to traverse the lethal shoals off the Outer Cape. Still, shipwrecks were common and the need for coastal vigilance never ceased.

With so many posts, one might wonder if these Cape Cod folk weren't a little paranoid over the fear of invasion. Actually, there was a sound basis for their concern: the Attack on Orleans. During the First World War, in 1918, a German U-boat surfaced off the "backside" of the Cape, near this tranquil village, and promptly began shelling Nauset Beach. A number of rounds struck the 140-foot steel tugboat, *Perth Amboy*, which was towing four barges of ordnance bound for Europe. All those barges were set afire. Twenty local Coast Guardsmen were able to rescue the crew aboard the tug with no injuries. The townspeople assembled on the high cliffs with clam rakes and rolling pins, prepared to resist any invasion. Several buzzing seaplanes from nearby Chatham Airbase (still under construction) appeared and dropped a few bundles of TNT in the direction of the sub. The dynamite splashed into the sea without exploding. As the planes turned back toward their base for more effective weapons, the U-boat (U-156) submerged and escaped, crossing the Gulf of Maine where she sank 21 fishing boats. Historians posit that U156 then high-tailed it across the Northern Passage on her way back to the German motherland and may have struck a mine—she was never heard of again. In total, U-156 had destroyed forty-four American vessels.

The raid on Orleans was the only incident during WWI where the Germans actually attacked America's home turf. Still, with that recent history, it is easy to understand how attentive the citizens of Orleans must have been twenty-five years later when wartime came around again.

By 1942, with the war fully raging, the Coast Guard organized a vast Beach Patrol. On the water, a civilian armada of commercial and private ships and yachts stood watch, to back up the Coast Guard fleet. During that year a German U-boat did sneak into Long Island Sound off New York City and launched a rubber inflatable under cover of night. Four specially trained saboteurs rowed ashore with explosive charges, but ultimately they were all apprehended. Another U-boat landed a sabotage party on the Florida coast, with similar results.

By the end of the year, as many as 50,000 military personnel and thousands of citizens beach-patrolled along the Atlantic seaboard, supported by a Beach Cavalry of 3,000 horses, and a canine force of over 2,000. School kids spent their weekends patrolling the beaches.

At night, Coast Guard personnel walked the shores armed with rifles, radios, and dogs. On the west coast a similar vigilance prevailed, with eyes focused on the Pacific.

Hitler had shown his intentions to infiltrate our homeland. He may have had success with a few small, undiscovered incursions, but the impenetrable chain of the Shore Patrol, led by folks like the Ormsby family, dissuaded any Nazi invasion.

* * * *

After the war, Chief Ralph Ormsby—who by then had been reassigned to the Brandt Point Coast Guard Station on Nantucket Island—was decorated with a Ribbon of Commendation for a heroic 1952 rescue operation. During an exceptionally violent storm, two large tankers were snapped in half off the Cape near Chatham. The sections of the sinking ships held surviving crewmen. Conditions on the sea were so treacherous that no aircraft could hover nearby, and no rescue ship could get near enough to the pitching hulks to rescue the crews.

Coast Guardsman Ralph Ormsby's crew was the first ordered into action. Ormsby commanded four Coast Guardsmen aboard a 36-foot lifesaving boat with a 90 horsepower engine. Off they plunged on the fifty-five mile crossing toward the site of the first stricken tanker, the *Fort Mercer*. With each sailor clutching to anything bolted down, the boat thrashed its way through seventy-foot seas in an attempt to rescue three dozen stranded sailors. Ormsby's crew spotted another tanker that had broken apart, the *Pendleton*, but the conditions were so horrific that Ormsby's boat was ordered back to port. Meanwhile, two more lifeboats from the Chatham Station were launched.

Later, testifying about the experience, Chief Ormsby recalled the perilous situation of the lifeboat, "The boat stood almost on end, with the waves breaking over her bow." The crews were doused for hours with frigid water.

Coast Guardsman Bernie Webber captained one of the Chatham lifeboats. After a terrorizing crossing, he reached the *Pendleton* and pulled the thirty-two seamen aboard. One was swept away. Webber miraculously got the overloaded craft back to Chatham. Coast Guard cutters eventually rescued the remaining crewmen off the floating hunks of the *Fort Mercer*, two by two, pulling them through the swells by lines tied to life rings. Twenty minutes after the final mariner was lifted to safety, the last piece of the severed tanker gurgled under. Coincidently, the entire episode unfolded in the same stretch of ocean where, thirty-four years prior, U-boat U-156 destroyed the *Perth Amboy* during the Attack on Orleans.

This wild rescue, known as "Two Tankers Down," is considered the greatest Coast Guard rescue of all time, and came to movie theatres in 2016 in the Hollywood thriller, *The Finest Hours*, starring Chris Pine as Bernie Webber.

Ralph Ormsby went on to serve as Chief of the Chatham Station from 1952 to 1954 and later served on the lightship *Nantucket*. His son John was drowned in a tragic diving accident while working on a crew salvaging the *Andrea Doria*.

Ralph's brother, Donald J. Ormsby, formerly stationed at Calhoon Hollow, transferred to the crew at the famed Highland Lighthouse Station, and became Chief Officer (the "lighthouse keeper") there from 1953 to 1956. One of his predecessors had been Bernie Webber, who was stationed there for a year during the war.

Like other Coast Guardsmen in the family (his father, his uncle, his brother), Donald was a family man, but under the administration of the Coast Guard, a crew of enlisted men now occupied the Highland Station keeper's house. The Chief lodged his family—his wife, Ida, and their five children, Dawn, Gary, Judi, Christopher, and Jenny—in a modest wood-frame home nearby on South Pamet Road.

Dawn was killed in a fiery auto collision just a few miles from the Highland Lighthouse. Gary spent a lifetime working for the National Park Service, tending the roads and grounds around the lighthouse. He was part of a 1996 engineering project, which moved the lighthouse back 500 feet from the edge of crumbling cliffs. Christopher graduated from the Massachusetts Maritime Academy as a stationary engineer. His first post-graduation assignment was aboard T2 tankers, the same class of tankers that broke apart during the monster storm of 1952. Jenny married the local judge's son and raised two daughters nearby, beneath the broad sweep of the lighthouse beam. Judi, at the age of eighteen in 1961, daughter of this multigenerational family of lighthouse heroes, found herself serving frappes and banana splits at the Dairy King on Route 6, just a crow's arc across the dunes from the lighthouse. That's where I met her.

Three years later we were married.

* * * *

During the late 1970s, while Judi and I were living in California and raising our three young ones, we returned to the Cape for a summer visit. By then both of Judi's parents had passed away, and her brother Garry and his wife, Sharon, had moved into the old family farmhouse on South Pamet Road.

One morning I arrived and found Garry with a bucket of mortar and a trowel in hand, tucking dabs of cement into voids in the mantelpiece above the wood stove. Polished brass gleamed from the bed of brick and fresh mortar.

"What's up, Gar?" I asked.

"Just finishing up," he said. "Got the old man's medals set into the brick here, you know, for 'posterity,' as they say. That's all that's left of him, a bit of bronze and a few old stories."

He finished tucking the last crumbs of cement around the badges and medals, using a bit of rag to wipe away any wispy streaks remaining on the surfaces, then headed off to rinse his tools. Left alone, I stooped to inspect the inscriptions cast in the medals—they all proclaimed the excellence of Coast Guard Chief Donald J. Ormsby in the art of marksmanship.

I had often wondered about Judi's father. He came from a family of Coast Guard heroes and lighthouse keepers and crewmen stationed on the tossing lightships moored in Nantucket Sound. But he was an enigma to me, and to Judi as well. Who was he? There is no glowing mention of him in any record books, other than the fact he once broke the fall of a young Coast Guardsman who had fallen from a scaffold while painting the tower. Unlike his father, uncle, and brother, he was not celebrated. In my brief encounters with him—I was the kid from away who gazed starry-eyed at his red-haired daughter—I knew him only as a glowering lumpy man who sat slumped alone in front of the TV, watching Red Sox games.

Now, all these years later, I think of those marksmanship medals mortared into the Ormsby hearth. Maybe there was more going on with this man I barely knew. I reviewed the reading and research I did on the role of the Coast Guard during the war, how the "coasties" patrolled the beaches with a dog or a horse or all alone, armed with a flashlight and rifle to fend off flotillas of submarines and storm clouds of Luftwaffe. Donald J. Ormsby, I now learned, had taught marksmanship to those same Coast Guardsmen patrolling the dark night shores of the lower Cape. I remembered how in 1918 the people of neighboring Orleans had gathered on the sandy bluffs with shotguns and rolling pins while U156 blasted their harbor to smithereens. I recalled the vigilance of the armed Coast Guardsmen on Long Island who swept up the German saboteurs moments after they stepped ashore. I remembered the tens of thousands of mariners who provided firepower for the corsair fleet ships patrolling the nation's beaches. These hallowed medals embedded in the family hearth proved Donald J. Ormsby must have taught all those fellows to shoot!

So, when we Burkes arrived on Isle au Haut in 1986, we landed with more than a lame dog and a crate of tools. We also brought with us the legacy of lighthouse keepers and Coast Guardsmen, a maritime heritage equal to that of Abbie Burgess, Esther Holbrook Robinson, Helen Smith Barter, and Mattie Belle Robinson Greenlaw—we landed with Judith Ormsby Burke, another resolute daughter in a long, long line of vigilant lighthouse keepers.

Chapter 17

Stories in the Shadow of the Lighthouse

Seventeen small cemeteries lie snuggled among the hills of this island. Some are hunkered along the shoulders of the village road, neatly tended. Others are buried deep in the woods, neglected, tombstones leaning or fallen, with lichen creeping across weathered chiseled names: Wife, Fisherman, Infant.

Consider, too, the centuries of Red Paint People and Penobscot Indians who came to hunt and harvest nature's bounty. There must be bits of their bone mixed into the ancient shell middens. Island explorers still find flint arrowheads and granite axes blended in with the stony beach rubble of Duck Harbor, Shark's Point Beach, Seal Trap, and along the Thorofare. Besides all these remnants, remember the burials at sea: sailors and soldiers and pirates shrouded in red, white, and blue, and the skull and crossbones, too. Even today, quiet boats—both large and small, classy and shabby—solemnly cruise by the lighthouse trailing ashy wakes.

What a wondrous and tragic amalgamation of spirits we have here around us, in our earth and water and air, and in the tree-crusted hills that shelter our own unfolding lives. We revere these slabs of graveyard stone, these scattered motes of ash and bone, the long forgotten eulogies wept beside shallow pits and swallowing sea, all common turf where we, too, shall someday be. Most of all, there's a special sorrow for those who passed before their expected demise, perhaps victims of mental illness, or high seas chicanery, or accidents, or broken hearts.

The rising sun casts the long shadow of the lighthouse across the mouth of the Thorofare, like a dark gateway where all must pass. Late in the day, this same sun moves to the western horizon where it thrusts its silhouette eastward toward the village heart. Over the centuries, this fateful shadow has been cast upon countless souls.

Here are the stories of just a few.

The Customs Man

Pulling the trigger of a blunderbuss has consequences—it's an irreversible act. Once the hammer snaps down, the dang thing is sure to go off. It's too late for the shooter to change his mind, or alter the trajectory of the shot, or make amends to the quivering victim bleeding to death at his feet. No badge-wearing bloke deserves to die for simply doing his job, but being a law enforcement agent on Isle au Haut has always been risky.

The murder of the customs agent took place on a dock in the Thorofare on a "dark and stormy November night" in 1808. As far as we know, it was the first murder (but not the last) to occur on Isle au Haut. And even though it happened a hundred years before the lighthouse was built, the perpetrators made their attack and escaped past the fog-curtained ledges of Robinson Point.

The characters in this confrontation had names you and I would never recognize, since both parties were non-islanders with no family roots here. The shooters, history tells us, were a band of ten armed smugglers from Buckston (today's Bucksport) aboard the schooner *Peggy*. They had arrived to seize a cargo of rice and flour impounded by United States customs officials—the required tariffs had not been paid. The dead man in the pool of blood was one of five U.S. Customs Agents guarding the impounded goods. Little more is known about the incident except that the smugglers tossed the body into the Thorofare and escaped. There being no local constable to apprehend them, they sailed away unimpeded. When the Customs Department in Castine sent reinforcements to Isle au Haut to pursue the miscreants, an uncooperative local population ignored them, perhaps feeling more in common with the outlaws. Ultimately, the agents did catch up to the *Peggy* in the Fox Islands Thorofare and hauled the fugitives off to the Castine jail. There, a mob of locals disguised as women overran the barracks and set the smugglers free.

The absence of any local government on Isle au Haut during those early years meant that there was no local constable. Isle au Haut was a loose appendage to nearby Deer Isle. In later years when the population increased to several hundred and the village was incorporated in 1874 with its own municipal government, Islanders still managed to get by splendidly without a lawman.

For many years, as an incorporated Maine Municipality, Isle au Haut was *supposed* to have a constable, but that was rarely the case. If you attended an annual town meeting on the last Monday morning in March, you would watch the town moderator ramble down through the warrant until they got to Article 18, where he read, "...to nominate a Constable to serve for the ensuing year..."

A brief moment of silence always followed.

Then, from a seat in the midst of the crowd came, "I nominate the Selectmen."

"Second," is voiced from somewhere else.

"Any other nominations?" prodded the moderator. "Hearing none, all in favor of the selectmen serving as constable for the ensuing year, signify in the usual manner." The habitual rise of clustered hands, a brief accenting hum. "All opposed?" asked the moderator. Silence. "Motion carries."

About twenty years ago, the townspeople figured they could save a fortune in ink and paper by eliminating the pretense of electing a constable. These days, you'll never hear that word uttered. So, in addition to the duties the Selectmen actually have (administrative, town payroll, etc.), the annual town meeting also assigns them any responsibility for riding wrangler over their fellow islanders. There are several town jobs—Animal Control Officer, Overseers of the Poor, even Fire Marshall—that, like Constable, convey some degree of responsibility for the behavior of fellow islanders. These are jobs no sane soul here would ever covet.

The consequences are too unnerving. It's got to do with island living. When you are surrounded by raging seas, buried in fog much of the year, encased in ice or stuck in mud for months at a time, far from the mainland, without ambulances, hospitals, municipal services, or Mom, you need to rely on whomever happens to be the next fellow coming down the road, or the boat nearest by. Think house fire. Think heart attack. Think sinking boat or missing child. Think the need for a hand to get your furnace working or to tow your boat to harbor. *You don't want any enemies.* No wonder folks shun any turncoat islander who hands out violations for un-leashed dogs, for burning brush without a permit, or for toking weed, or consuming too much beer. That way, everything stays copacetic. A fire—the entire town is there instantly. A disaster on the water—same thing. Slide off the road in the winter—no problem. And so on.

The downside, of course, is an occasional murder. Maybe it's worth the tradeoff.

The Unfortunate Mister Knowlton

At least the Customs Department collections fellow had the good fortune to die quickly; others, like William Knowlton perished much more slowly. He would have been within earshot of the lighthouse, too, had it been built by then, and the Keeper himself might have heard the screams. And had he seen poor Knowlton's dory come into the cove, he'd certainly have gone down to help.

By the early 1800s, William Knowlton's family had flourished and multiplied all along the Maine coast. In Deer Isle/Stonington they were noted seamen and merchants, especially well regarded for their skills as ship carpenters and builders. William moved to Isle au Haut in 1802, although much of his commerce was still centered in Stonington. A few Isle au Haut Knowltons were still listed on the 1850 U.S. Census, although William no longer would be among them.

It may have been the Robinson farmhouse he was building on the day of the accident, March 22, 1820. We know from The Day Before Yesterday, Clayton Gross's highly regarded history column in the local newspaper, the *Island Advantages*, that Mr. Knowlton was employed at that time to construct a house, although we don't know for whom.

In addition to being a carpenter, he was also an established expediter of freight and frequently transferred goods and supplies between the islands. So it's not surprising that on the tragic day he sailed into Robinson Cove to work on construction he had his dory laden with a massive iron wagon axle. Unfortunately for Mr. Knowlton, there was no safe place in the Cove to land such an awkward, unwieldy burden.

It wasn't until much later, after Charles Robinson had taken up residence there, that a landing point was erected. It was suitable only for high tides, so Charles could wrestle his traps aboard with his boots high and dry on solid decking. William Knowlton didn't have that advantage. With no neighbor waiting in the cove, no lighthouse keeper keeping a watchful eye on the comings and goings, and no secure landing point of any kind, he grounded his dory on a rising tide. Tumbled by millennia of tossing seas, the smoothed stones there can be glassy marbles, ready to scoot sideways from the pressure of any boot, with only a slimy coat of algae to soften their hammer-hard edges.

No human eyes were witness to whatever happened. But it wasn't long after Mr. Knowlton steered into the cove that folks saw his dory floating free in the Thorofare, its painter trailing. Within minutes, by land and sea, islanders appeared from all directions, like wasps zipping to the hive instinctively knowing it was all hands on deck, *pronto*, ASAP, S.O.S., STAT!

It was too late, however.

Only a coattail floated in the coming tide, and a boot toe broke the water's surface. One end of the axle poked skyward with the rise and fall of brine surging around it, cockeyed against the bottom, with its heft arched across the submerged still chest of Mr. William Knowlton.

People who believe in ghosts often say that untimely deaths leave wandering spirits that hang around for ages. Maybe they wait until they get retribution, or recognition that they mattered, or get purged by exorcists, or driven away by the smudging of sage and incantations by modern-day shamans. Or, in time, having had their fill of scaring the bejeebers out of innocent victims, they simply take their leave of their own volition.

Remembering that both the customs man and William Knowlton met their untimely deaths on the same shield of stone that came to support our lighthouse, isn't it likely that some hexed residue may have lingered, to complicate life for those who followed? Let's find out by moving ahead to the age after the tower was built, a time when crimson light was added to Robinson Point. That glow may have illuminated subsequent misfortunes.

The Second Time Around

If you ever get the chance to explore the boathouse at the lighthouse station, take a look at the peeling gilded frame holding the charcoal rendering of Frank and Elizabeth Barton. It shows a young couple with dazed expressions, gussied up for their wedding. He wears a coal black tie so broad and coarse it could have been fashioned from a welcome mat. She is fluffed up like a lemon chiffon pie, her teenage face taut with unsuppressed terror. On the morning after their nuptial night, she high-tailed it on the first departing boat to Rockland, never to return, leaving poor Frank behind with a partially eaten wedding cake, mired in a confusion of ungratified expectations.

Sally Greenlaw Bowen first showed me that sad rendering when we cleaned out the shed behind Mattie Belle's burned down farmhouse. Sally explained that Frank Barton was so unsettled by the speedy exit of his sixteen-hour bride that, even many years later, he remained distraught, reclusive, and tense. All he had left of his shattered dream was that lifeless smudge of carbon.

Jim Greenlaw remembers (at the age of six or seven) rowing with his grandfather, Charles Robinson, over to Kimball's Island, where Frank Barton had lived, to fetch some decent doors salvaged from a failed boarding house.

"Pretty sorry scene," said Jim. "Frank apparently cooked rarely. Oatmeal. Huge pot of it. Enough to feed him for a week. He'd fry up wads of it whenever he got hungry. The dried grit in the pot—at the end of the week he'd scrape that out and use it to fill his hand-rolled cigarettes."

"After some years went by, he needed a woman badly," Sally told me. "Fire burned in that man's belly—he had no way to extinguish it." The corners of her mouth curled upward ever so slightly and through

"Wedding portrait of Frank and Lizzie Barton. Charcoal on paper. Artist unknown. Circa 1904. Courtesy of Marshall Chapman. Photo restoration by William Brehm.

her thick eyeglasses a piercing directness filled the conversation between us. I understood her message completely.

"What became of him?" I asked.

"He struggled on for ages. Did some carpentry, some fishing. Bookkeeping, too. Lived in that dumpy little house behind the Crowells' place over on Kimball's Island. Pretty much stayed to himself, except at nights. I guess he was sort of a prowler. He really wanted to hook up with someone."

"Slinking around after hours? On Isle au Haut? Seems like pretty slim pickings," I said.

She remained silent for a moment. With those thick glasses and her stoic presence, I found it hard to read her. Then, unexpectedly, she burst out laughing. "Lord's sake, he wasn't the only love-starved soul on this rock!" she cackled.

Miss Lizzy Rich was another. She served as the island's spinster postmistresses and lived alone in a small frame house by the edge of the road. Her tiny front parlor served officially as the island's post office and unofficially as the local social center. There's where everyone convened to collect their mail, sales circulars, and Sears Roebuck catalogues, and whatever long-awaited parcel that might arrive on the early morning mail boat. Plans for the day were discussed there too, and there was always a bit of gossip to share or a date to be made for the next gathering of the Ladies' Stitch and Bitch Club.

At the center of the island's social life, Miss Lizzy reigned supreme. Being single, she was comfortable with all the island gents and a trusted confidante to all the ladies. Known for her prowess as a dancer, she spun herself silly at every town hall square dance. Leon Small squawked on the saxophone, Bernadine Barter squeezed the accordion, Noyes MacDonald tickled the ivories, and Stevie Bridges bellowed out the calls to "Lady of the Lake."

Miss Lizzy was inexhaustible. She swung every dancer till they were too dizzy to stand, she a whirling dervish of bright red checkered skirts and diaphanous petticoats, her Dairy Queen hairdo all akimbo and the stubby square heels of her patent leather shoes beating time with the music. She twirled the ladies, too, and promenaded the entire crowd 'round the hall till the dance floor seemed to smolder, the atmosphere saturated with sweat and laughter.

Was that where she and sad Frankie Barton first grabbed ahold of each other? Partners swinging? Sashaying home? Was there a cute little curtsy, a wink, a lingering warm hand on the small of the back? Or was it at the post office—that first moment—some insignificant piece of mail passing from hand to hand, fingertips brushing?

There were conventions to be honored, of course. Back then midnight romances were just as common as they are now, but a little more discretion was needed. For instance, Frank and Lizzy never dallied during daylight hours. It was expected that any rendezvous be plotted under the cover of night. Back in the 1950s, the island still had no electricity—hence, no streetlights or other bothersome illumination to expose their shenanigans. Since Lizzy lived in town and Frankie's abode was across the Thorofare on Kimball's, their trysts demanded lots of planning, but not so much as to be a challenge for a fellow with dripping libido and a gal with raging hormones.

Sometimes spontaneously, sometimes by arrangement, after sundown Frank Barton would drag his lead-patched skiff off the Kimball shore and launch her. As he rowed across the Thorofare, the red wink from the lighthouse to his starboard urged him on, his strokes becoming rapid as he neared the Landing Place. Two half hitches around a spruce tree and he was off, striding up to the road, through the village, past the island store, over Town Creek, more hurried now, more anxious. His dashing silhouette was framed by honeyed moonlight.

Her door was never locked. Her lantern was always burning and the tufted cotton twill bedspread with embroidered rabbits was always pulled down low. Among the tangled sheets and sweet feather pillows, sad Frankie Barton and dancing Miss Lizzy finally found their joy.

And so it went.

Years went by. Decades passed. How many midnight crossings? How many wondrous moments? Villagers knew, of course, the way they always do. But daytime interaction between the lovers honored traditional sensitivities. No hanky-panky during post office hours, no footsy-wootsy under the Revere Memorial Library table. When passing on the road they stuck to formal greetings.

"Good afternoon, Miss Lizzy."

"Why, the same to you, Mr. Barton. I hope you have a pleasant day."

Was it his age that finally led to the end on the frigid night of January 14, 1954? Or was it the nasty weather? At the age of 74, stooped and wind-swept, old Frankie Barton stood in the stern, heaving against the oars as he rowed back across the wind-tossed Thorofare. The weather had come around to the northeast, temperatures falling below zero, wind howling, slashing snow driving horizontally so hard the side of the skiff iced thickly, chisel-sharp breaking waves powerless to keep it clear. Every few strokes he'd pause to slough the snow from his face.

With the nor'easter howling and the tide sucking at his high-top boots, it took all he had to drag that leaded dory onto Kimball's shore. His muscles ached. His heart raced. His body craved rest. While the snow-gauzed eye of the lighthouse witnessed from across the water, step by aching step, he began the ascent toward his cabin. But his old man's stamina had run out; Frankie Barton seized at his chest and gulped his final breath. Soon, the crimson pulse from the lighthouse caressed only a gathering mound of snow.

* * * *

Six long, frigid days later, folks on the Isle au Haut side worried about Frankie. No one had seen him. The temperatures had been wicked. Stan Dodge, captain of the mail boat, took it upon himself to row over and check. Stan was a strapping man, and he mushed up through the drifts like a husky while searching the sky for signs of smoke from Frankie's chimney. Half way up the ice-sheathed hill, Stanley's search ceased. There was Frankie Barton, curled in an icy ball.

A serene smile graced his frozen face.

* * * *

The joys and tragedy of those who passed on the Shadow Side of the lighthouse will continue forever to inspire or haunt us. Less clear is the staying power of less documented tales—like the following account of The Legend of Joe-Pete Notch.

Chapter 18

The Legend of Joe-Pete Notch

If you had walked in to the lighthouse by the old trail prior to 1986, you would have come to a sharp rise in the path alongside Dead Man's Bog. Here, the bedrock jutted up through the quilt of spruce needles and ferns on each side of the path, creating a narrow gap about the width of a hayrick, a place Aubrey Greenlaw II called Joe-Pete Notch. Its namesake—according to Aubrey—"a two-thousand-pound bull moose, the last of the great ones to rove the swamps of Isle au Haut." For many years, one of his antlers hung from a stunted maple tree here at "The Notch," Aubrey's memorial to a tragic family mystery.

* * * *

In 1907, the lighthouse station had been built on a scant two acres of shore, without any right-of-way from the town road. There was a primitive buggy trail that twisted the quarter mile through the rocky outcroppings from the road to the old Robinson homestead, about half the distance in to the lighthouse. From the Robinson place, those last three hundred yards to the station were an obstacle course of glacial boulders, moss-covered cliffs, bayberry thickets, raspberries, and fallen spruce. Since the station had been built from the water, and since it was manned and serviced from the water, the U.S. Lighthouse Service had seen no need to provide a road to town for the lighthouse keeper's family.

This high spot by the Notch is where Aubrey Greenlaw pitched his tent during the summer of 1986, the year Judi and I purchased the lighthouse station and began to rent rooms to travelers. Aubrey kept an extra folding chair by his fire pit for any passing soul willing to stop and chat, as well as a bottle of Jack Daniels within easy reach. Often, after trekking to town to fetch the mail or pick up provisions at the Island Store, I'd stop here to catch my breath and gab awhile with Aubrey before climbing the hill to the inn.

Aubrey Greenlaw II was a dapper fellow, always dressed neatly, even while dwelling deep in the woods by the edge of a swamp, co-habitating with clouds of mosquitoes and the occasional snapping turtle. He conveyed his thoughts with the genteel delivery of an English countryman. He sported Bean boots and red checkered flannel shirts, but with no hint of the ragtag appearance of a Maine backwoodsman. His boots were mud-free from soles to uppers, the laces perfectly tied. His shirt was tucked in, and he was always clean-shaven. I wouldn't have been surprised to see him sitting among the lady slippers and skunk cabbage dressed with top hat and cummerbund.

"Yep, quite a character he was, that old Joe-Pete," Aubrey told me during one of my visits. He nodded toward the deteriorating antler dangling from the tree, what he referred to as "the memorial" to the great Joe-Pete. He added a measure to the canning jar he used as a drinking glass. "That was back when the Robinson place was first settled by my Granddad, Charles Robinson, before the lighthouse was ever built."

As daylight retreated into the forest around us and muted sounds began to emerge from the swamp, I watched the muscles tighten on old Aubrey's face, his eyes narrowing, his lips twitching just a little as he began to tell me the story. *Even then I wondered, would I be hearing fact or fiction?*

"That ornery moose was nothin' but trouble," he said. "Why, he ripped the laundry right off Miss Lizzie's line! Done it a bunch of times.

Rooted through folks' gardens, too, yanking up turnips and russet spuds. Worst of all, one time he waded into the harbor at low water and grappled up a mess of pot warp with an antler, hauled half a dozen traps ashore, ballast and all, with lobsters slapping their tails against the slats. Irville Barter watched the whole thing. Said Joe-Pete drug that tangled works up the beach and stomped in the traps, chomping on lobster and bait. Then he made his escape back to his hideout here. And back then, this patch of swamp was sanctuary for more than just a moose."

I eased into Aubrey's extra chair and made myself comfy. Something told me this would take a while.

"I'm surprised no one ever shot him," I said, offering unneeded encouragement for him to continue.

"Those were strange times," said Aubrey, sipping from the jar. "I guess everyone knew that moose was no ordinary critter. His mammoth size, his daring acts, the aura that seemed to surround him, it all added up to a powerful presence. Guess folks felt he had a right to be here just as much as anyone else."

He took another sip. A shiver of memory flickered in his eyes.

"Of course Cripple Crow might o' had something to do with it, too. Granddaddy Charles always said folks back then was as reticent about him as they was of the moose."

"Who was *he*?" I said.

"Penobscot Indians, they were, Crow and his family. They camped right here, right on this spot, drew water from the same dug well I use today," he said, gesturing with a nod toward the wellhead and bucket by the edge of his camp. "There were still whole families of them out here back in those years, during the summer months. Crow's was the last. Still hanging on when Granddad was here, in spite of the rugged treatment the villagers gave them. Some folks here didn't take kindly to Indian ways—just as soon wished they would paddle on."

"Same old story," I said.

"Yep," said Aubrey. Another sip.

"Sounds like Joe-Pete and the Crow family were all social outcasts," I said.

Aubrey nodded. "They weren't the only ones," he said. "Granddaddy was pretty much cast in the same mold. He was a fresh young fellow from Head Harbor. Elbow room was tight back then, fishin' grounds precious. Neighbors didn't take kindly to outliers pushing in."

I could relate to that. Judi and I had only a year on the island, and although villagers had generally been supportive toward us and our crazy new inn, we constantly got not-so-subtle reminders that we were new, different, and maybe not deserving of the same rights and respect as those with local blood in their veins.

Daylight was gone by then, the swamp dark and forbidding. Aubrey added a few sticks of spruce to the coals, urging the rebirth of modest flames. I slouched in my chair and waited.

"I guess each of them—Granddad, the moose, the Indian folks—they all shared a common link; rebels, they were—characters living on the perimeter. Sometimes, on evenings like this, when daylight faded and all the villagers were snug at home, that hulking moose would emerge from the swamp and join Crow and his family, right here by the fire."

"Was your grandfather there, too?" I asked.

"You betcha. He was still a bachelor then," said Aubrey. "Crow would fetch him whenever Joe-Pete came by. Must have been quite a scene: the giant moose, the Indian family with three little ones, and a lanky young lad from the other side of the island, all the island's outcasts gathered around the fire, sharing hopes and dreams."

Aubrey became quiet for a moment, remembering.

"Then came that horrid winter of 1883," he said, his grip tightening on the Mason jar.

* * * *

On August 26–27, 1883, the cataclysmic explosion of Krakatoa shook the earth. A picturesque island in the Sunda Strait, located between Java and Sumatra, was transformed overnight into a blinding thunderous Hades. The explosion was equal to the force of 13,000 Hiroshima bombs. 26 cubic miles of bedrock was blasted into the sky. The deafening catastrophe pounded the eardrums of people 3,000 miles away, annihilated somewhere between 36,000 and 120,000 souls, and filled the atmosphere with enough CO^2 and ash to darken the earth's skies for a decade. "Volcanic winter" reigned. That year in

Chicago, the thermometer plunged to minus 27 degrees and remained below zero for six consecutive days. The effect on Isle au Haut was comparable. Or worse.

Fortunately for Charles Robinson, he wasn't on the island that winter. He had gone off to Boston in search of opportunities to raise a little cash in order to develop his farm on Robinson Cove. Cripple Crow and his family weren't so lucky. With their tribe increasingly dispersed, and no home to return to, they had chosen to stay the winter on Isle au Haut, despite the isolation and friction from the community.

In the wake of the eruption of Krakatoa, the skies stayed ashen, the temperatures dropped. Around the globe, sunsets blazed with unbelievable brilliance: scarlet reds and oranges, purples and sulfured blues. This pallet of bloody hues inspired writers, poets, and painters. In Iceland, Edvard Munch painted "The Scream" prompted by the sunsets produced by Krakatoa. As those flaming summer sunsets slipped into fall and then to winter, temperatures at Robinson Cove began to turn scary.

By mid-December, Crow had already used his entire store of firewood and had to forage half-rotten frozen spruce and dead undergrowth to keep his family warm. The island deer starved and froze to death. Crow's search for snowshoe hare and squirrel became desperate. No loaf of bread or kettle of chowder ever appeared from the village.

In January of 1884, the salt water in Robinson Cove froze solid. The rise and fall of the tides fractured the ice and stacked it on the shore in ragged configurations, jumbled and broken, like the tumbled walls of some bombed-out city.

In the spring, Charles returned.

Fearful of how awful the winter had been, he went straightaway to the Notch to check on his friends. As he hiked past the last bits of melting ice and the sprouting shoots of skunk cabbage, a melancholy silence permeated. No raucous ravens greeted him, as they always had. The path was devoid of footprints, with no telltale sign of springtime hikers, not even the cloven tracks of deer, or the scurried markings of mice or voles. Something was dreadfully wrong.

Charles passed the bog. He made his way up the hill to the notch in the path. He stopped. He stared. Waiting there, still and cold as stone, Cripple Crow and his family rested, enveloped inside the decaying carcass of Joe-Pete, like an unholy nativity from some prehistoric pagan site. The creature was quilled with a dozen arrows and Crow's timber ax was squarely buried in the furry forehead. Nearby lay Crow's skinning knife, apparently cast aside once he and his family had eviscerated the huge creature and crawled inside. Moldering fingers still clutched the hide's edges in a failed attempt to use the body of the great moose to fend off the deadly winter.

Charles Robinson succumbed in the defrosting mud and wept. Eventually, after two days of agony, he managed to extricate the human remains from the cavernous ribcage. One by one, he lugged the bodies to the shore. Then he fetched a peapod, hefted each aboard, and rowed them across the Thorofare to Kimball Island. He knew a serene little clearing where there was enough soil to provide a proper burial.

"I was just a little fellow," said Aubrey, "all those years later when Gramps took me over to show me the spot. He made me promise to never show anyone. Guess he just wanted one other soul to know where the bones were hidden, just so the legacy survived."

"What about Joe-Pete's remains?" I asked.

Aubrey poured himself a little more whiskey and took a draw on the jar.

"Thar she blows!" he said, gesturing with his lips at the antler hanging from the maple. "That's all that's left. Critters made short work of the carrion, and the bones were spread through the bog by eagles and varmints."

"That antler's been dangling there since 1884?"

"No, Gramps kept it in the farmhouse shed; I'm the one who brought it here to the notch, but that was much later."

"Ummm," I said. "Must be more to the story?"

Aubrey readjusted himself in his chair and took another sip. It was late now, but I could tell he was in no hurry to finish.

"Gramps was still a young fellow back then, so he was shaken badly by the deaths. Struggled, drank a lot." He paused and swirled the jar, focusing on the sloshing amber liquid. "Finally, he started to recover. Eventually married a girl from Duck Harbor, twenty years his junior—Miss Lillian Hamilton. They had two little ones:

first a daughter, Mattie Belle—my mother—then Uncle Everett, who came two years later. Things went well for them. The Feds came along and bought a piece of his land to build the lighthouse station, fishing was good, and they had great neighbors. And of course they lucked out in 1936 when they got that same land back with all those added buildings."

"A story-book ending?" I said.

"You'd think so, I guess," he said. "But, you know, Jeff, I don't think he ever really got over the tragedy. That renegade team: Grandpa, the moose, those tough Indians—they were so close. All they had was each other. He missed them badly, right up to the end. Even then, when he died, it was as if there were still some haunting unfinished business."

It was dark now, and late. I needed to get back to the inn. Judi would be waiting impatiently for the butter and cream. But my chair refused to release me—no way could I excuse myself without hearing the rest of the story.

"What kind of *unfinished business*?" I said.

"Winters were fairly mild for years after the 'volcanic winter,' but there was a whopper of a winter a half century later, in 1936—I'm sure you heard of *that* one, everyone has, a real zinger." I remembered how Esther Robinson had told me about the record-breaking low temperature that winter. "Grandpa was still kicking along fine, already in his eighties. But thirty-six was so cold I think it took him back—back to 1884. He was a sorrowful mess after that. Died the following year, 1937."

"From some kind of connection with the past, you think," I said.

"Perhaps. After he passed and we buried him up on the hill, the following winter strange things started happening at the lighthouse."

I thought I knew a lot about the history of the lighthouse, but it sounded like I was about to learn more.

"I know by then the fog bell had been removed," I said. "The old lantern, too. They installed one of those acetylene rigs about then."

"Ayuh," said Aubrey. "Lousy damn thing. Didn't work half the time, unless Russell MacDonald went up there and frigged with it. But sometimes, when the lantern wasn't working, if it were really icy cold at night, my dear grandmother thought she saw the thing a-glowing. She was plenty old herself by then, of course, so we figured her imagination had gone a bit sketchy. But it kept happening. Others saw it too."

"What was going on?" I prodded.

"Nobody had an explanation. No one on the island anyway. Most of the summer folk thought it was nonsense. Except Bucky Fuller, of course."

"Buckminster Fuller, you mean? The genius synergetics guy? The one who did the geodesic domes, the Dymaxion car, all that?"

"Yep, the one and only 'Mr. Spaceship Earth.' His family had a summer place over on Bear Island. He explored these parts as a kid, always brimming with crazy ideas; had an answer for everything. Later, as an adult, when he became famous, he still came to Maine in the summer, to relax and pursue his wacky projects."

Aubrey paused and gazed into the bog, thinking.

"And…" I waited.

"I guess he heard all about the strange lighthouse on Isle au Haut," Aubrey continued, "the history, all about Cripple Crow and Joe-Pete, about Grandpappy's passing and how the beacon started to glow during cold winter nights. Took a fancy to the story and, as was his custom, started coming up with all sorts of theories. Triangles were his thing. Ol' Bucky not only had a proclivity for geodesic domes but he had an uncanny interest in the power triangles exert in peoples' lives. That jibes with a lot of other cultures too, where people believe triangles serve as concentration points for energy."

"Yeah, like sitting under one allows you to intensify your focus," I said.

"Yep. I guess Bucky did some map studies when he heard about our lighthouse's behavior. He figured out the coordinates of Joe-Pete Notch and where the Indians were buried over on Kimball's—over the years, I may have hinted too much about the location. He added the location of Gramp's grave, of course."

"Here, I'll show you," he said. He started clearing the clutter off the lobster crate he used for his camping table, leaving a selection of whisky jiggers and empty bottles to be used in his presentation.

I scooted my chair forward to get a better look.

Aubrey took an empty bottle and placed it near the edge of the crate.

"Let's say this marks where we are sitting: Joe-Pete Notch, the site of the deaths of the moose and Crow's family."

Charles Robinson near Joe Pete Notch. Circa 1900. Photo courtesy of Jim Greenlaw

Aubrey's gas lantern flickered slightly, illuminating the table, casting a long shadow from the bottle. He used a mug of shaving cream for his next prop, positioning it carefully on the far side of his imaginary map. "This is about where Gramps buried the Indians, across the Thorofare," he said, his thumb nudging the mug into its rightful position. He picked up a jigger and studied its glimmering facets, maybe assuring himself it qualified for the next assignment.

"Charles Robinson is buried here," he said, reaching across the crate and planting the jigger in place.

I studied the configuration. With the three objects in place—the empty bottle, the mug of shaving cream, and the whisky jigger—a perfect shape emerged: an equilateral triangle.

Aubrey reached over and grasped the lantern. His hand was shaking slightly. Carefully, calculatingly, determinedly, he lifted the lamp and moved it toward his makeshift map. Shadows quavered and dancing beams of light leapt like acrobats as the light descended. Aubrey lowered the lantern to the middle of the table.

"Here is the lighthouse," he said. "Dead center in the triangle."

"The nexus of three tombs!" I said.

Aubrey summed it up. "That mysterious glow from the lighthouse, it was generated by the remembrance of long ago times, the shared camaraderie of treasured friends, the energy from three points of light focused on their center point."

"Yes," I said, "triggered by frigid weather—a re-creation of the conditions that led to the demise of the moose and his friends."

"Yep," said Aubrey. "And the enduring power of a lighthouse that remembers and cares."

It was getting late. Judi would be wondering where I was. I had no flashlight and the climb along the darkened shore could be dicey. I thanked Aubrey for his hospitality, slung my knapsack onto my shoulder, and headed into the night. It was so dark I had to crane my neck and stare straight up so I could follow the strip of starry sky running between the treetops. At the shore, I began the uphill hike that twisted toward the station. From here on, I knew I was safe—every four seconds a ruby pulse illuminated my path.

* * * *

Aubrey The Second camped at Joe Pete Notch for only one more summer. He dropped in on me a few more times at the lighthouse, but his age was slowing him down. He passed away soon after.

I inherited the antler.

Chapter 19

Ghosts and Shamans

It's not my intention to hoodwink anyone into believing things contrary to their own inclinations. But in my attempt to write a comprehensive history of the lighthouse, I find it requisite to include some of the more mysterious incidents that made folks shudder, pack their bags and flee, or fall on their knees in wonder. More than just a pillar of brick with a flashing light bulb atop, this island lighthouse pulses with the heartbeat of accumulated stories. There are good experiences and bad, both terrifying and soothing. There's the tales told by fishermen on the landing, the epitaphs etched on tombstones, the impetus to get us up in the morning (or remain in bed with sheets pulled over our heads), the nebulous, fuzzy, glorious, confounding stuff that makes us see halos or scares us out of our pants. They are more than mere ghost stories, and include other things non-scientific, like the power of dousing rods, vaporous nighttime visitations, and the effect of unseen energy lines never plotted on any map.

During our years at the lighthouse, here are just a few of the head-scratching events that unfolded.

White Light

My dear wife, Judi, the lighthouse keeper's daughter, is a practical person. She's not prone to exaggeration. She dresses modestly, speaks directly, and doesn't succumb to gossip. She's a good listener, an astute negotiator and a peaceful woman who avoids attracting attention. Above all, Judi is a fearless materialist: she lives her life based on the facts of whatever she finds in her path.

During the night of August 15, 1988, while slumbering in our loft in the woodshed, she awoke in a flash of light.

She waited for morning before she told me.

"Jeff," she murmured, as we lay half awake with dawn creeping in around us. "The most amazing thing happened!"

I clutched at my pillow, rolled over, pulled the sheet over my eyes.

"Yeah…" I managed.

"In the middle of the night…something woke me…a colorful light…like fireworks, only brighter…*much* brighter…"

"Huh…" I said.

Judi doesn't fabricate. She sticks to the facts. Her announcement of a nocturnal visitation was—frankly—extremely unsettling. I pulled the sheet away from my face. "Whadaya mean?" I said.

My initial dismay was relieved when I realized she was bathed in peace—she lay in the morning light serene and beaming, like some bedclothes-enshrined Madonna.

"It was wonderful," she said, "I could feel the warmth, the light…I opened my eyes…the whole house swirled with sparkling glitter… waves of it, like the aurora borealis…"

"Really!" I said.

"At first I wanted to wake you, to share it with you," she said, "but I couldn't. It was so special…I needed to lay there in the light, as if… as if it were meant for only me."

That was almost thirty years ago. It's never happened again. We've talked about that experience many times since, but no other instance of such profound waking has ever occurred. That experience changed her, made her more accepting, more grateful, a gemstone smoothed of rough edges. It doesn't matters what "it" was, nor from where "it" came. "It" simply happened.

The Pantry Ghost

Lisa Louise Turner is a native islander: teacher, tax collector, knitter, and cook. Lisa also happens to be the Secretary/Treasurer of the Isle au Haut Lighthouse Committee, so I know her in many roles and have grown familiar with her idiosyncrasies, her moods, and what makes her tick. For more than a decade she worked for us at the lighthouse inn, as chef, as dishwasher, as hostess, as cleaner, as manager, and as advisor to Judi and me on the nature of island life. She's smart and dependable—her opinion means a lot.

During the years Lisa labored in the kitchen pantry whipping up cake batter and washing out kettles, she became intimately familiar with every square inch of that tiny nook. "It's haunted," she said, many times. She knew from the moment she first set foot in there. A "foreboding feeling," I think is the way she described it.

"It isn't scary, though," she said. "Not like some horrid thing is going to leap out of the cupboard and strangle me. Mostly it's a sound, sort of an incessant whine, like someone complaining."

No one else ever heard it. Only Lisa.

"I got used to it," she said. "It's like a dull toothache that never goes away. I'm not particularly superstitious, but I gotta say, that sound's no earthly utterance. Something ugly happened in that corner!"

Even though no one else could hear it, Lisa's analysis was strengthened when Jules Pelletier came to stay at the inn. Jules hailed from Louisiana, an artist and philosopher and devotee of the occult. Around his neck he wore a dangling silver medallion that reflected light like a diamond. According to Jules, the shiny facets of the medallion sorted life into profound flashes of insight, revelations he used to tell fortunes, or predict the future, or douse for water.

One evening after dinner, he explained that he often used the medallion to survey homes for energy points. He was unaware of Lisa's pantry predicament, so I asked him if he'd be good enough to check the house for problems, just to double-check Lisa's suspicions. He said he would be tickled to do it.

The next morning, after the breakfast dishes had been cleared away and the other guests had all gone trekking, Jules appeared in the kitchen with the medallion swinging from his outstretched hand. Lisa was cleaning the refrigerator. She watched him intensely without mentioning her troubling relationship with the pantry.

Jules wended his way around the kitchen. The dangling medallion pirouetted on the end of the chain. Around the counters they went and past the refrigerator, pausing here and there at each cabinet door, at every baseboard corner, like a hound dog sniffing bushes.

"This is the way we do it," he whispered. "Higher Power does the searching—all I do is hang on. It leads me along, twisting and dipping, giving answers to questions properly posed."

He had risen early, he said, and had already toured the other rooms. The medallion had evaluated every square foot of the hallway and the living room, with little of note to report. In the dining room, however, one particular corner tested positive as a potent energy zone, a perfect spot to meditate or recover from harrowing experiences, he explained. I smiled when he told me, knowing it was the dog's preferred snoozing spot.

"Can you ask it to check out the pantry?" I said.

"You bet," he said, turning toward the sink, the medallion gyrating and bobbing.

The instant Jules passed into the pantry, the medallion went berserk. First it would spin on its chain. Then it would jerk. Then it pendulously swung in arcs, or so it seemed to me. Jules's face was a mask of confusion.

"Holy moly," he said. "I've never seen *this* before…this spot is *really* toxic, worst I've ever seen! It's not just the movements that speak; I can feel it in my belly—this corner seethes with rancid karma!"

Jules asked us a million questions. He wanted to know about the history of the station: Had any crimes been committed here, any suicides or childhood disasters, that sort of thing. Try as we could, neither Judi nor I nor Lisa could conjure any answer for the medallion's behavior.

Jules scratched his head. "I suppose we could try smudging," he said. "Know any good witches out here? Someone handy with sage smoke and incantations? That ought to drive the bastard out."

"A few, maybe, but the gals out here are the redemptive sort—more pledged to follow the *Buddha Path,* not keen on purging and punitive stuff."

"Too bad," said Jules. "Well, then, how about a good ol' exorcism? That's less vindictive, and cleaner, too—no need to dirty the pantry walls."

I considered that for a moment. "Yeah, but out here, all we have is a gaggle of Congregationalists. The Reverend Ted doesn't have the authority to splatter holy water and shake a cross—we'll need the heavy-duty Catholic folks for that kind of magic, a Bishop, or Cardinal, or even a Duke."

While Jules and I continued our plotting, Lisa remained in the pantry finishing up the dishes, contributing nothing to the conversation on how to purge the ghost. With no solution for the screwy phenomenon, Jules and I soon wandered off to tend to other tasks, leaving Lisa alone.

Her hands in soapy water, a sardonic smile spread across her face. The eerie sound returned, moved closer to her ear, now stood right beside her. She dried the last of the plates and silverware, and used her dishcloth to give the countertop a final swipe. Then she noted down the hours she had worked in the little blue notebook by the cookie jar, collected her jacket, and headed out the door. Halfway across the dooryard, she slowed, turned a bit to look back at the Keeper's House before trudging down the hill toward the rest of her day, wagging her head and thinking.

"I'll never understand these mainland folks," she thought out loud, "the way they're never satisfied with the island, with their citified ways of thinking. They hate ticks. They bitch about the deer eating their damn arugula. The mosquitoes drive them batty. For Christ's sake, they can't even tolerate yer average household spirit!"

The Man on the End of the Bed

For most people, waking up after an afternoon nap and finding a strange man sitting on the foot of your bed would be a disquieting experience.

It wasn't that way for Rosemary Flanders.

"I could feel the weight sink into the mattress," she said, "a little nudge that woke me. With the late afternoon sun warming the room, the dinner preparation clatter coming from the kitchen, and the sweet memories of a morning hike still fresh in mind, I figured another delight was in order. I stretched and yawned a little—I remember that—then let my eyelids drift open."

"What did you see?" I asked.

I had poured her a cup of sparkling cider, the way I did for guests before dinner. Asking them about their day's events was routine for an innkeeper, but the intruder in Rosemary's room was pretty disturbing.

She took a sip.

"A kind face, and handsome, too, but it was the kindness that mattered. He wore fisherman's gear, you know, the high rubber boots, the floppy old-fashioned canvas hat, all that."

"But how did it make you *feel*?" I asked, worried. "Weren't you a bit concerned?"

"Not at all. In fact, it's been the highlight of my vacation, the best part of all! Oh, goodness, don't get me wrong—nothing untoward happened—it was all very proper," she giggled.

Dowsing Does It

I've had mixed results with dowsing rods. For example, my rusty old set (crafted from a length of unearthed copper cable) did a commendable job when it located Gracie's lost cat. On the other hand, when Jules used his fancy medallion to choose a spot for our well to be drilled, the resulting vein the well driller found produced only a dribble of unusable water. Regarding the efficacy of dowsing, however, we learned one good rule: The more strongly a dowser believes in the technique, the better it works. Jenny Tremble was the perfect example.

The Jenny drama played out on an otherwise typical evening at the inn. As usual, after dinner the guests drifted into the living room and eased themselves onto the sofa or into easy chairs for a chance to let their bellies settle, a time to chat and banter—the last golden hour of leisure before retiring for the night. Also, for me, this was the orchestrated occasion to perform my innkeeper ritual: answering the usual questions and telling a story or two. I waited in the kitchen with our dishwasher, Heather, for the dust to settle, for each sated guest to snuggle in with a current bestseller, a bedtime toddy, or a comforting conversation to close out the evening. Equipped with my favorite coffee mug, at just the right moment, I ambled in and lit the gaslight.

"How was your supper?" I addressed the bunch.

"Unbelievable."

"Finest kind."

"Filled to the scuppers."

"Oh, so yummy."

At first there was only small talk, listing home towns, professions, that sort of stuff, but sooner or later, some curious guest would ask how we came here, or who were our most famous guests, or how many ships have run aground here, how many lives lost. Then, just like clockwork, someone else would pop the inevitable question: "What about ghosts? Certainly you must have them? And stories of strange events—this place is crawling with mystery. What can you tell us about all that?"

On this particular evening of the Jenny Tremble drama, I had started out by explaining that we have a dearth of potable water. By that time, I had rigged up a shallow well pump that provided murky water suitable for washing dishes and flushing johns, but we were still lugging our drinking water by jerry can from a neighbor's well.

"Have you tried dowsing?" one fellow asked. "They say that works great for finding water."

"Yep," says another. "Back in the old days, that's how my granddaddy chose his well site. I believe he used an applewood stick."

In addition to these two gentle folk and several others, we also had two couples from Kansas City. Brash and tipsy, their rudeness dominated the living room. The wives sat squished together on the sofa, slurping Chablis and admiring their fingernails, while their beer-guzzling husbands occupied cushy overstuffed chairs, looking aggressive and casting disapproving glances at the pro-dowsing people.

"Not a lick of logic to that dowsing stuff," sniffed the stouter of the two. He wore a Kansas City Chiefs sweatshirt, extra large, but not expansive enough to enrobe his entire belly. Swallowed deep in the folds of the overstuffed chair, his squinty eyes hovered at the same level as his knees. His focus darted back and forth at the other guests, evaluating them to decipher who agreed with him and who did not. His pal was balding and skinny, his neck long and landmarked with ridged blue veins and an oversized Adam's apple. It undulated every time he spoke.

"Dowsing doesn't work," this thin man declared, dispensing his opinion with the authority of a drill sergeant.

"Never has," said his chubby buddy.

With these two intimidators laying down the law, others became hesitant to pursue the conversation.

To combat their negative assessments, I added my own well-rehearsed story about using my dousing rods to find Gracie's lost cat. While I spoke, the two nonbelievers scowled from their upholstered bunker. The wives looked offended, as if hearing a dowsing opinion different from their own might be causing them bodily harm.

Jenny Tremble was spellbound. She sat on the piano stool by the woodstove, hands folded properly in her lap. Her poufy hairdo sat atop her head like a nesting hen, held in place with hairspray and lighthouse barrettes. With every twist in the conversation, she shifted her posture to best hear the dowsing arguments. Her fingers began to fidget, as if she were an anxious clerk craving pen and steno pad. Inquisitive eyes glinted with fascination.

Other guests politely listened while I recounted my experience. I told how I found the rusty wire, how I fashioned the rods on my boathouse workbench, how I turned the measured lengths on the anvil while forging the metal with my hammer. I remembered feeling the power grow, the burgeoning warmth in the metal, the tingling sensation in my hands when I finally grasped them.

Mesmerized by the story, my audience listened. I described the subsequent search for the missing cat, the rods swinging in my hands like compass needles, pulling me through the woods. Gracie's cat sprang out of the bushes into my arms.

But the drama of my story was dashed by a chortling interruption.

"Yeah, yeah, yeah," sneered the fat man. "If you can dowse like that, why not produce gold, or oil, or blue chip stocks? Why waste your time on scruffy cats?"

The other guy snickered, too. "Dowsing doesn't work. Never has. Never will. Any fool can find water if they dig deep enough."

Jenny Tremble spoke out.

"Sounds fantastic to me. What a wondrous gift it is, coaxing water from rock."

The Kansas City folk snorted.

Despite the uncomfortable atmosphere created by the Midwestern naysayers, something bloomed in Jenny's demeanor. Like a rose opening its petals, this demure young secretary straightened herself on the piano stool and emitted an aura so strong it brightened the interest of everyone, except for the cranky Kansans, of course.

"I want to try it," she timidly said.

She sat more upright now, her feet planted squarely on the floor, her hands grasping her knees, ready to rise, eyes flashing determination, emitting the unfettered faith of one just converted.

"I want to do it!" she said again, with more conviction. "I want to dowse for water! Now!"

All around the room, shocked guests gaped. They thought she was nuts…but they also admired her.

"Let's try it out," she said, rising to her feet. "Why not see for ourselves?" She turned and looked at me, smiling. "Where are your dowsing rods?"

Taken back by losing center stage, the fat man and his buddy fought to regain higher ground.

"But…but, you can't do that!" said the buzzard-necked guy, hovering on the arm of the chair. "It's freezing outside…and black as coal."

"Yeah, and how could you prove anything anyway? You got a backhoe out there running, ready to dig a hole?" said his pal, laughter belching from his belly so fiercely that waves of jellied flesh roiled beneath his football jersey. "Besides, you got no permit to drill!" He laughed even harder, slapping his knee for emphasis, hoping his bravado would deflate her gumption.

But she stood there in the aura of the gaslight, glowing like a haloed goddess, her shining eyes waiting for a response from me.

"I'll go get the rods," I said.

Into the night I scurried, down the path to the boathouse, knowing the way by habit. Lifting the rods off the nail where they dwelt, I returned straightaway to the dining room where all were anxiously waiting. Jenny Tremble still stood by the woodstove, serene and confident; the Kansas duo still guzzled beer and chortled. All the other guests waited, enthralled by the unfolding drama.

As I passed the rods on to Jenny, a tangible current sparked between us. I showed her how to hold them loosely so they could pivot at will, how to give them the freedom to lead the way. The other guests, myself, the very walls around us seemed to glow a little brighter as soon as she took hold of them.

"Betcha can't even find water in the toilet," said Mr. Raptor-man.

"Hold on, folks, get ready for a tsunami," said Mr. Football Jersey.

Jenny took a few tentative steps, like a child learning to walk, the rods dangling and limp in her hands. She circled the living room, stepping around chair legs and the sprawled feet of watchers. With each pace she took she gained confidence. The rods stiffened slightly and became parallel with the floor. Their tips sniffed along as Jenny Tremble circled. The rest of us were reserved, silent, focused on her journey. Even the hardcore resistance seemed becalmed, out of respect for what was happening.

She crept into the dining room. Here the dowsing rods pulled her around the tables, pausing occasionally before moving further. The rods were ramrod straight now, a team of draft horses working in tandem. Past the windows they pulled, around the crowd of silent chairs, past the china cupboard and the coffee decanters, through the doorway into the hall, through the foyer and past the stairs. The rods remained unwavering. Behind Jenny Tremble trailed the rest of us: me, the dishwasher, and the other guests. Even the naysayers poked along, shaking their heads and waiting for what they believed would be unmitigated failure.

Into the kitchen our procession went. Jenny Tremble moved to the center of the room, slowing, as if she sensed a trophy fish tugging at the bait. Suddenly, she came to a halt. Due to her unexpected braking, the caravan behind her piled into one another.

"Oh, my golly!" she said. "Come look at this!" We craned our necks and jostled around her, all stretching to gawk: The dousing rods had swung across each other, frozen in a rigid "X."

"The spot!" said Jenny Tremble.

"Bingo!" said Heather.

"Oh, God!" said guest after guest after guest. "She's found water!"

Still loitering in the foyer, the Kansas City Four stood apart from the clamor, their eyes broadcasting accusations. "Prove it," one said.

"I have nothing to prove," said Jenny Tremble. "For me, joy comes from believing. My body felt the tingle, the scent of water. As sure as the migration of swallows, those dousing rods led me to H_2O. How deep? Doesn't matter—could be in China for all I know. But one thing is certain: I felt truth throb in that metal, and I'll never let that go."

The crowd broke loose in accolades for Jenny Tremble. From the foyer came only snickering and hushed vulgar words.

Me? I stood alone at the basement door, my hand upon the knob.

"Ladies and gentlemen, I have an announcement to make," I said. "Please tie your shoes snugly and follow me. We'll take a little tour now, of the lighthouse catacombs. You folks from Kansas, you come first. Be careful not to bump your head descending. It's kinda hazardous down here."

The Kansas Four bulled their way to the doorway, with the others lined up behind. I turned on my flashlight, twisted the doorknob and pushed. From below, the darkness opened to swallow us as I led the Kansans down, keeping my light trained on the wooden steps so they could see their way. Once securely planted on the cellar floor, they waited in the blackness while I returned the beam to the staircase so the others could clamber down. Once all were safely waiting, little was required to wrap up the evening. I swiveled the flashlight around to the cellar space directly below the kitchen, where the beam illuminated a massive red brick wall that partitioned off a quarter of the basement.

"What's with the wall?" someone said.

"Ladies and Gentlemen," I announced, "this is the old lighthouse cistern, a thirty-five-hundred-gallon tank brimming with rain water, fed by downspouts from the roof. It's our reserve, in case we ever run dry, or need to fight a fire, a vast lagoon a mere three feet under the kitchen floor."

Jenny Tremble was jubilant.

"You gotta believe if you want it to work," she said.

Jeffrey Takes a Hit

In the fall of 2005, I was struck with a nasty heart attack.

I had been one of those "low risk" candidates, the lucky ones who had no medical "indicators." We had sold our house in Orland where we had lived during the winters for the years our son Matthew went to high school in Blue Hill. I was there that day to remove the last truckload of belongings, so the new owner could move in.

It was one of those achingly beautiful autumn days. The air was fresh and cool, and the October sun sat low yet warm, while the maples released cascades of fiery leaves that swirled across the yard, piling up against the hedgerows like Thanksgiving displays in department store windows.

Most of my truck was already loaded, but the last few feet and the tailgate I had saved for the weightiest item: our waterlogged five-foot-diameter redwood hot tub. A two-by-four was perfect to tip it over on its side. Since it was round, rolling it over to the end of the truck was easy. Here came the problem, though: How would I lift the dang thing up and into the truck bed? It was the final thing to be loaded. I would be done for the day. It would be the last trip down this familiar old driveway. Then, on to new horizons.

Charged with energy and ambition, I figured, "Oh, what the hell," and scrunched down low with my knees bent—that's how you do it, right, so you don't pop a vertebra or blow out a kneecap? I strained, I grunted, I heaved and lifted, and just as I had hoped, the nasty thing rose like a monster from the Black Lagoon and slipped perfectly into place.

"Whew," I said out loud to myself. "That's sure satisfying."

Funny, though, my body didn't feel so good about it.

I felt vaguely dizzy. And hot, even though the late autumn air had required a wooly jacket.

Looking around to make sure everything had been accounted for, I gave our old house a "Namaste" bow and slid into the driver's seat. Then, I got out again to remove my jacket. Damn, was it hot!

Getting back in was laborious. I clutched at the wheel and sagged into the seat. In my stomach the discomfort of heartburn arose (I'd suffered from GERD from the age of nine, although it wasn't diagnosed till 40 years later).

But it wasn't stomach acid. It was different. Not a single hot burning point, more widespread, more…more scary.

The truck floated down the drive, almost driving itself, I, merely a dazed passenger along for the ride. As if by autopilot, the Toyota followed Route 75 north to U.S. 1, peeling off to the East toward the double-lane highway that would carry me through Blue Hill and down to Stonington.

I was sweating now. The glare from the sky seemed blinding.

I better stop and get some Tums, I thought. Hadn't that always helped an aching belly?

At the turn-off to Blue Hill there's a Texaco convenience store where they would have the good old cure. But the Toyota didn't stop there. We crawled on through the twists and turns of the two-lane, slower now, barely traveling. But now—unlike the previous moments—only a single thought kept me moving forward: *There's a hospital in Blue Hill.*

Most of the rest is hazy. I remember somehow ending up in the hospital parking lot where I pulled as far back as I could. I didn't want my overloaded rig blocking the emergency entrance.

The truck door opened somehow, and my body leaned after it. When my feet found pavement, I almost went down. I staggered over what felt like acres of blacktop like a delirious cowboy crossing the Mojave. Step by struggling step, the emergency room doors got closer.

Inside…emptiness. No rushing hospital hubbub noise. No "stat" codes bleating from intercoms. No aides pushing gurneys with sheet-covered bodies. No one anywhere: I was doomed.

I stood there tottering.

From the back of the room, a faraway voice sounded.

"Yes, may I help you?" I think she said.

She rose like a hazy phantom from her desk and drifted a few steps toward me.

Then she may have hollered, "Oh, my God!"

Only faint memories then: a gaggle of white coats, nitro pills, an injection perhaps. I remember crying. Then, a surreal flight by helicopter to the Maine Medical Center in Bangor.

* * * *

Joyous strains from Vivaldi's *The Four Seasons* woke me. Nurses and aides rushed about putting exotic equipment away, coiling up tubes and stowing supplies. A sweet young woman who patted my hand and told me, "Everything will be just fine," pushed me to a recovery room.

At some point during this foggy drama, a doctor arrived by my bedside. Before addressing me, he scanned the clipboard he carried, circled something in pencil and cleared his throat. He looked at me over the top of his glasses.

"Mr. Burke, I'm Doctor Dashane."

"What happened?" I asked.

"Three plugged arteries. The lower descending one was the worst—ninety-five percent blocked. Let me show you."

He leaned backwards against my bed and cradled the clipboard, poked at the drawing with his pencil, and explained.

"Almost shut off completely right here." He tapped the diagram. The corner of his mouth gave a little twist, a coded message that seemed to say, "You nearly bit the dust!"

"That was the worst one, but you can see up here and over here, two more highly constricted passages. I put stents in the lower descending artery and this one, too. You'll have to come back again for me to do the third."

"Am I going to be all right?"

"There's some damage, but you should be okay. 'Course you'll need to make some lifestyle changes and stay on medication. You're a 'heart patient' now; life will be different from now on, but you'll be fine."

Cripes, I thought. Last thing I needed. I'm a washout at 63? No more fun. No more cheeseburgers. No more sex.

Before they let me go, they signed me up for rehab, diet classes, and new prescriptions. Geez, I realized, this disaster is going to screw up my life forever! Worst of all, they're making me come back for yet another stent!

* * * *

The next two weeks were hell. I felt like crap. My strength was gone. I faced a future of sorrow and loss. I'd never be the same. My life would be miserable, boring, and short. But most of all, I was terrified.

* * * *

On the day before my scheduled admission for the third stent, Judi and I arrived early at the Town Landing. Dense fog filled the harbor that morning, as thick and weighty as my mood. These past days, since my heart attack, I hadn't been able to think about anything

The Isle au Haut Lighthouse Station Today, photo Courtesy of Meghan Cooper.

except my plunge into misery, disability, and, ultimately, death.

A guest at the Keeper's House was also leaving on the same boat, so we had given him a ride to the dock. This fellow professed to be a shaman: Doc Purington is what he called himself, a tall gangly fellow with a limp and a twangy lisp that reminded me of "Chester" on the old *Gunsmoke* show. During appetizers he had cured every guest of one ailment or another. Doc had asked each to stand directly in front of him. He would evaluate their posture, put his bony hands on their shoulders, then place an index finger on their solar plexus, while his other hand scurried across their bellies like a spindly spider, feeling, sensing, and prodding deeply. Then he would shake his hands, as if he were casting off pus extruded from their bellies. Later, each guest told me that heat had emanated from his fingertips, and a vibrating energy penetrated their flesh. Without exception, each insisted afterward that their neck no longer ached, or the dull pain in the lower back had vanished. (Yes, stuff like this happens all the time at the Keeper's House—this isn't like any normal bed and breakfast!)

Now, here was Doc, hitching a ride with us to Stonington. He asked where Judi and I were going. I told him about my recent heart attack and that now I was returning to the hospital for yet another stent.

"Want me to heal you?" he said.

"Sure," I said. At this point, I was willing to try anything to get those sawbones out of my life.

Just then, a voice called out.

"Hey, Jeff. You guys need a lift back to America?" It was George Cole, one of the island's summer residents. He stood in the stern of his boat, ready to cast off—his offer would save us the mail boat fare and get us to Stonington quickly. We climbed aboard with our overnight bags (Doc carried only a Navajo tote filled with talismans, Kachina dolls, and rattles). George purred off just as the mail boat came into view through the north end of the harbor.

George's boat is no ordinary boat. Made by Hinckley Company in Southwest Harbor, it is renowned as the "jet picnic boat." That means it's designed to get a bunch of summer rusticators to pretty places quickly, in comfort, and with impressive speed and luxury. She's named *Tír na nÓg* (from Irish mythology, meaning "magical place," and often used to refer to "the land of youth" or "where one never gets old"). This boat is 36 feet of gleaming fiberglass, polished brass, and richly rubbed teak. Beneath her deck, a pair of Yanmar 370-horsepower diesel engines force 160 gallons of water per second through a propulsion jet. With no propeller, she draws only two feet of water and could practically scoot along on wet grass. She can cruise without straining at 29 knots (about 33 miles per hour), gliding over choppy seas as if they were a putting green. Landing at crowded docks? Never a problem: The craft's water jet ejectors swivel beneath the cabin so the captain can aim them in any direction, pushing the boat sideways into a dock space no longer than the boat itself. Galley, head, lounge area, she has it all, with jaw-dropping technology to boot. This baby sports Loran, radar, GPS, chart plotters, Sirius satellite radios capable of tuning to hundreds of bands, automatic winching anchors, and self-cleaning johns. The problem is one needs to be an engineering genius just to get her started.

The fog was starting to lift. When George turned the thing on we could hardly tell she was running. He eased silently away from the dock.

My shaman buddy, Doc, was busy prepping me for my treatment. First, he had me lie back in my cushy deck chair. Then he unfolded a glittering tapestry from his medicine bag, tucked it under my chin and smoothed it across my chest. Over my heart he centered a pyramid of black tourmaline. "Excellent healing powers," he said. His hand dipped once more into the bag, this time retrieving a gourd intricately decorated with aboriginal symbols. He shook it. The dry seeds inside rattled. In circular patterns he waved it back and forth low over my chest.

"You'll be just fine," he said.

Then he began to chant.

"Oh-gan-a-wee, whid-a-wee, sud-a-wee, moo..."

Meanwhile, George had navigated *Tír na nÓg* into the channel and eased the throttle forward.

"Oh-gan-a-wee, whid-a-wee, sud-a-wee, moo. "

George activated his rotating radar, flipped on the panel of pulsing screens—a string of flickering, beeps and neon glowing permeated the cabin.

"Oh-gan-a-wee, whid-a-wee, sud-a-wee, moo..."

Doc's incantations gathered passion and increased volume. George's flying saucer gathered speed and rose in the water. Two separate forces competing. Palpable tension. We raced toward crossing the bar, this caterwauling consortium of technology and magic, flying along on wings of spray wide enough to irrigate the Corn Belt.

"Oh-gan-a-wee, whid-a-wee, sud-a-wee, moo..."

George, backed by his phalanx of whirling antennas and flashing electronics, swiveled his captain's chair around to face us.

"Hey," he barked at Doc. "Your voodoo shit better not fuck up my navigation system."

We all broke into hysterical laughter—Judi and me, Doc, and even George. "You'll be just fine," they all hooted.

As we crossed the bar, the last frail strand of fog lifted, exposing the lighthouse at the south end of the harbor. George veered due North towards Stonington. Just before Kimball Island shifted across our stern and hid the lighthouse from view, I think I saw the lantern wink. And like the fog that parted, the sense of dread about my health also magically lifted.

I realized then, I *would* be fine.

Chapter 20

How the Lighthouse Changed My Life

I grew up a sad kid in a middle-class, lily-white suburb of Columbus, Ohio. In school, I was the perennial academic failure, and the instigator of trouble. Cowboy boots and a saxophone exemplified my persona, plus hanging out with the beer-guzzling crowd. I won election as President of the Grandview Heights High School Booster Club because all the other candidates split the vote for who was most popular. I was different.

As President, during my first student body assembly, I had my buddy, Gene, blast his 12-gauge shotgun behind the curtains, and I failed to introduce Gretchen Tangleman to lead the Pledge of Allegiance. The faculty became so alarmed by my behavior that the annual musical production was cancelled, rather than to allow Jeffrey to produce and direct it. By the time I graduated, the police had busted me on three separate occasions.

The saxophone thing never went anywhere (I couldn't play the blues).

And I graduated (barely) at the bottom of my class.

At Ohio State, I changed my major every quarter, although my academic probation never wavered.

I wasn't cut out for Business Administration.

Fine Arts sailed by in a similar fashion: I couldn't draw.

Education was out of the question: *Me* teaching school?

But I sure could drink! That was my sole subject of interest.

In 1964, I got married, moved near campus, and joined a Free Speech sit-in that paralyzed the administration building. That helped. Out of nowhere, history courses started making sense, seemed intriguing, and stimulated my learning appetite.

A week after graduation, Judi and I headed for Puerto Rico for Peace Corps training. For the following two years we served in the mountains of Venezuela, organizing co-ops and latrine-digging projects.

We also started publishing a volunteer newsletter, *Boca Abierta*. Volume #1, Issue #1 (and the *only* one) featured articles about the expanding war in Vietnam. Since the Peace Corps is an arm of the U.S. State Department, I was busted again; the director hauled us off to Caracas where we were threatened with expulsion.

After the Peace Corps, we moved with Peter, our newborn son, to New York City and worked for the Welfare Department. That lasted three months (the summer of 1968). "Let's give California a whirl," we said. That led to myriad social and political upheavals: graduate school at Berkeley, factory organizing, and hippie communes. During the first seven years of Peter's life, we lived in seventeen different houses. I worked in the sheet metal industry, became a custom furniture maker, and worked as a technical teacher for Johnson's War on Poverty. I got busted again, for "inciting to riot" at the Oakland Unemployment Office.

I quit drinking in 1978. Even sober, my life still stumbled along in much the same pattern.

I tried graduate school again—still unrewarding. Other than to my family, I held no allegiance to anything.

"Let's move to Maine," said Judi.

"Groovy," I said.

Fourteen-year-old Peter rushed to pack.

"I'm not going!" protested twelve-year-old Dawn.

"What's Maine?" said seven-year-old Matthew.

Off we went again—yet another search for Nirvana.

* * * *

One wintery October morning in 1985, I stepped off the mail boat on Isle au Haut and saw the lighthouse for the first time. I didn't realize then that this tower would change my life.

When I was younger, I had lived day-to-day, year-to-year, decade-to-decade. Now, the lighthouse grounded me to a life mission. All those frustrated cravings I had in my early years—art and music, organizing people, wondering about how to make a difference in how we live together, what makes us tick, and how we solve our problems. The lighthouse now provided a theater, a canvas, a place that brought it all together for me, and a stage to share the same opportunity with thousands of other seekers.

We hosted a young patient dying of cancer who shared her struggles with us.

We hosted a childless couple from Philadelphia trapped in stagnant lives. They moved to Maine and adopted a baby from China.

We hosted a vice president of a Wall Street bank, who quit her career and got a job stocking shelves at Trader Joe's.

We hosted a Vietnam veteran filled with rage who taught us about the stresses that tore his life apart.

For twenty-five years I stood on the lighthouse landing, the tower waiting behind me, and welcomed these guests, saw the light burning in their eyes as they landed, looking past me toward the tower. Like me, they too found some resolution here in the presence of the lighthouse.

* * * *

Thirty-two years later—now in my dotage—here I am retired, past owner of the Keeper's House Inn, and living nearby with my bride of fifty-four years. Yet, I'm still attached by umbilical cord to the lighthouse, a parent unable to let go. After all, I'm the dad that sired the rebirth of this place, and I'm proud of the attention she garners from every passing boat. I'll do anything to keep her sturdy. Someday, somewhere down the road, our joint venture may dim, but it will never vanish.

I am a man who has always wanted to make a difference. The *Lighthouse and Me* became a joint venture. One life. One guiding cairn of stone. One brief encounter on a five-billion-year-old orb hurtling through space.

The lighthouse, which shines for so many, will always be my beacon.

Epilogue

Sooner or later I knew this writing project would come down to groveling and pandering. But before I fall on my knees and start begging, let me simply say, "Thanks for joining me for this tour through time, through the cold hard facts and the wild imaginations."

Now, as Chair of The Town of Isle au Haut Lighthouse Committee, I have work to do—we have a lighthouse to save. The bricks are crumbling, the foundation is endangered, and the lantern room is rusting so badly that shards are falling into the ocean. The disintegrating steel girders that hold the lighthouse together are compromised so badly they must be replaced. And the carrying timbers that support the walkway linking the tower to land are shot, compromised by weather and oxidized anchor pins. Plus, we are committed to bringing the fog bell back and rebuilding all the righteous old characteristics that made this lighthouse so special.

It won't be cheap. Since the Isle au Haut Lighthouse is on the National Register of Historic Places, those picky folks at the State Historic Preservation Office demand the highest standards. We have to match the original mortar that lies between the bricks, for instance, and to replace the missing wood doors that gave access to the bell, we're compelled to use old-growth straight-grained oak having at least eleven growth rings per inch (imagine that!). Plus, there's the future to take into account, and the need for an endowment fund to always keep her tidy.

If you'd like to support this effort, you can be a lighthouse, too! Send your tax-deductible contribution to:

Town of Isle au Haut, Lighthouse Fund
Attention: Lisa Turner, Secretary/Treasurer
P.O. Box 41
Isle au Haut, Maine 04645

Or donate online at:

Friends of Isle au Haut Lighthouse,
www.isleauhautlighthouse.org

All donations are fully tax deductible. Friends of Isle au Haut Lighthouse is an IRS registered 501(c)3 not-for-profit organization, #81-2019159.

Finally, thank you for reading my book. I hope you enjoyed it.

Keep the light shining,
Jeff

Isle au Haut, Maine,
September 23, 2017

Camden Public Library
Camden, Maine

387.155 Bur
Burke, Jeffrey
The lighthouse & me: history,
memoir & imaginatio